PHILLY BARKER

BARKER

IS ON THE CASE

ALSO BY JOANNE TRACEY

The Philly Barker series
Philly Barker Investigates
Philly Barker Is On The Case

The Melbourne series (contemporary romance)
Baby, It's You
Big Girls Don't Cry
I Want You Back
Careful What You Wish For
It's In The Stars
Christmas At Mannus Ridge *(coming soon)*

Escape To The Country series
Wish You Were Here
Happy Ever After
The Little Café By The Lake
Escape To Curlew Cottage

JOANNE TRACEY

PHILLY BARKER
IS ON THE CASE

A PHILLY BARKER MYSTERY

First published in Australia in 2023

by Joanne Tracey

https://joannetracey.com

Copyright © Joanne Tracey 2023

Print ISBN 978-0-6450735-9-1

Ebook ISBN 978-0-6450735-8-4

Cover design by Enni Tuomisalo of Yummy Book Covers

The right of the author to be identified as the author of this work has been asserted in accordance with the *Copyright Amendment (Moral Rights) Act* 2000.

 A catalogue record for this book is available from the National Library of Australia

For Kali –

the inspiration behind Balthazar

Prologue

I'd seen a dead body before; several, in fact. Over the course of twenty years in the police force – with most of those years spent in London – the occasional corpse was, sadly, part of the job. Poor Bally, however, had not and was now barking furiously at the inert lump he'd found behind the barn. I took a step closer and then another, a gasp escaping at the realisation that under the dusting of snow dark clothes were visible … and black shoes …

Regardless of the number of dead bodies you've been forced to see, you never quite get used to it. I certainly hadn't. Besides, it had been many years since I'd been on the force and longer than that since I'd been confronted with a violent death. And even from this distance, the rusty stains in the snow left me with no doubt that this person had met with a violent ending.

With a trepidatious glance around the silent barnyard, I whistled softly for Balthazar. With one final bark, he retreated a few steps from the corpse, his tail uncharacteristically lowered, his breath coming in anxious pants that hung like smoke in the cold February morning air.

I stepped towards him and paused with my hand on his collar, willing myself to moderate my breathing so I could hear beyond the pounding of my heart. In, hold, out, hold. In, hold, out, hold. The bleating of sheep floated on the air from a field towards the moors, but otherwise, all was silent. Bally's liquid eyes turned towards me as if to say, what do we do now?

'I don't know,' I whispered, reaching down to hold him against my leg.

A scrabbling sound to my left startled me. I turned quickly; a blackbird was scratching in the brambly hedgerow. The breath I'd held onto whooshed out.

The crunch of gravel under my boots reverberated through the crisp morning air as I walked carefully towards the lump. A quick glance behind to the farmhouse showed no sign of activity, not even a steady stream of puffy smoke from the chimney. What Yorkshireman would allow his fire to go out on a raw morning like this?

Only last week, farmer Albert Horsley was telling me how his wood-burning cooker could heat the main part of the house. 'It's only Jess and me these days, lass,' he'd said, reaching down to stroke the sheepdog's head. 'And we're happy to sit around the table after our tea.' Albert would never have let the fire go out. Not willingly.

That was something else that was missing – Jess. She'd

never leave Albert's side. Where was she?

Ordering Bally to sit, I slowly stepped closer to the snow-covered body, afraid of who I'd see but knowing I needed to see it.

When I finally reached it, I couldn't stop a gasp as I stared down into the wide-open eyes of the victim. A gaping wound in the middle of his forehead indicated the cause of death. This, I was certain, was no accident.

With shaking hands, I reached for the phone in the back pocket of my jeans and punched in a number.

'Robbie? It's me, Philly. I'm at Albert Horsley's place.' I paused and added, 'There's been a murder.'

Chapter One

Nine days earlier ...

'Is it my imagination or is February really the longest month of the year?' Isobel Mayfield sighed loudly as she slid into the Victorian mahogany spoon-back chair in my shop at Chipwell Barn Antiques. As she collapsed back into the chair, today's shawl of choice – black velvet, presumably to match her mood – fell softly around her, a perfect frame for the chair's cream opulence. Cat-like Bell, who had her own shop – vintage fashion, fabrics and accessories – in what we all referred to as The Barn, had the ability to make even a slump appear elegant.

'You know the old saying: Thirty days hath September, April, June and November. All the rest have thirty-one – except February, which has fifty-eight – and the good news is, we're only still in the first week.' I placed the Georgian silver butter knife I'd been dusting back on a shelf filled with more silverware and smiled indulgently across at her.

'No one's coming out in this weather,' she moaned, her

long fingers tracing the intricate scrolls on the chair's arm. 'I can count the number of customers I've had today on one hand.'

'Tell me about it.' I closed the glass door on the cabinet, wiping away a rogue fingerprint with the cloth and pushed my glasses onto the top of my head . 'Why do you think I've resorted to rearranging cabinets? Sometimes I wonder whether we wouldn't be better off closing our doors for a few weeks at this time of the year.'

Bell shrugged a slim shoulder as she slung one long black-leather-clad leg over the chair's padded arm, pointing her toe in the ballet flats that were her usual choice for days in the shop. 'Don't worry.' She noticed my grimace. 'I won't mark it, and Simon will still be able to sell it.'

Simon Bridges, the furniture trader in The Barn, also provided chairs for Bell's and my shops and the occasional chaise longue or settee for the café; the only catch being that we couldn't get too attached to them. These days, I barely raised an eyebrow as Simon carried one chair away and wheeled another in to replace it.

That was how it went here in the barn. A conglomerate of antique dealers, we each had our own market niche. I mainly traded in general antiques – vintage china, kitchenalia, silverware, jewellery, art and books. General bric-a-brac, I suppose. In the shop beside mine were the Ashton brothers, Ambrose and Eugene, septuagenarian tweed-loving dealers of what were collectively termed militaria. Whether you were searching for military uniforms, badges, medals, memorabilia or even items made from old gun shells (which the brothers called 'trench ware'), the Ashtons were known throughout Yorkshire as being the men to see. Unfortunately, this meant that just before Christmas last year, when would-be art thieves had attempted to persuade me to hand over documents I wasn't inclined to give them, they were able to use a set of duelling pistols from the Ashtons' cabinets in an attempt to persuade me to do as they wished. It had been the brothers' cranky cat, Rochester (who ruled the roost in their shop from his basket beside Ambrose's sturdy mahogany campaign desk) who had gotten us out of that particular pickle.

Simon's furniture took up the space at the rear of the barn and across from him were Tamsin and Henry Proctor, whose vintage garden furniture and accessories spread out from their shop into the garden behind the building. With expansive views across the green patchwork of hedgerow and tree-lined fields of the Howardian Hills, tables out here were in high demand by café patrons in the summer months. The Proctors had locked their shop for the time being; no one, they said, wanted to buy garden furniture in January and February, so each year, when the January sales were finished, the shop was closed until the spring rush began in March with new stock they'd collected on their annual travels to France. Perhaps they had the right idea.

'Anyone for tea and an Eccles cake?' The final member

of our collective, Ginny Wilding, popped in, her bright yellow knit jumper with a giant hot pink heart in the centre like a ray of sunshine in the February gloom. Ginny ran the barn's tea shop, and people came from miles away just to have one of her scones, superb sausage rolls, the ever-present parkin or other baked treats. Good business for her was good business for the rest of us – especially during the times when competition for tables was fierce and patrons were forced to take a number and wait. Waiting often moved to browsing, so I had some of my best sales days when the café was busy.

Eyeing Bell lolling in the cream chair, Ginny added, 'Careful you don't mark that. Remember how upset Simon was when he thought Philly had covered it in blood the night Rochester had to rescue her?'

'He was only worried about the chair once he knew I was unharmed,' I clarified when Bell merely raised a well-groomed brow. 'Besides, not a drop was spilt on the upholstery.'

'Even so, I'm surprised he's trusting you with a cream chair.' Ginny chuckled. 'There's a reason why you rarely wear white.'

I grinned my agreement; there was no point arguing with her. I spent my workdays going through people's dusty attics or barns, rummaging through boxes at auction, or polishing my wares in the shop. White, on me, rarely stayed white; it's why my work uniform was usually jeans, Chelsea boots, and a long-sleeved T-shirt or jumper; although I did swap the T-shirt for a button-down shirt and blazer on auction days.

Rather than contemplate the possibility of Bell leaving a mark on the cream upholstery (and making a mental note to ask Simon to swap it for something I'd be less likely to damage), I homed in on the important part of Ginny's entrance. 'Eccles cake? Whenever you bake them, you're always sold out by lunchtime. Has the café been quiet too?' I pushed aside a pile of books I'd been meaning to find shelf space for and perched on the edge of my desk.

'Have you been outside today?' she asked sardonically. 'It's proper parky.'

'I took Bally out to do his business a couple of hours ago, and even he looked up as if to say, "I can hold on, you know."' As if he knew I was talking about him, Balthazar looked up, his tail thumping twice on the floor. 'But if you have Eccles cakes going, I'll help you out.'

Ginny beamed, her dimples flashing. When it came to Ginny, a smile was never far away, but there was little she enjoyed more in the world than feeding people. 'Bell?'

Bell screwed up her nose delicately. 'No thanks, sweetie.'

'Will Ambrose and Eugene be back this afternoon?' Ginny asked hopefully.

'I don't think so. They've gone to an auction in Bradford. I'm supposed to be keeping an eye on their shop, but so far …' I shrugged.

'Simon?'

'God, you are desperate to get rid of those pastries, aren't you?' drawled Bell, one hand absently stroking Bally's head. Ginny flashed a wry smile in her direction. 'I have no idea. He's doing a delivery this afternoon in Thornton-le-Dale. Someone has bought enough furniture from him to fit out their dining room, sitting room and entrance hall.'

'Second home or short-term rental?' I asked, the demand for both having risen in the area since covid lockdowns.

'No idea, but it's certainly left him low on stock.' Bell rose from the chair in one fluid movement. 'Well, I'm closing for the day, girls. I'll leave you two to it.'

As she sauntered out the door, I said to Ginny, 'Unless you're also knocking off early, I guess it's just the three of us.' I inclined my head to indicate Bally was part of that team. 'And I'll hang around until five in case anyone does come in or call through.'

That was another thing about The Barn, as one or another of us was often out attending auctions, house clearances or responding to calls from customers asking us to pop around to check out what they had to sell us, we all kept an eye on the phone and each other's shops.

'I have a date with Richard, but I'll make tea and stay for a while longer,' Ginny announced, leaving me to get back to my cabinets, Bally following her out in the hope of securing some of what always smelt so good in the café.

It was only a minute or so later when Bally was back, but this time accompanied by a black-and-white sheepdog who, he'd quickly decided, judging by the amount of excited mutual sniffing and tail wagging, was friend, not foe. Behind the dogs shuffled an older man carrying a box that appeared to be in danger of self-destructing.

'Here'—I reached for the box—'let me take this for you.'

'Ta, lass.' He puffed out heavily, took his woollen flat cap from his head, gripped it against his chest and leant back against my desk.

It took a moment before he caught his breath. 'Can I help you?'

'Aye, if you're Philly Barker.' He ran his hand over the stubble of white hair covering his head.

The sheepdog was sniffing at my feet; I held my hand open to allow it to smell before ruffling behind its ears. 'I'm Philly. How can I help you?'

'The name's Albert.' He held out a weathered hand for me to shake. 'Albert Horsley, and that's Jess.' At the sound of her name, the dog's tail wagged before heading off to conduct a sniff test of the shop, Bally close behind. 'Iris Metcalfe was saying you might be interested in some bits and pieces I was wanting to sell.' He dipped his head towards the box.

I'd recently bought some silverware and a few other pieces from Iris. Iris had mentioned she had a few friends who might have some similar items they wanted to part with.

'Iris is a good judge of character, and she said you'd give me a fair price.'

Even though his words indicated one thing, his eyes narrowed warily; I didn't take it personally; there were plenty of unscrupulous dealers in our game.

'I'm pleased to meet you, Mr Horsley, and I'm happy to have a look. But why don't you take your coat off and sit down.' I directed him to the chair Bell had recently vacated. 'I'll see if I can't rustle us up a brew.'

'Call me Albert.' He eyed the cream lounge with suspicion. 'I'm too mucky for that chair.' When he brushed the brown thick-gauge cord of his trousers, a little cloud of dust followed.

Suppressing a grin, I pulled the oak pre-Second World War captain's chair from behind my desk. Stamped with a coronet and the marks of the Air Ministry, it was on loan from Ambrose and Eugene. 'I know what you mean – I'm scared to sit in it too. Use this chair instead, and I'll see about a brew.'

'No'—he waved the offer away—'I won't be staying. It's raw out there tonight, and I want to get home before it's dark, but you take your time looking through the box. It might be summat, or it might be nowt.' His gaze fell to his weathered leather boots. 'If you're interested, I have more at home. I'm a mile or so this side of Dunthrop.'

Guessing it would embarrass him to have me go through the contents of his box while in the room, I said, 'How about I have a look and come up with a fair price? Leave me your address, and I'll call by next time I'm at Iris's.' He scribbled the details down on the paper I handed him.

'That would be grand.' Putting his cap back on, he whistled quietly for Jess.

'I'll see you soon, Albert.' I gave the dog another ruffle behind her ears. 'And you too, Jess.'

Touching his cap lightly in a farewell, the pair ambled out.

Albert and Jess had no sooner left than Ginny was back – with a bear-like man in a rumpled suit and an arch glance at me. 'Look who I found lurking about. We go all afternoon without seeing anyone, and now it's busier than Kings Cross Station.'

'Robbie!' I replaced the layer of newspaper that had been protecting the contents of Albert's box and turned to greet him. 'You didn't mention you'd be out this way.'

I'd met Detective Inspector Robbie Dawkins late last year when he'd called at The Barn to enquire about some fake Clarice Cliff pottery that had been doing the rounds of the antique stores and salerooms. A widower a few years older than me, Robbie and I had become good friends, and Robbie was now a frequent visitor at the barn. Despite Ginny's teasing, and although both Robbie and I were single, neither of us were interested (for now at least) in taking our relationship further than friendship.

'You'll be wanting a brew, Robbie?' Ginny guessed.

'Aye.' Nodding, he rubbed his large hands together, a grateful smile on his face as he shed his heavy coat, brushing off the drops of sleet that still clung to it before hanging it from the 1930s hat and coat stand behind my desk. 'Thanks, Ginny.'

Once she'd disappeared into the café, I sat back on the edge of my desk. 'So what brings you here today?'

Bally was jumping around him in joyful welcome, and Robbie leant down to ruffle his head. 'A break-in at a farm out Lower Kirby way.' He loosened his navy tie and undid the top button of his white shirt, breathing an audible sigh of relief as he did so. 'The complainant thinks it happened yesterday but only noticed this morning.'

'Really? What was taken?' Many of the farmhouses in the district had been in the same family for years. I couldn't imagine there'd be much of value to attract thieves.

My scepticism must've shown on my face. 'Interesting that you ask,' he said wryly. Patting at the chest pocket of his white shirt, he pulled out a black-covered notebook and his glasses. Snapping open the elastic that held it together, he moistened his forefinger with his tongue and flipped through the pages. With a cheeky grin in my direction that chased the crags on his face away, he said, 'I might as well tell you in case anyone comes in trying to off-load it.'

'Or in case I see it up for auction at Young's in York.' I returned his smile and gestured to the chair Bell had recently vacated. He eyed it warily – I must get Simon to swap it for something more practical – before sitting down with the voluptuous sigh of a man who'd spent the day out in the elements.

'Right.' He referred to his notebook. 'The usual silverware – spoons, servers, sugar tongs, that sort of stuff.' He waved at my cabinet in illustration. 'You know what it's like on these farms that have been in the family for years – no one really has a definitive list of what they have.'

I nodded my understanding, picked up a pen and idly tapped it against the desk. 'But they always know when it's missing.'

'Aye, they do.' He referred to his notebook. 'All the thief had to do was pick up the chocolate boxes it was stored in – the ones with drawers you used to get your assorted chocolates in.' He looked up from his notes. 'Do you remember those?'

I shook my head. 'No, our choccies didn't come in anything so posh as that in Australia. But I know the ones you're talking about – Terry's used them in the sixties. They're very collectible. In fact, I saw one the other week – it was being used to store the owner's silverware too.' I flicked at my chin as I remembered. 'She had quite the collection of vintage biscuit tins and chocolate boxes – most of them from Terry's of York.'

The chocolate company used to be based in nearby York and was, for a time, one of the largest employers in the district.

Robbie chuckled, the low rumbling bringing a smile to my face. 'This lady also had another box taken that held some jewellery. An engagement ring, a couple of lockets, a pair of wedding rings.'

I smiled ruefully; most farmhouses in the region would have a tin just like that holding their precious bits and pieces. I'd seen one of those the other week too – a round cardboard box dating back to the 1920s that used to hold chocolate burnt almonds and now contained jewellery much as Robbie had described.

'Then there was'—his forehead furrowed as he read from the page—'something called a firefly cage?'

My pen stalled. 'A firefly cage? I don't suppose it was Iris Metcalfe's place that was robbed?'

Robbie shook his head in disbelief. 'How on earth could you know that?'

Ginny chose that moment to appear with a tray of tea things and a plate of Eccles cakes. I cleared some space on my desk for her to place the tray down, and as she poured the tea, I ducked next door to the café for another chair.

'Have a seat and join us, Ginny. Robbie was telling me about a robbery over at Iris Metcalfe's.'

Robbie had just taken a bite of the flaky pastry, and while his mouth was too full to protest, he raised his eyebrows at me sardonically, a gesture I chose to ignore.

'Actually,' he said once he'd swallowed. 'You were about to tell me how you knew it was Iris Metcalfe's place I was talking about. By the way, Ginny, these are excellent. Are they new on your menu?'

Ginny beamed at the compliment, both dimples on full display. 'Thanks. I don't make them often but had some fruit mince leftover from Christmas, so figured this was as good a way as any to use it up.' She looked between the two of us. 'But if this is business, I'll leave you to it.'

'Stay where you are, Ginny.' Robbie wiped a crumb of pastry from his mouth with the back of his hand. 'There doesn't seem to be any secrets here.'

'If you're sure,' she said hesitantly.

'So Philly … How did you know it was the Metcalfe place I was talking about?'

I sipped at my tea and shrugged lightly. 'I was out at Iris's a week or so ago. She needed to sell some pieces to help with expenses and showed me those boxes. The jewellery belonged to her parents, and I knew she didn't want to part with it, so I didn't buy it from her. I did buy some other bits and pieces from her, though – a silver card box, an Edwardian vesta case with a lovely enamel picture of a hound that will be very collectible with the horse and hounds set, and an oak hat block that Bell is using for displays in her shop. There was also a rather nice painting I think I'll take to auction rather than sell here. Victorian oil – horses and hounds, that sort of thing.' I nibbled at my bottom lip. 'She showed me the firefly cage but seemed reluctant to part with it, so I encouraged her to hold onto it as long as possible. It was a nice piece, and I'd need the right buyer.' I screwed up my nose as I thought back to the conversation. 'She remembered playing with it when her grandmother was still alive. Apparently, her great-uncle wasn't into farming sheep and wanted to see the world – or something like that – and he brought it back from his travels. It must've been quite the thing to travel to the Far East back in those days. Anyway, I gave her a fair price for everything I bought, so hopefully, it's enough to see her right for now. The last thing I wanted was some unscrupulous dealer coming in and giving her a pittance for it all.'

A slight frown hung on Robbie's face. 'But what exactly is a firefly cage?'

I stood and walked around my desk, sliding into the captain's chair. Opening my laptop and retrieving my glasses from their position on my head, I beckoned to Robbie to come closer. He rose to stand behind me. Ginny shuffled in alongside me to look over my shoulder. 'I remember the first time I heard of them – it was on an episode of an old TV show, *Lovejoy*. You might've seen it? Late eighties, early nineties?'

He shrugged a shoulder. 'I vaguely recall the name but don't think I ever watched it.'

'Fair enough. Lovejoy was a roguish antique dealer

in Essex, I think. Or was it Norfolk?' I shook my head; it didn't matter. 'He was also a womaniser, and the whole thing would be seen as being politically incorrect these days, but whatever. Anyway'—my fingers tapped away at the keys—'that's where I first heard of a firefly cage. The only ones I've ever seen, though, up to now, anyway, have been in paintings like this one.' I bought up a picture from The Met's collection by a Japanese artist. The subject was a courtesan and her attendant carrying a cage of fireflies.

'That's beautiful,' said Ginny. 'Both the painting and the box.'

'See how the attendant is holding a box?' I pointed to the box on the screen, and Robbie nodded, eyes staring at the screen. 'That's a firefly cage. You can't see from this, but it probably would've been lacquered with gold and silver designs, the sides a tight mesh. Some of them were quite intricately decorated.' I showed him a few examples; Ginny continued to peer over our shoulders. 'They used to catch the fireflies and keep them in these boxes.'

'The poor things,' exclaimed Ginny.

'I know, it all sounds quite cruel now – and it's been illegal for nearly a century in Japan – but they gave off light like fairy lights. I read somewhere that they're a metaphor for passionate love or the souls of fallen soldiers.'

'Can you remember what Iris's cage looked like?' Robbie asked.

I nodded. 'It wasn't as intricate as some of the

examples I just showed you. The top and the bottom were made of black lacquer, with some gold swirls on the top a bit like this.' I pulled across a writing pad and roughly sketched a rectangular box, the sides hatched with metal gauze, a lantern-style top with a handle for carrying.

'Would you know it again if you saw it?'

I grinned back at him. 'I might forget a face, Inspector Dawkins, but I never forget an antique.'

His eyes remained fixed on my drawing. 'Why didn't you buy the box from her too?'

'She wanted me to, but I had no idea what to value it at. I told her that – and that I'd check in with some of the auctioneers I knew to see what estimate they'd put on it. As I said, though, it deserved to go to a collector or someone who'd really appreciate it. It's too beautiful and rare to go into a general sale. My hope was that I'd match it to a buyer; I'd still get a premium on the sale, but she'd also get what it was worth. Anyway, the proceeds from what I did buy will see her through her immediate crisis; hopefully, it's bought her some time to decide what she wants to do.' I grimaced. 'As things have turned out, though, maybe I should've given her a price for everything.'

Robbie looked up from his notebook. 'Hold on; you said she needed time to decide what she wants to do ... about what?'

'About selling up. She didn't mention it?' When Robbie continued to look blank, I clarified. 'She's been offered good money to sell the farm, really good money, but it's the only home she's ever known, so naturally, she's not sure what to do.'

'Does she have any relatives?' asked Ginny, who had now sat on the edge of the desk beside me.

'Her sister passed away a few years ago, and her children – a niece and a nephew, I think – are up Middlesborough way. They're not close – although she did say they're very keen for her to sell up and go into an aged care home.'

'I bet they are,' muttered Ginny.

I nodded in understanding. 'Yes, even Iris said as much. She told me they weren't interested in the farm but just wanted to get their hands on the money.'

'I would've thought she'd be too old to run the farm properly now, though,' said Robbie. 'She'd have to be in her midseventies.'

'Seventy-six and let me tell you, she's still switched on. She's leased the paddocks and the barns to her neighbour – he runs sheep on them – so all she has to worry about is the farmhouse. From what she alluded to when I was out there, she's had some unexpected expenses – big ones.'

Ginny laughed one of her belly laughs – the ones that brought a smile to anyone listening. 'What?' I asked, lost as to what I'd said that had prompted Ginny's laughter.

'Is there anyone who doesn't tell you everything, Philly?'

I had the grace to at least appear sheepish. 'Not really,

no. Anyway, her boiler blew unexpectedly, and the repair was more than she could afford; and, let's face it, who can be without a boiler at this time of the year? So I helped her out and left her with enough in case she has some more problems. It didn't seem right for her to part with family heirlooms when she didn't really need to.'

Usually difficult to read, the expression on Robbie's face could've been admiration. 'You're a good woman, Philomena Barker. A lot of less scrupulous dealers would've taken advantage of her.'

Warmth filled my cheeks. 'I only did what any decent person would do. I told her I'd call by in a week or so, though, if she wanted to talk through her options with anyone.' Ginny's grin widened as she noticed the gleam in my eyes. 'After all, if I'd taken those goods off her hands, she wouldn't have had anything there worth stealing. When you think about it like that,' I mused, 'it's almost like I owe her.' I wrinkled my nose as I ran through the items Iris had shown me, the jewellery Robbie said had been stolen. 'It would probably be best to let Catherine know to be on the lookout in case anything comes into the auction room,' I mused.

'The thought hadn't crossed my mind.' The sarcasm in Robbie's tone was balanced by his knowing smile.

'I probably should come with you when you do that. After all,' I added, with a butter-wouldn't-melt-in-my-mouth expression, 'I can probably give a more succinct description of the missing goods than you can.'

Robbie chuckled and shook his head. 'Because you never forget an antique.'

'Exactly.' I glanced at my watch. 'Anyway, I'm not sure about you lot, but I say we close up.'

Ginny gathered our teacups and plates, waving away Robbie and my offers of help. 'I can do this. I'll see you tomorrow, Philly, and I'll see you around, Robbie.'

While I totalled up my meagre sales for the day, Robbie began rummaging through the box Albert had left.

'What do you think?' I asked, closing the lid of my laptop. 'Anything decent in there?'

'I wouldn't have a clue. Where did it come from?'

'Albert Horsley – he has a farm out near Dunthrop. Dropped it in just before you arrived and wants me to go and have a look at some of the other things he has at his farm. Iris told him what I'd done for her.'

'Careful, Philly, or you and your soft heart will be financing the boiler repairs of half the pensioners in North Yorkshire.' Even though he said it with a wry smile, I recognised the warning for what it was.

'Maybe, I only buy what I know I can sell. And besides, you never know what treasures could be hiding in here.' I pushed aside the crumpled newspaper acting as a rudimentary padding for the box's contents. 'I told him I'd visit and have a proper look around, although I suspect it's more the company he's after than a valuation.' A stoneware spirit jug caught my eye, and I removed it from the box.

'Although this is rather nice.' I turned it upside down, squinting to locate the maker's mark on the base, before pulling my trusty loupe from my jeans pocket. 'Doulton Lambeth … a lovely salt glaze … late nineteeth century …'—I looked up and grinned at him—'this *is* nice.'

Robbie smiled as he correctly guessed that if he didn't move me along, I'd become stuck in the box and we'd never leave. With some reluctance and a wry grin, I placed the jug back in the box and pushed it away. 'I'll look through it properly tomorrow.'

While I locked my shop Robbie checked that all the other shops in the barn were secure. It was something he'd fallen in the habit of doing since that night just before Christmas when a would-be art thief threatened the Ashtons and me at gunpoint – although when I say gunpoint, it was an antique pistol that had been decommissioned, but that was a detail I wasn't certain of at the time. I did, however, appreciate his concern for my welfare.

'Feel like a pint and a bite to eat?' I asked as we walked to our respective cars.

'Sounds good.' He held the door of my ancient Land Rover, Libby, open for Bally to jump in.

'I'll just need to quickly change my top,' I said, noticing the dust marks on the bottom of my loose-fitting long-sleeved tee.

'No problems, I'll follow you down.' He held up a hand of acknowledgement and climbed into his car.

Chapter Two

Home for me was half a mile away in Chipwell, a small village in North Yorkshire consisting of a church, a few dozen houses that were, like mine, mostly constructed from the local limestone, and an eighteenth-century pub just a few doors down from where I lived – The Chipwell Arms. I could, of course, have easily walked to The Barn – and did so more often in summer when the daylight hours were longer – but I was often bringing boxes to and from home or running out to attend auctions or inspect house clearances, so it was far easier to have Libby.

Robbie pulled up behind me and followed me into the house, nodding with approval when I disarmed the burglar alarm he (and my ex-husband, Stewart) pressured me into installing a couple of months ago.

Keeping his coat on, Robbie took Bally out through the French doors into the garden to do his business. It hadn't long finished raining, and the puddles on the concrete path were glinting with the reflections from the kitchen lights. Robbie huddled into his coat and rubbed his hands together, his breath visible. He turned and saw me watching him, the moisture on the windows softening the features of his face and lessening the bags under his eyes. He raised his eyebrows in a silent question, and I held up my hand in acknowledgement that this wasn't getting us any closer to supper and ran lightly up the stairs.

After swapping the dirty top for a tight-fitting charcoal shirt, I examined my reflection in the mirror behind my door. Despite indulging (probably too often) in Ginny's treats, my job was an active one and that, as well as daily walks with Balthazar, was enough to keep me in reasonable condition with everything more or less still in the right place – albeit softer than it used to be. I was, however, fully aware that at my height – a few inches over five feet – it wouldn't take much to change that situation.

There was more ash than blonde in my hair these days, but as I kept it short, it all blended into each other. I tucked the little wings that stuck out at the side back behind my ears. Besides, what did it matter if my jaw was slacker than it used to be, if my cheeks weren't as pinchable as they used to be, if there were more shadows under my blue eyes. It's not as if there was anyone in my life I needed to impress. Before I could stop it, an image of Robbie came into my mind, and just as quickly, I pushed it back out, reminding myself that it wouldn't do to be thinking like that. A quick slick of lipstick and I was ready.

When I walked back into the kitchen, Robbie was on

the phone. Leaning against the kitchen bench looking out into the dark garden he didn't at first notice I'd come back into the room.

'Yes, sir.' His lips curved into a half-smile as he spied my reflection in the glass doors. 'I understand.'

Guessing the caller to be Stewart – my ex-husband and Robbie's chief superintendent – I bent down to acknowledge Bally, who was jumping all over me as if I'd been missing for hours rather than minutes.

'I'm sure I can manage it on my own although …' Robbie hesitated and then, with his eyes on me, added, 'I was thinking I could use Philly's expertise on this one. She knows the complainant and was at the house only a week ago, so she has a good understanding of what was stolen.' At his silent question, I nodded. 'She could help identify any recovered items as well.' A pause. 'I'm with her now. Did you want to speak to her?'

He handed the phone over. 'What can I do for you, Stewart? Please don't ask me to pick your children up again; as much as I adore Misty and Reuben, I don't fancy driving tonight. Where's Alison?'

'It's nothing to do with the children.' He sounded affronted and I couldn't hide my grin at how easy he was to rile. 'Besides, that was just the one time I asked you to do that, and Alison still hasn't let me hear the end of it. Nor have Misty and Reuben, but for different reasons, I suspect.' A smile came into his tone. 'They can't wait to repeat the experience – and with hot chocolate and Ginny's muffins, why wouldn't they? But no, it's not the kids. This investigation of Robbie's, are you okay with what he's proposed? I can't spare anyone to help him out and this close to his retirement …' Stewart didn't need to finish the sentence: this close to retirement, Stewart wouldn't want Robbie to take on anything new that would need to be handed over.

'The shop is quiet at the minute, so that's fine.'

'That's good then. There was something else though …' Stewart sounded uncharacteristically hesitant. 'I wanted to talk to you about Robbie.'

Involuntarily, my gaze swung across to the detective, who raised a questioning brow. 'What about?' I asked evasively. When Robbie and I first became friends, Stewart didn't exactly warn me off him – we'd been divorced for over ten years, so it was, after all, none of his business who I saw – but he did ask me to tread carefully. Robbie's wife had passed away some years before, and Stewart hadn't wanted to see him hurt again. Since then, Robbie had been a comfortable part of my life and even attended the family Christmas dinner at my son's house. We remained, however, strictly friends.

'It's just about his retirement dinner …'

'What about it?' I held one finger in the air to let Robbie know I'd only be another moment.

'Has he asked you to go with him?'

'Really, Stewart? We're having this discussion? The answer is yes, but I don't see what concern it is of yours.' Robbie grinned at the exasperation on my face, the action smoothing out the crags, making him look younger than the sixty-one I knew him to be.

'Maybe we should have this conversation later.' Stewart was sounding frustrated, although he had no right to be. This was none of his business.

'Maybe we shouldn't have this conversation at all,' I retorted.

'I'm not asking for *that* reason; it's good the two of you have become such good friends. It's just that Alison will be there too and having two Mrs Barkers might be a bit strange. Plus, there's the issue that Robbie hasn't dated since his wife passed and it could start some rumours in the office.'

'Oh, for goodness sake, Stewart. That's ridiculous, and if it's all you've got to worry about at present, you really need something else to occupy you. How long has it been since you had a decent murder on your patch?'

Robbie let out a surprised snort of laughter and leant down to scratch behind Bally's ears.

'Don't even wish that on me, Philly,' Stewart said seriously. 'I can't be doing with the paperwork or the overtime expense; we've got budgets to meet, you know.'

I let out a short laugh. 'Does Alison even know that you were going to mention this?' At his silence, I chortled again. 'Ha! She doesn't know, does she!'

He mumbled something indistinctly.

'What was that?' My initial annoyance was giving way, and I could see the funny side of the conversation. Deciding to put him out of his misery, I said, 'Don't worry, Stewart, I'll talk it over with him and make a call after that, okay?'

His exhalation of relief came down the line. 'Thanks, Philly. I know it might seem ridiculous to you, but he hasn't had an easy run, and I'd hate for him to leave the job on an uncomfortable footing.'

On the job, Stewart wasn't known for his soft side, but under that gruff exterior, he was a kind man. Despite our divorce, even I couldn't accuse him of being uncaring, and I liked that he cared so much about Robbie.

'It's fine, Stewart. Anyway, we're on our way out, so I'll talk to you later.'

Handing the phone back to Robbie, I whistled for Bally, picked up the house keys and my handbag and turned to Robbie. 'Let's go.'

'Was that about me?' Robbie asked, holding the front door open for me.

'Uh huh.'

'And the retirement dinner?'

Nodding, I turned slightly to glance at him in the darkness, the streetlights casting enough light to see his lips quirking up at the corner.

'Is the problem that both his ex-wife and his current wife will be there, or that I've asked you to come with me?'

It was still amusing how, despite attending several events together now and regularly sharing a meal at the pub, we were careful not to use the 'd' word. We were two people who enjoyed each other's company, but that didn't make what we were doing 'dating'.

I hesitated briefly, contemplating avoiding the question, but opted instead for honesty. 'He says both, but I suspect it's the latter rather than the former.' The corner of my mouth turned up in a wry smile. 'He's concerned that your colleagues might think we're dating.' I rolled my eyes to illustrate how ridiculous it sounded and to hide my discomfort.

Robbie merely looked amused as he paused in the doorway of the Arms. 'Does it concern you? After all, while I know you get on well with Alison—'

'Now,' I cut in. 'I get on well with her now, but it's taken a long time to get to that stage.' While I'd blamed Alison for many years for both her youth and my broken marriage, these days, I was at peace with it and, by extension, her. We'd never be best friends, but as Stewart and I shared two adult children – Ryan and Chloe – and were grandparents to Ryan's children, Ada and Alfie, if I avoided Alison, it would mean absenting myself from family Christmases, birthdays and other events. And I wasn't prepared to, as my mother would've said, cut my nose off to spite my face.

'Even so,' Robbie continued, 'it can't be comfortable being at a social event like this one with her – it will be a different scenario to being at a family gathering.' The lines on his forehead deepened. 'If you're not comfortable with that, I'd understand.'

'Not at all,' I said breezily. 'I know what coppers are like when it comes to gossip, and Stewart and I are old news – so old I'm sure there are officers who don't know that Alison used to be Stewart's secretary rather than his wife. No'—I shook my head—'I'm not worried about that; I'm more concerned about you. It is, after all, your night, and I don't want it spoilt by gossipy speculation about us.'

He grinned at that, his teeth catching his lower lip as he let out a sardonic half chuckle. 'I wouldn't have asked you if I was worried about that.' Pulling the wrought iron handle on the heavy oak door, Robbie stood aside so Bally and I could enter, the spaniel bounding ahead. 'Let them talk. If they're talking about us, they're leaving some other bugger alone.' He hung his coat and scarf from the overloaded hooks in the entrance, waiting as I shrugged out of mine before hanging those too. 'Now, what'll it be? Your usual?'

I examined his face for any sign of something else – discomfort maybe – and on finding none, nodded my thanks and made my way to a round wooden table, Bally already settled on the rug by the fire left there for dogs.

For a miserable Tuesday night in February, the bar was surprisingly busy, and judging by Josie's bustle, the dining room off to the side was full. I smiled reassuringly at her as she rushed past, her arms laden with plates of varying emptiness and narrowly missing Holly, the other server, heading into the room with full plates of food – and Robbie carrying our drinks. All three grinned an apology at each other and continued on their way.

Robbie placed our drinks on the table with an exaggerated exhalation of relief and pulled a couple of cardboard coasters from his pocket, tossing them on the table. 'It's proper busy in here tonight. Lynn was telling me the dining room is fully booked.' Roger and Lynn Marsh had been the proprietors of the Arms for the last two decades, arriving in the village soon after Stewart and I did. Lynn had told me there were times they were still treated as incomers because they'd originally come from down south. Stewart and I had fitted in much more easily – he'd been born in a village not far from here, and as I was Australian, I was still excused for my mistakes. 'Aye, lass,' the old-timers would say, 'you weren't to know, being from down under and that.' I still had to hide my giggles whenever anyone referred to me as a 'lass', but I supposed that to anyone over seventy, anyone under sixty (and I was only *just* under sixty) was a lass.

'It's not even trivia night.' I took a sip of my red wine, the Rioja filling my nose with scents of cherry and plum and my chest with warmth.

'Apparently, it's a big group from London – about a dozen couples. They've booked all the short-term rentals in the village for the week.'

'If it's that many people, they've probably taken all the rentals in the next village too.'

'Aye.' His smile was sardonic as he took a large mouthful of his ale, wiping his mouth with the back of his hand. 'Now, about before – are you fine about me suggesting you help with the case? It's not something I'd normally do, but knowing you'd already be planning a visit to York to see Catherine about that firefly cage, I figured if you were going to be involved, we might as well do it properly.'

Catherine Young was the auctioneer at Young and Johnsons in York. I'd worked for her back when I was studying my fine arts degree after leaving the police force. That job at the auction house had been what started me out in this business.

'You mean you wanted to tell Stewart in advance so he doesn't hit the roof about me being involved?' I shook my head in exasperation. Stewart would never let me forget what happened last Christmas, even though I told him I'd been looking after myself perfectly capably in the years since he left me. 'Of course I'm fine about it, but I heard you say you were on your own for this one. No Sergeant Stanley?'

'Not this time; he's been allocated to the new DI.' As I would've asked him more about the new inspector, he said, 'But back to tomorrow, are you able to get anyone to watch the shop for you? I thought we could pay a call on Catherine and give her a list of what's been taken.'

'If the day is anything like today, it will be quiet again. Between the brothers Ashton and Bell, it'll be fine, but yes, I have a good idea about what was in those chocolate boxes.' I took another sip of my wine. 'And afterwards, we probably should call in on Iris – just to make sure she has no aftereffects from the robbery.'

Robbie grinned; he wasn't fooled by my attempted nonchalance. 'It's not exactly on the way back, but I'm guessing if I said no, you'd go out there anyway.'

Josie chose that moment to deliver our meals, saving me from having to respond. 'Kedgeree fishcakes for you, Philly, and gammon, chips and eggs for you, Robbie.' She placed the plates in front of us. 'With extra bread and butter for you to mop everything up.'

'Thanks, Josie.' Robbie grabbed some bread and pulled it in half. 'Just the way I like it.' When she left, he said, 'Pick you up at the shop? Around nine-ish?'

'Sounds good. Now, tell me, how did the robbers get into the house?'

Robbie uttered a mirthless laugh.

'Let me guess … through the unlocked front door?'

Robbie rolled his eyes, his mouth too full to answer.

Chapter Three

'Philly!' Catherine was supervising the hanging of a painting in her York showroom when Robbie and I arrived the following morning. 'And Inspector Dawkins too. I'll be right with you.' To her assistant Becky, who was up the ladder, she said, 'A little more to the right. Perfect!'

Smiling her satisfaction, she walked across to us, her black heels click-clacking on the concrete floor. She greeted me with a double air kiss and Robbie with a handshake. 'To what do I owe this unexpected pleasure? Don't tell me you've unearthed another valuable painting.'

Late last year, an unattributed late nineteenth-century oil painting of Whitby I'd acquired in a box of odds and sods at auction had turned out to be quite valuable. It was still locked away in the vault and would be auctioned in March as one of the headline pieces in Catherine's quarterly fine art auction – and had been attracting quite a lot of advance interest. I looked across at Robbie, my raised eyebrows asking his permission to speak for him. 'Unfortunately, no,' I said. 'It's rather more serious than that.'

'Given the presence of the inspector, I thought it might be. You need me to be on the lookout for some stolen property? Please don't tell me it's stolen silver.'

I lifted a shoulder. 'It's silver.' As Catherine was about to groan and tell me it was almost impossible to identify unless there was something special about the silver, I added, 'And a nineteenth-century lacquerware firefly cage.'

Catherine's finely drawn eyebrows disappeared under the steel-grey fringe of her short, straight bob. 'Are you sure?' I nodded. 'You'd better come into the office and tell me all about it.'

While Catherine was always impeccably groomed, her office was anything but. The floor was littered with boxes and piles of books, and against one wall leant a stack of framed prints. She pointed us towards two office chairs and sat behind her oak desk. I lifted the pile of paperwork on mine and added it to the piles on her desk. Robbie did the same, but when he sat down, his chair immediately sank with a groan. 'I think the gas might've gone on that one.' Catherine grimaced, pushing her black-rimmed glasses back onto the bridge of her nose. 'If you fiddle with it, it should come good.'

Robbie played about with the handles and adjusted the seated at a more appropriate level.

'Have you got a list of everything that was stolen?' Robbie passed across a printed sheet, and we waited as Catherine ran her eyes quickly over it. 'No offence, but this is more comprehensive than what you guys usually bring to us. Normally I get a list that reads something like "silver spoons, silver knives" … This one at least tells me what sort of spoon and what sort of knife. You've even mentioned hallmarks on a few.' She looked up from the sheet and smiled her approval.

'I can't take the credit,' said Robbie. 'It just so happened that Philly had been out at the property recently and—'

'And Philly has a photographic memory when it comes to antiques,' finished Catherine. 'Anything exceptional about any of this?' The question was directed at me.

I shook my head. 'Not really. It's the same sort of thing that gets handed down in these families. A few nice pieces but nothing worth a lot on its own. The chocolate boxes she stored them in are quite collectible, but again, I'd say every farmhouse of a certain vintage in these parts would have some of them tucked away in their loft or their shed full of tarnished silverware, or nuts and bolts.'

'I remember my mother used one to store her sewing things in,' Robbie mused.

Catherine chuckled in response. 'We get several through here. I have a domed baroque style one from the fifties in the next general sale.'

'What have you got on it?'

She shrugged. 'Twenty to forty pounds. Fifty on a good day, but they must be in fabulous condition, and this one is average.' She glanced again at the printed sheet before pushing it aside and steepling her fingers under her chin. 'I'll keep an eye out for you in case someone comes in, but with the amount of silver we get through, the likelihood of identifying any of it ...' She didn't need to finish her sentence. 'What I really want to hear about is the firefly cage.'

I handed over the rough sketch I'd drawn for Robbie. 'The owner's uncle – it could have been a great-uncle – was in the merchant navy and brought it back from his travels in the East. Probably won it in a poker game or something. She remembers her grandmother keeping letters and cards in it – it sat on her bedside table.' I paused before adding. 'I feel guilty because she'd wanted me to buy it off her and while I told her I'd ask around to see if I could find a collector, I could tell she didn't want to part with it.'

'It's not your fault,' said Robbie.

'I know, but ...' I shook my head. 'I have no idea how much it's worth – maybe a couple of hundred in a general sale, but to a collector, it could be a lot more than that – maybe up to a thousand pounds.'

Catherine nodded sagely. 'To the right person. Was there any gold or silver in the lacquer?'

'A little gold dust in the swirls. It wouldn't have originally come from a wealthy family, I don't think – probably the Japanese nineteenth-century equivalent of middle-class – but then, I don't know a lot about oriental antiques.'

'Perhaps,' she mused, her red-tipped nails tapping on the desk. 'But I trust your instincts. The best I can do is keep an eye out for you. I might miss a stolen Stilton scoop, but I'm unlikely to miss something like this.'

'Thanks, Catherine, that would be a help.' Robbie retrieved his wallet from inside his jacket breast. 'Here's my card in case anything does come up.'

She leant across the desk to take it. 'I'll call you if it does.' She cast a conspiratorial glance at me.

'Preferably before you call Philly,' Robbie countered, failing to completely hide his wry smile.

We stood to leave. 'Do you mind if I have a quick mooch around before we go?'

'I wouldn't expect anything less, Philly. You'll be at the next sale?'

'Absolutely. I'll see you then.'

Back in Robbie's car – after a quick scout around the auction house – with the heater blaring, I said, 'Right, what's next on your list?'

'I can drop you back at the barn if you like ...' A quick glance my way and he added in a more resigned tone, 'Or we can call in and see Iris Metcalfe first.'

'Now, that's a good idea. After all, what else would you be doing this close to retirement?'

'Aye, you have a point there.'

Something in his voice made me examine his profile more closely. While his gaze was focused on the road ahead, something in the set of his jaw made me think he was aware of my stare and was determined not to show any emotion. Perhaps he needed some encouragement to confide in me.

'What's wrong? Have they banished you to the detective equivalent of traffic control?'

The corner of his mouth turned up slightly. 'Something like that. They have me trying to tidy up some cold cases – mostly robberies and the like.'

'Let me guess – Stewart doesn't want to give you anything you then have to hand over to someone else.'

He nodded and added a shrug of resignation.

'Has anyone come into your role?'

There was that little twinge in his lips again. 'Aye. A new inspector from Oxford by the name of Chris Whitely.'

'Hmmm, that's a change – Oxford to Yorkshire. I'm guessing he's young and ambitious?'

Robbie lifted his shoulder lightly. 'Weren't we all at that age?'

'I suppose … Stewart certainly was.'

Up ahead, the bells were clanging and the barriers were coming down at the Kirkham Abbey rail crossing. Across the river, on the other side of the old stone bridge, a herd of dirty-white Charolais cows lay in the weak winter sun, and beyond them stood the ruins of the old priory.

'I take it the robbery of an old woman on a farm in the middle of nowhere doesn't figure highly on the new inspector's priorities,' I said wryly.

He didn't answer immediately, the rattle of the train as it sped through giving him time to frame his answer.

'The likelihood of finding the perpetrator is low,' he finally said, turning to face me. 'And you're not going to make your mark chasing unsolvable robberies.'

'But they figure it will give you something to do for the next week or so. Is that why Sergeant Stanley isn't on this case too?' The bells stopped their clanging, and the gate slowly opened.

'He needs to get used to working for Whitely, and as you say, I don't need him on this job.' We were moving again so Robbie turned away from my gaze.

There it was again, that weary tone. 'Are you regretting retiring?'

He glanced quickly across at me, his face set in its usual inscrutable arrangement. With his eyes back on the road, his shoulders lowered as if he'd decided to confide in me. 'Maybe, I know it's time, but …'

'You'll miss having a purpose?' I said softly.

'Aye,' he admitted. 'The chief super says I can come back from time to time as a consultant, but I can't see Whitely being too thrilled about that.' He paused, remaining focused on the sweeping bend in the road. 'I know nowt else but being a copper.' I reached over and gave his arm a light, awkward pat. He flashed me a tight, forced smile in response. 'I might have to come and help you out from time to time.'

'I've always wanted an apprentice.'

He chuckled softly. 'You don't think I'm too old to teach?'

I pretended to consider the question seriously. 'A little set in your ways perhaps, but you can always make the tea.'

His chuckle turned into a laugh, and the awkwardness was gone. Although our chat was light for the rest of the short drive, it somehow felt like our relationship had moved to a new level of trust.

As we pulled off the hedge-lined lane and parked outside the old stone farmhouse, Iris came out to meet us, wiping her hands against the faded floral apron she wore over her navy woollen jumper and grey trousers. Her initially wary expression lightened when she recognised us. 'Philly! And Inspector Dawkins. This is a surprise … Don't tell me you've already found my things.'

'I'm sorry, Mrs Metcalfe, not yet.' Robbie stepped forward with his hand outstretched, which she took. 'I hope you don't mind, but I've brought Philly in on this case to help me.'

'Call me Iris,' the older lady said. 'I'm always happy to see Philly.' I kissed her weather-worn cheek. 'Oh be off with you.' Her smile was warm and welcoming, considering what she'd been through.

'Don't go thinking Robbie, sorry Inspector Dawkins, was talking out of school, Iris. He'd dropped in for a brew and told me he'd been out this way investigating a robbery. When he mentioned the firefly cage, I guessed it was you. I'm so sorry – I should've taken it all off your hands when I was last here.'

'It's not your fault, pet.' She squeezed my hand. 'You thought you were doing me a favour. I had to tell that other pushy bugger who turned up here that I didn't want to sell, but you knew what was best for me.'

My breath caught in my throat and I raised my eyes to meet Robbie's. His hand had instinctively gone for the notebook and pen he kept in the chest pocket of his shirt. Vaguely, I noticed the blue blob of ink in the bottom corner of the pocket and suppressed a grin. It must be an occupational hazard.

'What other bugger, Iris? You told me that someone had made you an offer to buy the farm, but you didn't mention someone wanted to buy your silver. When was this?'

'What am I doing keeping you out here in the cold? Come inside the pair of you. There's a brew on and some scones not long from the oven. I was going to take some down to Albert Horsley – he and Jess, that dog of his, love my scones, they do. Did Albert come and see you?'

We followed Iris into the kitchen. 'He did. I promised I'd call in and see him in the next few days, so if you like, I can drop some over after we've finished here.' Not knowing whether I'd see exasperation on his face I couldn't look at Robbie as I said it.

'Could you, pet? That would be grand. It's right parky out there again today.'

'It would be no trouble at all,' I assured her. 'If I didn't need to be out, I don't think I'd want to stray too far from the warmth either.'

As Iris set out the tea things and a plate of fruit scones, creamy butter and homemade damson jam, I looked across at Robbie, who simply shook his head, although his resigned grin told me he wasn't cross about this change of plan.

'You were telling us about the person who offered to buy your things,' I prompted, buttering a scone. 'When was that?'

'Aye, well, it was just a couple of days after you were here.' Iris began pouring the tea.

'Not the same person who made an offer on the farm?' I asked.

'No. He was all suited up. I remember because it had been raining and he trod in a puddle of muck near the gate. Dirtied those nice shiny shoes of his, it did.' She frowned as if forcing herself to remember the details. 'He wasn't from up here – somewhere down south, I'd reckon.'

'The man who wanted to buy your silver?' Robbie asked, reaching for another scone.

'No, the man who wanted to buy my farm.' Iris spoke as if she were scolding an inattentive schoolboy. 'The one who wanted to buy my silver was from around here.' She frowned again and took a sip from her teacup. 'Not from here, exactly, but definitely a Yorkshireman. He was older too, maybe your age, Philly, but trying to make out he was younger – you know the type.'

I nodded; I did know the type. 'Did he just turn up?'

'Aye. Pulled up where you've parked today and knocked at the door as bold as brass.'

'Did you notice what type of car he was driving?' Robbie had a way of making even a pointed question sound almost conversational.

She bobbed her chin. 'It was a Land Rover, but much newer than yours, Philly. Black, I think.' She tilted her head as she remembered. 'Nay, not black, dark grey.'

'Did you invite him into the cottage?' Robbie brushed a crumb from his notebook, pen poised to record her answer.

'I didn't want to let him in, but he asked for a glass of water, and I couldn't say no, could I?'

I shook my head. 'No, you couldn't. Can you remember exactly what he said?'

Iris's eyes narrowed on me. 'Are you thinking he might have something to do with the robbery?'

I glanced at Robbie. 'Perhaps. It does seem a coincidence that he turns up and then a few days later ...' I reached for the teapot and poured more tea for her.

'Thanks, pet. Now, what did he say?'

'Take your time,' Robbie said, his tone gentle.

'I might be seventy-six, lad, but I'm still as sharp as a tack,' she scolded. 'I told him he'd better come in and gave him some water from the tap. I had a batch of teacakes I'd just taken from the oven – it was my day to go and see Esme, you see.' As my brows raised in silent question, she elaborated. 'Esme Hall – she's Albert Horsley's sister, you know. Lost her husband a few years back and had a fall a month or so ago. Tripped over a ladder in the shed, she did. Said she'd gone to investigate an intruder.' Iris scoffed at the possibility. 'I'll 'appen there was no intruder; more like she'd had an extra sherry and forgotten the ladder was there.' It was all I could do not to smile. 'I like to visit her on Monday so it must've been Monday before last that he was here.' I glanced again at Robbie, who nodded almost imperceptibly.

'Did you tell him you were on your way out?' I tried to keep my tone casual as if the answer didn't really matter.

'Aye. He saw the teacakes and said they looked good and hinted that I give him one, but I wasn't having any of that. I said I was on my way out and they were for a friend who was poorly so he wouldn't be getting any. Then so he didn't get too comfortable, I asked him what he was doing here.' She took another sip of her tea. 'At first, he ignored my question and asked what was wrong with my friend, and I said that she'd had a fall and Monday was my day for visiting her.' Here Iris paused again. 'Why is it that when you're younger you fall over, but when you're old, falling over is having a fall?' She didn't seem to be expecting an answer, so I shrugged in response. 'I asked him again, direct like. I said, "What are you doing here?" and I gave him one of my stares – the ones that mean I don't have time for any funny business.' She demonstrated the stare.

'It would be enough to scare me.' I laughed.

'It worked on him too. He told me he worked for a York auction house and heard I was interested in selling some of my antiques.' As I was about to interrupt and ask how he'd heard that and reassure her I'd said nothing, she added. 'Of course I told him that was rubbish and what made him think I even had anything to sell. Well, his tone changed then; he put his hands up as if I'd got him on that one and he dropped the charming act. Then he said he hadn't heard anything, but the auction house he worked for had suggested he might like to call in on some of the farms in the area and see if they had anything they wanted to sell. Then he said the person he worked for was more honest than most dealers who wouldn't give me a good price for what I had. Don't worry, though, Philly, I stood up for you and said the dealer I work with was so honest she'd refused to take some of my silver and our mum's rings because she could tell I didn't really want to part with them.'

I smiled my thanks, but my mind was whirring with questions.

'He said that you must be one of the few trustworthy dealers in the area and that he'd leave me to get on with my day. Before he left, he asked me to have another think about whether I wanted to part with my treasures because there's no use for those old things these days and my grandchildren certainly wouldn't appreciate them. "Why shouldn't you have the money now?" he said. I didn't tell him I didn't have any grandchildren, but I told him I'd think about it – not because I was going to think seriously about it, of course, but more because I wanted to get rid of him so I could go and see Esme. I knew she'd be worried if I was late, you see.'

I inclined my head. 'Did he happen to tell you his name?'

'He did. Ron someone or other. Jackson? In fact'—she pursed her lips—'he left me a card. Now, where did I put it?'

She pulled down a folk-art letter holder from on top of the fridge and rifled through the contents. 'If we know his name, it should be easy to find him, and then I can get my stuff back.'

'If it was the same person,' I said cautiously.

'I was sure I put it here.' Iris tipped the brochures out of the letter holder. 'But it's not here now.' She looked up, her faded blue gaze on Robbie. 'Maybe he took it when he broke in – so I wouldn't be able to identify him.'

'Did he see you put it away?' Robbie's expression gave nothing away, but there was concern in his voice. This was sounding very much like a well-planned burglary.

Her gaze fell. 'Aye. I told him I wouldn't be needing it

but would keep it anyway. I only took it to get rid of him.' Her voice, which had been strong as she told her story, was beginning to waver.

I stood and patted her arm lightly. 'Don't go thinking any of this is your fault, Iris. You weren't to know.' I handed her the brochures and other business cards to return to the holder. Most were takeaway menus from Malton restaurants, and I wondered how often she'd used them. One was for an Indian takeaway that had closed years ago.

'What Philly said is right.' Robbie's tone was kind. 'These people know what they're doing. Can you remember what this Ron Jackson looked like?'

Iris sat back at the kitchen table, her momentary wobble over. 'As I said, he was about your age, Philly – midfifties, I suppose.' I preened at the thought of looking younger than my almost sixty. Iris ran her eyes up and down the length of Robbie. 'About the inspector's height, I'd say, grey hair, but cut short at the front … maybe a bit too long at the back.' Her brow furrowed and her nose wrinkled as she cast her mind back. 'He was wearing grey suit pants with black shoes – scruffy though, not clean like the real estate agent. He had one of them sleeveless jumpers on – black wool, it was – and a black overcoat – a bit like yours, Inspector.'

Robbie nodded as he scribbled in his notebook. 'What about his build? Was he fat, thin?'

Iris's teeth caught the side of her lower lip. 'Average for a man his age.' She chuckled to herself. 'Would fancy a pint and a plate of ham, chips and eggs, I'd say.'

Robbie pretended not to notice my grin, closed his notebook and took his glasses off. 'Thanks for that, Iris; you've given us more to go on.' He stood and shrugged his jacket back on. 'Don't forget to warn your friends about this character.'

'I won't,' Iris said solemnly. 'Let me know when you collar him,' she said with a completely straight face. I had to turn away to hide a giggle that threatened to escape at her turn of phrase. 'And don't forget the scones for Albert,' she added, standing to wrap them in a clean tea towel. 'Tell him I'll pick this up when I see him next week.'

'Will do, Iris.' I kissed her lightly on the cheek. 'You take care now.'

'Mind how you go, Philly. You too, Inspector.'

Chapter Four

Before speaking, I waited until we were on the lane that joined the road back towards Chipwell. 'You think this isn't an isolated incident, don't you?'

'Aye, I do.'

'He was smart enough to have a business card to make his visit look legitimate, but also to remember to take it back in case anyone links his visit with the robbery.'

Robbie nodded. 'I'll check the records when I'm back and see if there are any others who have been broken into in a similar way.'

'Don't let DI Whitely know; he might try and steal your glory.' I laughed, but I was only half joking. The new inspector sounded like one of those numbers-driven policemen who might jump on the tail of an investigation if it meant he'd look good to his superior officer. Stewart had been an expert at it. Yet closing something like this would be the best way for Robbie to finish his career.

He cast me a quick sideways glance but didn't contradict me. 'That's Dunthrop up ahead,' he said. 'You're going to need to direct me from here; I have no idea where we're going.'

I shook my head a little; I was getting way ahead of myself. At this point, we had an isolated robbery in an isolated cottage – there was no evidence it was anything bigger than that. 'You'll need to take a left up ahead.'

As we pulled up to a stop outside the Horsley farmhouse, Jess rose to her feet from where she'd been lying in the weak winter sun on the gravelled courtyard and barked.

Albert appeared from inside the house and shuffled across to the dog. 'There's a good girl, Jess. It's just Philly Barker.' Ruffling the dog's head, he called, 'Ow do, pet? I wasn't expecting to see you again so soon. And who's this you've brought with you?'

'This is Inspector Robbie Dawkins, Albert. Robbie and I have just come from Iris Metcalfe's.' I lifted the tea-towel-wrapped bundle in my hands. 'I told her I was going to call in on you and she sent these with me.' After handing the scones to Albert, I bent to pat the dog, who greeted me like a long-lost friend.

'Iris told me she'd had some trouble,' Albert said, shaking Robbie's hand. 'Is that what took you out there?'

Robbie nodded. 'Yes, and Philly came along because she knew the pieces that had been stolen.'

Albert pursed his lips and shook his head slowly. 'It's a bad business when you're not safe in your own home.

You'd better be coming in then.'

'Do you lock your doors when you go out?' I asked as we followed him into the house. Like Iris's cottage, we entered through a boot room, a brown wax jacket, an olive waxed gilet and a tweed jacket hung on hooks, a few woollen flat caps beside them, and straight into the kitchen. A round oak table stood on a faded rug, an equally faded upholstered chair sat in one corner close to the fire, the walnut occasional table beside it with a pipe and a rolled up newspaper hinting it was Albert's favoured place to sit. An oversized oak dresser full of plates took up almost the entirety of another wall.

'Nay, pet. I've never locked them in all the years I've been here, and I'm not going to start now. Besides'—he gave his dog's head another affectionate ruffle—'Jess here would see anyone off, and at this time of the year, I'm unlikely to stray far from the fire.'

I opened my mouth to say more, but at a warning look from Robbie, I shut it again; I would've been wasting my breath.

'You'll be wanting a brew?' Albert had already put the kettle on the hob.

'Aye, that would be grand.' Robbie's tone was one of resignation. Yorkshire hospitality being as it was, no was not an acceptable answer.

'Have you had a look in that box I left you?' Albert asked.

'Not yet. I was going to do it this morning, but ...' I opened my hands wide and shrugged.

'No rush, pet. It's just a few bits and bobs, but our Jenny wants me to start clearing out the barn and the other sheds. That husband of hers probably has his eyes set on a barn conversion or summat. I said to her, he'll have to wait until I'm gone, he will.'

'Maybe she's just concerned about you having a fall,' I suggested. If they were anything like the sheds I inspected after the owners had passed away, I could only imagine what was in there. The messy pile of paperwork and newspapers on the dresser gave me a hint that the shed wouldn't be likely to be any tidier.

'One of them buggers were around here the other day wanting to buy the place,' Albert said as he put some of the scones onto a plate, wrapping the remainder to keep them fresh. 'I sent him on his way quick smart. Wouldn't be surprised if our Jenny's Jim had given him the word. Barn conversion ...' He shook his head as though the very phrase was abhorrent to him. 'Said I'd get good money, he did. Summat about how there was a market for holiday lets and second homes and the like.'

'Iris said she'd had someone come by making a similar offer,' I said tentatively.

'Oh aye, she mentioned that. Esme did too.' Albert shakily set the tea things on the table, an assortment of china cups that rattled in their mismatched saucers. Meakin,

I guessed, serviceable but not particularly collectible. I didn't hold out hope of finding much in the box he'd brought into me, but Iris had referred him ...

'Let me pour,' I offered, hoping he wouldn't be insulted by my offer.

'Aye.' His smile was small and grateful.

'I don't suppose ...' I glanced quickly at Robbie, who gave me a tiny nod. 'I don't suppose someone has been around wanting to buy antiques from you? A Ron Jackson?'

He pulled on his white-whiskered chin. 'There was someone who came by ... That might've been his name. I didn't let him in, though.'

'When was he here?' Robbie leant forward, warming his hands on the teacup.

'Last week some time.' He shook his head as if frustrated by his inability to remember the details. 'Sometimes the days all seem the same. I told Iris about it, and that was when she told me about you. Said if I wanted to sell anything, I should talk to you first. She said you'd do me a fair price.'

I smiled gratefully. 'I'm glad she did.'

'Would you know him again if you saw him?' Robbie reached again for his notepad and glasses.

Albert scratched idly at his whiskered jaw, the lines on his forehead deep. 'Aye. I've seen him since and recognised him alright then ...' I resisted the urge to prompt him and glanced across at Robbie, who appeared relaxed but alert.

It was an expression I was getting to know well. Albert nodded to himself, a triumphant half smile curving his lips as the pieces slid into place. 'That was it – it was at The White Horse. He was talking to Gordon Willoughby – he's got a horse place down the road a bit. Wych Tree Farm.'

Robbie jotted the name in his notebook. 'Did it look as though this Gordon Willoughby knew him?'

Albert shook his head. 'Couldn't say, but Gordon would bend the ear of anyone who bought him a pint.'

'When you say he has a horse place, did you mean racing stables?' I wouldn't have thought racing stables would be a good target. There'd bound to be people coming and going all the time.

'Nay, one of those e-questrian places.' He elongated the e. 'Riding and whatnot.' He narrowed his eyes. 'Are you thinking he's the one – this Ron Jackson character – who broke into Iris's place?'

Robbie caught my eye, his brows rising.

'You do, don't you? So that would mean the Willoughby place could be next.' Thoughts whirled across his face.

'I don't think we can speculate in that direction yet,' warned Robbie. 'This man might have absolutely nothing to do with what happened to Iris.'

The look of pure innocence that came over Albert's face told me he didn't believe a word of it – and that he would be straight on the phone to Iris as soon as we left the premises. That would be all we needed – a posse of elderly

Yorkshire farmers on the rampage.

And that's exactly what Robbie said not long after in the car when we'd said our goodbyes and left Albert and Jess. 'He'll be straight on the phone to Iris, won't he?'

'Probably.' I didn't tell him that Iris had probably already phoned every other elderly farmer she knew in the district too.

'That's all we need.' His sigh was resigned.

'Look on the bright side. If any of their friends have received a visit from Ron Jackson, they'll know to be on their guard. And if they haven't yet, they'll know to call you if they do.'

'As long as they call me,' he said with a brief but meaningful glance in my direction. 'And don't try to take the law into their own hands or bypass me to go straight to you.'

I couldn't suppress my grin at the idea of Iris, Albert, and any of their cronies brandishing rolling pins at a cowering Ron Jackson. 'If they do call me …'

'Which we both know they will …'

'I'll be sure to let you know.'

He let out a little snort of disbelief and shook his head once. 'Of course you will.'

'So what's on your agenda for this afternoon?' I asked, deliberately changing the subject.

'I'll head back to the station and check the records for any unsolved robberies that look similar to Iris's,' he said.

'What about you?'

I shrugged. 'The usual. I'll look through that box of Albert's, and then I thought Bally and I might try somewhere different for supper tonight.'

Even though his eyes hadn't strayed from the road, from the set of his jaw, I could tell they would've been suspicious. 'And where would that be?' His voice sounded weary as if he already knew the answer but had decided to ask anyway.

'The White Horse at Dunthrop,' I replied with my shiniest halo on. 'I've heard good things about it.'

'I don't suppose there's any point in me asking you not to go?'

'I don't know why you wouldn't want me to.' The halo gleamed brightly.

'In that case, what time do you want me to pick you up?'

Chapter Five

By two in the afternoon, the sun had given up its battle against the rain that had been threatening all day, and like yesterday, customers were few and far between. Simon had gone to Beverley for an auction, and Bell had taken the afternoon off to join him. While we all knew they'd been dating for a few months now, they'd both kept quiet about it at first and even now were acting in a 'nothing to see here' sort of way. Bell because she didn't believe anyone else had the right to her business and Simon because I don't think he quite believed that after having a crush on her for so long, she'd finally said yes.

In any case, I'd told her that between Eugene, Ambrose and myself, we'd manage to look after her shop – although so far, I'd served just one customer, selling a black wool cloche.

With the shop all tidy and in order and my to-do list ticked off, I pulled Albert's box from the shelf and carefully placed it on my desk before the bottom fell out. 'That was lucky,' I said to Balthazar, who raised his head briefly before dropping it back onto his paws. 'Now, what do we have in here?'

'Talking to yourself again, Philly?' Eugene walked in. Always immaculately attired, today's tweed suit – right down to the waistcoat with a little gold chain across the front – reminded me of moorland heather in full bloom.

I chuckled. 'There's no one else to talk to this afternoon. What are you two up to?'

'We bought a few larger pieces at yesterday's auction, so Ambrose has decided we need to move the stock around to accommodate it.'

'Which means Ambrose will be directing traffic and you'll be moving furniture and displays.' I pictured Ambrose sitting behind the massive mahogany campaign desk ordering Eugene around. At seventy-five and two years older and several inches portlier than his sprightlier brother – relatively speaking, of course – Ambrose regarded the ability to order his younger brother around as his birthright. He looked so downcast I took pity on him. 'Do you want some help?'

'Would you mind terribly?'

'Not at all. I was just going to have a look through this box, but I can do that any time.' I whistled for Bally, and we both headed to the adjacent shop, Bally keeping plenty of distance between himself and where Rochester was curled up in his basket behind Ambrose's desk.

'Philly! Has that brother of mine brought you in to

help?' Ambrose, resplendent in woodland tweed, peered over the wire-rimmed glasses that sat low on his nose.

'It was no bother; besides, I get a first look at your newest purchases. That has to be worth the effort of moving a few pieces around.'

'And hanging a few pictures.' Eugene pointed to the pile of timber-framed maps resting against one of the glass cabinets.

I looked at the stepladder and sighed; I should have known I'd be roped into ladder-climbing activities. Pulling out one of the maps, I examined it. 'What is this? It looks like a normal map, but … Is that German writing?'

'It is indeed – both a regular map and with German writing. It is, in fact, a Second World War bomber map. The Germans reproduced our maps and overlaid them with strategic information. We managed to pick up six of them yesterday.' Ambrose had his thumbs in the fob pockets of his waistcoat and was puffed with pride.

'We've been waiting for a lot like this to come on the market.' Eugene lifted one of the maps and traced its contours with his finger. 'We were lucky that yesterday was such a dreadful day – it kept some of the other serious bidders away.'

'Their loss.' I wiped at some dust on the edge of the frame.

'Indeed,' said Ambrose. 'Now, lass, I was thinking you could hang them in a line on that wall.' He pointed towards a roll-topped tambour writing desk. 'And that writing desk could be moved to that wall.' He pointed in the opposite direction.

I met Eugene's eyes and rolled mine.

It was another two hours before Bally and I made our escape back to my shop, and I'd no sooner pulled an item from Albert's box before my first customers of the afternoon arrived. The four women shared they were on a girl's trip and had been into York shopping and for tea at Betty's and had called in on their way back to their accommodation in nearby Westow.

One excitedly saw the little stoneware jug I'd taken from Albert's box and simply had to have it – as well as an assortment of Victorian jelly moulds. I also sold a Troika vase I'd never really liked and some vintage duck decoys for a ridiculous amount of money. Another of the party bought two scarves and a navy-blue forties tea dress from Bell's shop, while the fourth member of the group ummed and aahed over an art nouveau silver hat pin before buying a Scandinavian blue enamelled brooch.

With a happy sigh, I locked up after them and had another wistful look at Albert's box – which would need to wait until the following morning. After spending the afternoon up and down ladders and lugging furniture, books and boxes, I needed a shower and a change of clothes before heading back out this evening. I lifted my right arm and took a surreptitious sniff of my armpit. Yes, definitely a shower.

•

'I don't believe it,' muttered Robbie as we stepped into The White Horse that evening.

'What?' I cast my eye around the pub. An assortment of cooking utensils, enamel pots and mugs hung from timbered ceiling rafters, horse brasses lined the brick-walled fireplace, and various other agricultural implements were scattered here and there.

Robbie inclined his head and, with a wry smile, said, 'Look who's at that table.'

When I noticed who he'd seen, I couldn't help the laugh that burst from me.

'How about I get our drinks while you find out what they're up to,' he suggested, resignation written all over his face.

I made my way over to the pensioners sitting around the table closest to the fire. Bally had already beaten me there and was reacquainting himself with Jess.

'Albert and Iris ... what brings you here?' As if I didn't know.

Albert's ears coloured a soft pink, and he rubbed his hand over his stubbled head while Iris, forthright as ever, met my eyes, an obstinate tilt to her chin. 'We fancied a night out, didn't we?' She looked at her companions for agreement and introduced the third member of their little party. 'This is Esme, she's Albert's sister. Esme, this is Philly

— I told you about her. And that man at the bar is Inspector Dawkins – he's the policeman on the case.'

Again I suppressed a grin at her turn of phrase.

'We're on a stake-out, Philly.' Esme beamed, excitement written all over her face. She flinched suddenly and scowled at Iris. 'Why did you do that? That's my good leg. I had a fall, you see, Philly. Fell over a ladder that shouldn't have been there, I did.' She held her leg out and lifted the hem of her navy trousers so I could see the bandage around her mottled calf. 'It's been nearly a month, and I still need to go back to Doctor Dobson every week to have the dressing changed. When you get to my age, your skin takes a while to heal. I can take the dressing off and show you if you like?'

'No.' I chuckled, not wanting the sight to upset my appetite. 'That's fine. But what stake-out are you here for?'

Esme opened her mouth to answer, but Iris silenced her with a steely stare. 'Albert said he'd seen Ron Jackson in here, so we thought we'd do your policeman's job for you.'

As I would have said, 'He's not my policeman,' Iris narrowed her eyes and said, 'Are you advising on stolen antiques tonight too?'

I hoped the flush in my cheeks would be attributed to the heat of the fire, but Robbie was there.

'No, we're here as two friends having a night out,' he said. 'Not,' he added with his serious face on, 'that it's any business of yours.'

Iris, however, was unabashed and tapped the side of

her nose. 'Don't worry, Inspector, your secret is safe with us.'

With a sigh, Robbie handed me my glass of Rioja and addressed the elderly trio. 'If you three are doing what I think you're doing, you need to stop and leave it to us.'

'Do you mean we should leave it to you and Philly or you and the constabulary?' Iris looked as though butter wouldn't melt in her mouth. Albert was saying little but grinning widely as though it was the best night's entertainment he'd had in a long time. 'Anyway, we're here as three friends having a night out.'

Albert guffawed, and Esme said, 'But you said we were on a stake-out for Ron Jackson.'

Iris shook her head in a gesture of 'you can't get good help these days' and I laughed and said, 'We'll leave you to it.'

Robbie led me to a round wooden table far enough away from the bar that we wouldn't be heard, but angled so we could see anyone who came in.

'What are those three like?' Robbie rolled his eyes as he asked the question.

'I know, but it's perfectly harmless, and they're having a bit of fun. Besides, it's not as though they're interfering with your investigation.' I took a sip of wine, relishing the earthy warmth that spread across my chest. 'Is there an investigation?'

Robbie wiped the beer froth from the top of his lips with the back of his hand. 'Aye, there's an investigation.'

He hesitated only briefly before adding, 'I went through the files, and there are other cases, but …'

'No one has spent any time on them.'

He nodded. 'I can't say that I blame them – an isolated instance of a farmer leaving their door unlocked and having a few pieces of silver stolen …' He shrugged. 'They would simply have been lectured about locking their doors and told that someone would look into it. A few calls would be made; it would be written up and put to one side.' He grimaced. 'No, it's not something that would be prioritised.'

'Are there any similarities?'

'Just the fact that they tend to have been older people, living alone in relatively isolated farmhouses. There's no mention of anyone calling by looking for antiques in the days or weeks preceding the robberies, and there was no mention of anyone named Ron Jackson.' He frowned slightly, the furrows in his brow appearing deeper in the dim light. 'But then, no one probably thought to ask about that. I certainly didn't – it took you being there for Iris to offer it.'

'Did you mention it to Stewart?'

He nodded. 'Aye. I told him I think there's a pattern and I'd like to follow it up some more and that I'd like to keep you on as a consultant of sorts.'

'An antique consultant to the York constabulary. I like the sound of that. It will almost be like the old days when I was on the force.'

He chuckled at that. 'Hardly. But if you can get

someone to look after the shop … You have a way of getting people to open up to you. I wouldn't involve you if I thought there was any danger …'

'Bell will keep an eye on things. I need to finish looking through the box Albert left me, but other than that …' I didn't get to finish what I was saying as Iris claimed my attention, madly waving from their table and beckoning me over. Robbie and I exchanged a 'what now' look. 'I think I'm being summonsed.'

'While you're gone, I'll look through the menu.'

'And probably have ham, eggs and chips anyway.' I grinned at his predictability.

'Away with you.' He hid his smile in his pint glass.

'What's so important?' I said mock-sternly when I presented myself as requested at the pensioner's table.

'See that couple over there?' Albert pointed towards a man and a woman who had recently entered the bar.

'What about them?' Both around my age – late fifties – the woman had taken a seat at the table next to where Robbie and I were sitting while her companion was at the bar waiting to be served.

Albert leant forward in his seat so he could speak in a conspiratorial whisper. 'That's the man Ron Jackson was speaking to when I saw him. Gordon Willoughby.'

'Not that we know for sure that the man who called in at your place and came here for a beer is the same man who went to Iris's,' I reminded him.

Iris leant in. 'I think we all know it is. There can't be two Ron Jacksons running around wanting to buy antiques and then coming back to rob defenceless women.'

'We still don't have any evidence ...' Looking at the three disdainful faces before me, I didn't finish what I was going to say – they wouldn't have believed it any more than I did. 'Okay, I'll see if we can get him talking.'

Iris nodded approvingly. 'If you've got it under control, we'll leave you and Inspector Dawkins to it. Esme here needs to get home, and we haven't had our tea yet.'

'You can let us know how you go,' said Albert, rising to put his waxed jacket on.

'We'll make sure our friends are warned,' said Esme, reaching for the walker beside her chair.

I said my goodbyes and, seeing the man Albert had identified as Gordon Willoughby was still waiting at the bar, made my way there to replenish Robbie's and my drinks.

Other drinkers were sitting on bar stools, so I had to squeeze between them to get to the counter. As I did, I nudged Gordon Willoughby's elbow. 'I'm so sorry,' I said when he spun towards me, seemingly ready to say something to whoever had knocked him. Upon seeing it was a woman, however, his ruddy face softened into an easy smile.

'You're right. No harm. I hope you're not in a hurry, though, he's taking his time.' Clean-shaven – head as well as jaw – he had an open, approachable face and was dressed in jeans, brown dealer boots and a light blue cotton twill shirt under a navy wool jumper.

'Sorry to keep you waiting.' The barman was finally off the phone. 'What'll it be?'

My neighbour placed his order. 'Busy tonight, Marty?'

'Not too bad,' the barman replied in an Australian accent.

'It's been a while since I heard an accent like that,' I commented.

The barman grinned widely and passed the pint across to Gordon before pouring white wine into a glass. 'You're a long way from home, too.'

'I've been here for so many years, though, I reckon I've lost most of my accent.'

'You haven't,' said Gordon, paying the barman. 'It's still there.' He winked at me and took the drinks to where his wife waited.

I chuckled and gave Marty our order. 'Where are you from?'

'Brisbane,' he said. 'I came over here just before lockdown, and when I couldn't get home, decided to wait it out. Then I met Ellie – she works here too'—he sent a smile towards the pretty brunette carrying plates of food—'and didn't want to go home. Well, not yet anyway.'

'That's how I ended up staying,' I said. 'Met a man and the rest is history.'

'He must've made it worth it,' he said with a meaningful glance over at Robbie.

I leant in closer. 'Different man,' I said with a cheeky grin and, after paying, took my drinks back to our table, leaving Marty laughing.

'What was that about?' Robbie asked.

'Oh, just a joke with the barman,' I dismissed. 'Are you ready to order?'

We'd almost finished our meals when the man Albert had identified as Gordon Willoughby turned around and began talking to us. 'How long has it been since you were in Australia?' he asked.

Even though we had chatted lightly at the bar his abrupt question surprised me and I had to think through my answer. 'Umm, it would have to be about five years. My daughter lives over there.'

He nodded thoughtfully. 'Is it true that everything stops for the Melbourne Cup?'

Robbie frowned slightly, probably, like me, wondering where this line of enquiry was going.

'I don't know if it still does – it certainly used to. These days there's a lot more controversy about the race, though, so not everyone gets into it the way they did when I was growing up.'

At this, his wife turned around, an apologetic look on her face. 'I'm so sorry.' To her husband, she said, 'Gordon, these people were trying to have a quiet dinner.'

'No, it's okay. In fact'—I glanced quickly at Robbie—'why don't you join us?'

Robbie gestured towards the empty chairs. 'Please do.'

'If you're sure …' Gordon grabbed his beer and was out of his chair and into one of the spares at our table. His companion was slower to follow. 'Gordon Willoughby,' he said. 'And this is my wife, Marlene.'

'Nice to meet you.' Robbie extended his hand. 'I'm Robbie Dawkins, and this is my friend, Philly Barker.'

After the introductions, an uncomfortable silence settled over the table. Robbie was the first to break it. 'You were asking about the Melbourne Cup; does that mean you're into horse racing?'

'Of sorts,' replied Gordon. 'We have an equestrian centre – Wych Tree Farm. Have you heard of it?'

'Can't say I have,' said Robbie. 'Is it a riding stable?'

'We have riding stables,' said Marlene, 'and a dressage ring.'

'But we also spell racehorses – that's where we lease our paddocks out to owners to graze their horses. Some owners use it for short let-ups to freshen a horse in training, and others might need an extended break after a long racing campaign. We also have facilities for broodmares and foals too.'

From the way he spoke, it was clear Gordon was used to being the centre of any conversation. Marlene had the attitude of a woman who was more accustomed to sitting back and letting her husband do all the talking. Slightly built and dressed in jeans with a pale printed shirt, she seemed the sort of woman who would blend into wherever she was without being noticed.

'That must keep you both very busy,' I commented, mentally filing away the information.

'It does. Marlene looks after the stables and the riding school, but the racehorses are my thing. And now we're getting into holiday letting as well … there's plenty to keep us occupied.'

'Holiday lets? That can be a lot of work,' I prompted.

'We only have a couple at the moment,' said Gordon. 'Outbuildings that we've converted, but I'm looking for more. That's where the money is these days – in barn conversions for short-term lets.'

As Gordon espoused further on his subject, Robbie smiled tightly and took a mouthful of his beer.

Marlene, who had been sitting back listening, addressed me. 'I feel as though I know you, Philly – or at least your name … What do you do?'

'I'm an antique dealer. I have a shop in Chipwell Barn Antiques.'

'Of course!' Marlene slapped her thigh lightly. 'I love your shop. Gordon, that was where I bought your Christmas present a couple of years ago. It was of a chestnut horse with a jockey. The background had white racing barriers in it. You probably sell so much you don't remember it.'

'No, I do recall it – a nineteenth-century English racehorse in the style of George Stubbs.' I'd bought the painting cheaply at auction and had made a nice profit on the sale.

'Philly never forgets an antique,' said Robbie wryly.

'Particularly when it was such a nice piece. If you're into horsey antiques, I have a rather lovely Edwardian vesta case with an enamel picture of a hound that's come in and another oil – a hunting scene, early twentieth century.'

'I'll have to drop by,' Marlene said, her finger tracing the stem of her wine glass. 'You'd think that after working with horses every day, we'd be over them, but I do have a nice collection of equestrian-related antiques. You should come by and see it one day.'

'I'd like that,' I said.

'That's a great idea. You can tell us which pieces are worth anything. After all, if Marlene here is going to buy more, I might need to off-load some so we have room in the display cabinet.' Gordon laughed heartily at his joke.

It wasn't long after that Robbie said, 'Well, Philly, I know we've both got a busy day ahead, so I'd better get you home.'

Marlene looked at her watch. 'Goodness, is that the time? I've got a full day tomorrow too.'

'It's been lovely to meet you both,' I said, leaning down to pick up my bag from the floor.

'Don't forget to drop by sometime to see my collection,' said Marlene, slipping her handbag over her shoulder. 'I'd really like your opinion.'

'Actually'—Gordon slid his chair under the table— 'what are you both doing on Sunday?' He sent a glance to his wife, who smiled and nodded. 'Come by for a drink, and we'll show you around. Let's say four.'

'That's very kind of you. Robbie?'

'Aye, we'll see you then,' said Robbie.

'I might drop by the shop to look at the items you mentioned before that,' said Marlene.

'I look forward to seeing you; if you like, I can give you a call if those items sell.'

She opened her handbag and handed me a card. 'Great idea. Here's my card with our details on it.'

We said our goodbyes, re-donned our jackets, roused Bally from his position by the fire (it's a dog's life) and stepped out into the night. A light drizzle was falling, the drops seeming suspended in the light above the pub sign.

'They seem friendly,' I ventured as we headed towards the car park.

'Hmmm,' said Robbie. 'Very friendly and, dare I say it, a little too friendly?'

'Is that just your copper's inbuilt suspicion showing?' I laughed so he wouldn't take me seriously, but his profile didn't change.

'Maybe. Probably … we'll see …'

Chapter Six

After checking that Bell was happy to keep an eye on the shop – and Bally – while I was out with Robbie, the first order of business for the next morning was to finally look through the box Albert had left. Aside from the stoneware jug I'd already sold, the rest were odd bits of china, a couple of commemorative spoons, and a plate from the last coronation. It was all readily saleable but nothing special.

It wasn't until I pulled out the last newspaper-wrapped piece that I found it – a solid oak ashtray with a horseshoe on the top and a little carved mouse sitting on the side. Being simple, practical, beautiful and exceptionally crafted, it was a perfect example of the Arts and Crafts movement. My heart did a happy dance, and I was still grinning when Simon loped in. Dressed in his usual jeans, band T-shirt and flannel shirt – today's band was something obscure I'd never heard of – Simon reminded me of a dog who didn't quite know how tall he was and, as a result, forever bumped into things.

When he saw what I was holding, his cheerful greeting

smile froze. 'Is that what I think it is?'

'If you're thinking it's a Mouseman ashtray, then yes.' My fingers traced the smooth lines of the heavy oak ashtray.

Robert 'Mousey' Thompson had been a furniture maker from Kilburn – about twenty-five miles north-west of Chipwell. His signature was a small carved mouse on every piece. Although he passed away midway through the last century, the factory was still operating and pieces from his lifetime were highly collectible.

Simon slipped his reading glasses on, the cord that kept them around his neck so he wouldn't lose them hanging loosely against his shirt. 'This is an old one – and quite rare. He stopped carving the paws in the thirties – they had a habit of breaking off … This one, though, is in nice condition.' He looked up, his grin matching mine. 'The horseshoe on top is a racing slipper, so I'd say it was originally a commissioned piece – and will go down nicely with the horsey set.'

'What would you put on it? I was thinking a couple of hundred.'

'As a value?' I nodded. He tapped his bottom lip. 'Yes, three hundred on a good day, but to a collector, possibly more.' He let the glasses hang from their chain. 'If it were me, I'd take this to auction – it would be the best chance of getting top price. Where did it come from?'

'A customer of mine out near Dunthrop. It was in a box of items he wanted me to look at. I want to make sure I give him a good price.'

'Do you know if he has more? I have customers who would pay good money for anything from, say, the thirties through to the sixties.'

Simon's face lit up with excitement, something I hadn't seen in quite a while. 'I doubt it … but I'll check next time I'm out there.'

'That would be grand. On another note, Bell tells me you're involved in some investigation with that policeman of yours.' His mop of curly grey hair flopped over his eyes, and he pushed his glasses onto the top of his head to keep it out of the way. 'Maybe I'd better swap that cream chair for another that won't show the blood.'

'Oh, haha. I'll have you know I didn't get a drop on the last one, but seriously, if you have something else, please do swap it over. I'm paranoid about getting this one all dusty.'

His mouth curved into a wry smile. 'I'll see what I can do.' With a wave, he was off.

To ensure the ashtray wouldn't get sold until after I'd had a chance to talk to Albert, I placed it under lock and key in the storeroom and priced everything else for display and sale.

Robbie arrived just before ten, and once we were in the car and on our way, he filled me in on the day's schedule. 'Our first stop this morning is near Birdslip – Eddie Mayne. He placed a complaint three weeks ago, although the problem is he doesn't know *when* he was robbed, only that he was.'

'Another one who routinely leaves his door open and just happened to notice that his box of treasures was gone?'

'Something like that,' agreed Robbie. 'Assorted silverware and some jet jewellery. He kept it in—'

'—a Terry's of York chocolate box?' Robbie nodded ruefully. Over the years I'd seen so many chocolate boxes or biscuit tins filled with assorted jewellery and other trinkets. 'If it was jet, I'd say the jewellery would be Victorian mourning jewellery, but I'll know more when I talk to him. Who else do we have?'

'Jane King from Upper Kirby. She lodged her complaint last week. Lost her mother's dressing table set – whatever that means – and assorted silverware.'

'Have you memorised the cases?' It was impressive how he could just rattle the details off.

'There wasn't much to memorise.' A sardonic tilt pulled his lips. 'The attending officers took the barest of details – which is what I suspect this individual is banking on. He doesn't take very much and what he does take is easily transported and not readily identifiable.'

'So if Iris hadn't been robbed and Stewart hadn't put you on the detective version of garden leave, he might've continued to get away with it.'

'He still could; after all, I nearly made the same mistake. I wouldn't have made the connection between someone scouting the house for antiques if I hadn't taken you with me that day.'

He took his eyes off the road briefly and smiled gratefully at me, his approval filling me with a warm glow.

'Who else do we have on the list?'

'Delwyn Ross – also from Upper Kirby. She was robbed last Wednesday.'

I shook my head. 'I can't believe that no one put these together! If it is Ron Jackson, he's quite confident.'

'Yes, which means he's liable to take more risks – and when he takes more risks, he'll make more mistakes.'

Eddie Mayne was almost a carbon copy of Albert Horsley – except that where Albert had a stubbled jaw, Eddie had a thick white beard. Other than that, they were cut from the same Yorkshire plaid. Eddie's dog, Lassie, an elderly golden labrador, came out to meet us when we arrived and treated us as long-expected guests.

'I thought you buggers were going to do nowt,' he said to Robbie once we'd introduced ourselves, explained the purpose for our visit and were seated with the ubiquitous cup of tea before us. 'And now you've brought an antiques expert out with you.'

'Philly's helping me with this one as it can be difficult to identify the stolen antiques,' Robbie explained.

'Well, it's about time people like me were taken seriously. You buggers are usually only interested in city crimes.'

'Are you able to tell me about the items that were taken?' I jumped in before Eddie could get into the woes of the ordinary man ignored in favour of big city issues.

'As I told the other bugger what was here, it was my grandmother's and my mother's things. It mightn't be too much to you, lass, but they meant a lot to me.'

I smiled gently at him. 'I'm sure they did. Robbie tells me you stored them in a Terry's chocolate box?'

'Aye, it was shaped like a treasure chest, and when I was a boy, that's what I thought it was – full of treasure. All my mother's precious things were in there, but as I said to that other bugger who came here wanting to buy them, they're probably worth nowt but to me.'

Robbie lifted his head slowly and reached for his notebook. 'Did you mention this to DC Park? That someone else was here wanting to buy them?'

'He didn't ask, did he.'

'I don't suppose this man told you his name?' I ventured.

'Aye, it was Ron someone or other … He even left me a business card. I put it right here on the dresser.' He sorted through the piles of correspondence on the old oak kitchen cupboard. 'It *was* right here.'

I met Robbie's eyes, that card was long gone.

'Have you seen it since the robbery?' Robbie asked, that familiar crease returning between his brows.

'No …' His eyes narrowed. 'Do you think he was the bugger that took my stuff?'

'Possibly,' Robbie conceded.

'So he took his own business card too, in case I worked it out? Crafty bugger.' He pulled at his beard, a tone that could almost be respect in his voice.

'What did he look like?' I asked.

Eddie's description matched what we'd already been given of Ron Jackson.

'Did he come into the house?' Robbie asked.

Eddie nodded. 'Said he was parched and would I mind giving him a glass of water. I couldn't say no, so I let him in, even though I was getting ready to head into town. It was my shopping day, you see.'

'Did you mention that to him?' Robbie's expression was impassive, but Eddie didn't miss a beat.

'You mean that's how he knew to come back when he did?'

Robbie nodded, and Eddie's face fell with dismay. 'Reckon as how it's my own stupid fault, then.'

Not wanting him to dwell on his mistake, I said, 'Eddie, can we go back to the jewellery? What did it look like?'

He recovered quickly. 'My mother's wedding ring was in there – just a plain gold band. There was also a black brooch with a gold flower on it. Jet, it was. And a ring that was also black – but I don't think it was the same stuff – with some shiny stones around the outside. They looked like diamonds, but our mam said they weren't.'

I took my phone out and googled Victorian mourning jewellery. 'Did it look like this?' The picture I showed him was of a striking black enamel ring rimmed with marcasite.

'Aye, like that. And another with the same stones in it.

It was silver, though. I could draw it for you.' He pulled a sheet from the notebook stuck on the fridge and roughly sketched two rings and a rectangular brooch with a stylised gold flower.

'Thanks for this, Eddie, it's useful. You said there was some silver as well?'

'Aye, it's harder to know with that – some bits and bobs. Spoons, and tongs and the like.'

'Any special patterns on any of it?'

'The spoons had a square shape at the end. There was also a wee dish with a Yorkshire rose on the bottom and a little blue charm with "Yorkshire" written on it and the rose.'

'Was it regimental? Like a medal?'

He shook his head. 'No, but come to think on it, my father's medals were in there too. This one was more like what you'd buy in a gift shop.'

Robbie's pen scratched across his notebook as he captured the details.

'Is there anything else you can think of?' Lassie nudged at my hand; I obliged and scratched her head.

'Nay. I reckon that's all.'

Robbie put his notebook into his top pocket and rose from his seat. 'Well, thanks for your time, Eddie; I'll be in touch.'

As we went to leave, something else occurred to me. 'Has anyone else been around?'

Eddie tugged at the end of his beard. 'There was that bugger wanting to know if I was of a mind to sell up. Said he could get me a good price if I wanted to. I sent him packing – my sister's boys will sell it soon enough when I'm gone. He can wait until then.'

'Have you heard from him since?' Robbie held the front door open.

'Nay.'

After saying our goodbyes, we climbed back into the car. 'This real estate guy has a habit of turning up everywhere we go,' I commented. 'It could just be a coincidence.'

'Aye, Philly, he does. And I don't believe in coincidences.'

'No, nor do I.'

The following two visits went much as the first did. We consumed more tea, and each had an almost identical story: Ron Jackson had shown up wanting to buy antiques and, on being told there were none for sale, requested a glass of water to get inside the house and into a conversation. Details of the householder's routine were accidentally disclosed, and Ron left after leaving his business card – something which each of the householders had thought lent legitimacy to the encounter – only to have the card not be there when they'd been prompted by us to look for it. When asked, each had also said they'd had a visit from a real estate agent in the days or week before.

Back at The Barn (where, fortunately, there were still a couple of portions of Ginny's cauliflower, cider and cheese soup left), we debriefed.

'The real estate agent has to have something to do with it,' I said. 'It can't possibly be a coincidence. Maybe he's the one who's doing the scouting. Maybe it's not Ron Jackson.' I was clutching at straws, but I really couldn't see how else the two could be linked.

'The real estate agent is definitely involved – I just don't know how.' Robbie dunked a piece of scone into his soup. 'I don't think he's the one doing the robberies, though. For starters, he never got through the front door of any of the houses, and whoever is robbing these people knows their routine – largely because they've told him.'

'If the real estate agent is involved, though, we're back to square one. No one has a name for him or a decent description. He's just described as being middle-aged and well dressed. That's it. It could be anyone.'

'I know,' Robbie conceded. 'I still think the key is Ron Jackson. The real estate guy is a distraction, to be sure, but I don't think he has anything to do with the robberies.'

'Hmmm.' I wiped the last piece of my scone around the bowl to pick up every last trace of soup. 'We're going to have to go back to update Catherine with this new list, aren't we?'

Nodding, he wiped his mouth with a paper serviette. 'I can do that if you've got other things you need to do this afternoon.'

'Thanks, Robbie. I know we're quiet at the moment, but I don't want to push Bell's friendship too far, and I need to get back out to see Albert and pay him for what he's already given me. Did I tell you what was in that box?'

Robbie grinned as my shoulders lifted at the memory of the little ashtray. 'No, but I've seen that look on your face before, so it must be something special.'

'Oh, it is.'

To his credit, he listened patiently as I told him about the piece, an indulgent smile on his face. When I'd finished sharing and our conversation wound up, he rose and slid his chair under the table. 'I'd better be off. I'll let you know if anything else comes up; otherwise, I'll see you Sunday.' At my blank stare, he added, 'Wych Tree Farm ... remember?'

I shook my head, frustrated with my forgetfulness. 'Of course. I'll see you then.'

Chapter Seven

The rest of the afternoon sped by in a blur. Simon took the cream chair away and replaced it with an Arts and Crafts high-backed oak armchair from the beginning of the last century. With its peacock green upholstered seat and back and sinuous arms and legs, it was a beautiful piece of furniture and much less prone to be damaged.

'In the style of JS Henry,' Simon told me. 'But about two thousand quid cheaper. And the fabric is reproduction Christopher Dresser and won't show any blood.' He winked and earned himself a playful punch on the arm.

Bell took the opportunity of me being around to duck out to Chipwell Hall, where Lady Cunningham had been supervising a clean-out of the attics and had found some old trunks containing clothes and fabrics owned by the previous two Lady Cunninghams she thought Bell might be interested in. Since the events of last December, Lady Cunningham's lady-of-the-manor persona had slipped, and she and Bell were developing an unlikely friendship, largely thanks to a shared interest in fashion.

The Ashtons had a small group of war historians visiting from Australia that kept them busy for the afternoon, and while business wasn't exactly booming, between Bell's shop and mine, Bally and I had enough customers to keep us occupied.

It was after five and the sun was almost down when I pulled up at Albert's farm. As the sun dipped, so too did the temperature, and I jammed a woollen beanie onto my head and donned a scarf and gloves for the short walk across the cobbled yard to the kitchen door. Jess was barking inside.

'Eh up, Philly. Ow do, pet?' Albert came to the door before I could knock, Jess pushing past me to greet Bally. 'Are you coming in, then? It's right raw out there.'

'Thanks, Albert.' I rubbed my hands together. 'I wouldn't be surprised if there's not a hard frost tonight.'

'Aye. I reckon you'd be right. You'd be wanting a brew?'

'Ta. I brought you some of Ginny's parkin too.'

The older man took the offered box of sticky ginger slice and smiled his thanks. I removed my outdoor layers and hung them from the hooks in the boot room before moving into the kitchen to stand in front of the fire, my palms held up against the flames. 'That's better.' The warmth flowed through my hands and into the rest of me.

'What brings you out here, pet?' Albert poured hot water into the crazed china teapot.

'I've had a look through the box you left me and wanted to pay you for it.' I named a price that made his eyes widen.

'Away with you, pet. That's too much.' He frowned suddenly. 'I'm not needing any charity, Philly.'

'And I'm not here to offer it. There was a piece in that box that I can sell for quite a bit, so this is a fair price but still leaves me with some profit.'

Still frowning, he set the teapot on the table. 'Do you mind getting us a couple of cups from there?' He bobbed his head towards the old dresser.

'Sure.' I retrieved the cups with their matching saucers and poured our tea. 'It was the ashtray. The one with the mouse on it.'

He looked up at me, brow furrowed. 'That wee thing? With the horseshoe on the top?' I nodded. 'Well, then.' He shook his head, his lips pursed in disbelief. 'If I'd have known that mouse was worth summat, I would've shown you the others.'

'The others? You have more pieces by the same craftsman? Robert Thompson?' The words had to squeak out past my now-racing-with-excitement heart.

'Oh aye.' Albert nodded solemnly. 'My uncle used to do some work for him out at Kilburn – The Mouseman, they called him. When Uncle Bert died – he was Albert too, you see, pet – our dad brought all his things here. There's another ashtray and a few other bits around here. I don't know how he came to have it, though, although there was talk he was given it as payment for jobs. Back then, he was just starting out.' Pinching at his whiskered chin, he tilted his head to the side. 'Happens there's a table in the shed and that'—he flicked his thumb towards the dresser—'has a mouse on it somewhere too. It would be a bugger to find under that lot, though.' His smile was wry as he eyed the piles of papers that had made their home there. 'Although if it's worth a bit, it might go towards those roof repairs I'll be needing soon.'

'Do you mind?' I stood and waited for him to nod before I pushed one of the piles away to reveal the side of the dresser. There it was, running along the edge of the oak, its tail streaming behind it. With my breath quickening, I traced its tiny body with my finger; it had been beautifully carved.

'If you want to sell, I think the proceeds would easily pay for your roof repairs and more besides. I'd like to see the table too.'

'Sup up, then,' he said, and I swallowed the rest of my tea as instructed. 'We'll need the torch out there; the outside light is broken.' As he said that, he looked away, but not before I saw what could've been concern on his face.

'Is everything okay, Albert?'

'Aye.' He nodded once. 'Just kids laikin' about, I expect. There's a bit of it about. Nowt to worry yourself about, pet.'

Making it clear he didn't want to discuss the issue further, he pulled his jacket off the hook and shrugged it on over his woolly jumper. I did the same and followed the bouncing light of his torch out of the house, across the uneven cobbles of the courtyard to the old stone-built barn.

Upon reaching the door, he removed the padlock hanging loosely from the latch. 'That's not even secured, Albert,' I chided. 'What's the point of having a padlock if the keys are still hanging from it?'

'There's nowt here to be bothered stealing, pet.' Albert lifted the wrought iron latch and slid the heavy wooden door open. Reaching inside, he flicked the switch, and a dull light filled the shed – which was all I'd feared it to be. If we'd been here in daylight, I was sure I'd be able to see the layers of dust and cobwebs (and their inhabitants) more clearly, but for now, I was grateful I couldn't.

'It's under here.' He moved aside an assortment of rusty tools and lifted a dense canvas tarpaulin to display a heavy refectory-style oak table.

Simon would be able to date it more accurately, but judging from the subtle surface rippling of the hand adzed top that was apparent even in this light and under the conditions Albert had kept in, I'd place it at somewhere in the thirties. The little hairs on the back of my neck that bristled whenever I was in the vicinity of something very special stood to attention. 'Albert, this is a beautiful piece … stunning, in fact.' I used the torch on my phone and crouched down to inspect the base and legs, running my hand down the solid, turned legs to find the mouse. Yes, there it was. While it would need to be examined in daylight, it looked to be in sound condition.

I straightened and wiped my hands on my denim-clad thighs. 'If you want to sell, I can refer you to my colleague Simon. He'd make sure you get the best price for it, but honestly, Albert, it shouldn't be sitting out here; a table this beautiful deserves to be pride of place.' I stroked the top, marvelling at the patina of age. A little careful TLC and this would look amazing. 'It's such a pity you don't have the chairs that go with it.'

Albert frowned, his eyes going to the shed roof, his thumb and forefinger pinching his chin in a gesture I recognised as his thinking face. 'There could be some around somewhere – in the loft, maybe.' He shook his head. 'We're not going to find them tonight, though. If you want to bring this Simon of yours out for a look, he's welcome to come. I can't say how it's doing anyone good sitting out here.'

I pulled the tarpaulin back over the table – more reverently than it had been removed. 'I'll organise it for you, but do me a favour and keep the door padlocked. If I'm right, this is very valuable indeed.'

'Aye, pet. I'll do that,' he grudgingly agreed.

'And find somewhere else for these tools.' I picked up a mahogany-handled extension table crank. With its iron handle and hexagon-shaped end, I'd guess it didn't belong with the table under the tarpaulin. I set it back carefully on top, an issue, perhaps, for another time. 'In fact, how about I come out on Monday when the shop is shut and help you sort through this? If anything, it'll mean I don't need to worry about you having a fall.'

Albert's eyes were suspiciously moist. 'You don't need to be doing that, pet. I'm sure you've got better things to do on your day off than spend it with an old bugger like me.'

'That's as maybe,' I conceded, 'but jobs like this can be rewarding, and besides, I happen to have a soft spot for old buggers like you. After all, who knows what we'll find.' I smiled gently at him. 'Anyway, we should be getting back inside so Bally and I can leave you and Jess to have your tea.'

I shoved my hands into my jacket pockets and waited for Albert to switch the light off and slide the door shut, flicking the padlock in place with a decisive click, the sound amplified by the dark and the cold. Jess and Bally were sitting patiently waiting for us, but just as we turned to walk back across the yard to the house, I heard something that sounded like metal against stone … followed by footsteps. I held up my hand to stop Albert from going further and strained to hear. The dogs, however, had also heard and began barking. As the footsteps – for it was footsteps – pounded away down the lane, Albert and I attempted to control our dogs.

'Jess!'

'Bally!'

Both hesitated just long enough for whoever it was to climb into the car they'd parked halfway down the lane and then ran after the intruder, with me following. The vehicle

– which looked to be a dark-coloured four-wheel drive – drove off, not turning its lights on until it was far enough away for me not to read the registration plates.

The dogs, prouder of their protection work rather than their disobedience, bounced around me for congratulation on seeing the intruder off. Hands on hips, I dragged in some deep breaths before returning to the courtyard where I'd left Albert. The vehicle had driven off almost immediately which meant someone had been waiting for him … but why?

'Are you alright, pet?' Albert met me on my way back up the lane. 'You went haring off after them.' Judging by his breathing he must have shuffled after the dogs and me.

'I'm fine, just a tad out of breath – it's been a while since I ran anywhere.' I attempted to laugh it off and gasped for a breath at the same time. 'Has anything like that happened before?'

While I couldn't see his expression in the darkness, Albert gave a brief nod. 'Aye, pet. The last time was when my outside light was smashed.'

'The last time? There's been more than once?'

'Aye. There was a right commotion one night a week or so back. I thought it might have been foxes, but when I came out the next morning, something had been in my woodpile. It took me quite a bit to get it restacked, let me tell you. Then a few nights later, the light and tonight … I thought it was probably kids laikin' around … especially since Iris said she's had some trouble and Esme has too.'

Despite my lack of confidence, I put on a reassuring smile and spoke with conviction. 'It probably was kids, but we frightened them off tonight, so let's hope they won't be back. Why don't you go inside and I'll take the torch and the dogs and check around the outside of the shed – see that nothing's been damaged.'

Even though I'd seen the intruder – or intruders – drive off, I still held my breath, my heart hammering, as I stepped carefully around the barn. Swinging the torch in a wide arc, all looked untouched until the beam glinted off something metallic and cylindrical. It was only when I bent closer that I realised it was an aerosol paint can, obviously dropped in haste when the would-be vandal heard our voices. Using a clean tissue from my pocket, I gingerly picked it up, taking care not to touch it more than needed, and dropped it in one of the doggy poo bags that were always in my jacket pockets. Who knows, Robbie might be able to get some fingerprints from it.

Looking at the aerosol can, maybe it was kids skylarking about … although wayward kids didn't usually go around in four-wheel drives and why target a barn so far off the main road? Then there was the matter of Iris and Esme … Esme had said that when she fell, it was because a ladder was where she didn't remember it being …

Back in the kitchen's warmth, Albert had made a fresh brew. 'Unless you'd like something a bit stronger, pet.'

'No, thanks, tea will be fine.' I opened the bag so he could see the paint can. 'I think they had plans to redecorate your barn wall – and not in a good way.'

'You could be right.' He shook his head, his lips pursed. 'Are you going to give it to that policeman of yours to cheek for prints?'

His eyes had that same gleam I'd seen earlier – and in Iris's at the pub the other night. Now that the immediate danger had passed, I bet he'd be straight on the phone to Iris to tell her all about it. Speaking of which ... 'You mentioned Iris had had some trouble too; why didn't she tell Robbie and me?'

He shrugged. 'Probably because you didn't ask. Same as how I didn't tell you either. The thing is, pet, when you get to our age, you don't want to admit that maybe things like that shake you up.'

I held his stare until his eyes dropped, confident I understood. Both Albert and Iris prided themselves on their independence – and both had dug their heels in about staying on their farm as long as they could. Albert, without words, was telling me that nothing would drive him away.

'Right then, if you're sure you're okay, I'll leave you to your tea. I'll talk to Robbie about what's happened here and to Simon about the table, and I'll see you on Monday?' I drained my tea and stood to go.

'Aye, pet, that would be grand.'

'And please, Albert, lock your doors at night. I don't

want to be losing sleep worrying about you.' I kissed his whiskered cheek and chuckled when he coloured.

As I drove home, I phoned Robbie – hands-free of course – and filled him in on the evening's shenanigans.

At the end of the telling, he was silent for long enough for me to worry we'd been cut off. 'Robbie?'

'I'm deciding how to tell you I wished you'd phoned me before checking the property on your own in the dark in a way that won't have you angry with me for treating you like someone who can't look after herself,' he finally said slowly, his tone serious.

'You know that all came out loud, don't you?' Picturing his wry smile, I chuckled. 'Seriously though, Robbie, there was no danger – I'd already seen him – or them – drive off. And I had the dogs with me.'

'Balthazar the protective cocker spaniel and Jess the sheepdog – yes, they'd be enough to frighten off any would-be assailant.'

'Maybe not, but their barks sound bigger than they are and would certainly make someone think twice. Besides, as I said, I'd assessed the situation, and there was no need for you to come out there. I found something though – an aerosol paint can. Don't worry, I made sure to pick it up with a tissue, barely touched it, in fact, and I've put it in a poo bag.' I glanced in the rear-view mirror. The car that had been behind me since leaving Dunthrop was still there.

'In a poo bag? That will be a new one for the fingerprint boys. If it was a paint can, maybe it was just kids larking about.'

'Perhaps. It concerned me, though, that Iris has had some similar trouble as well.' I slowed to take the turn towards Chipwell. The headlights behind me did the same thing. 'And I think Esme has too.'

'Iris? Why didn't she tell us?'

'I asked Albert the same question.'

'Let me guess – because we didn't ask.' Robbie's exasperated sigh was audible.

'Pretty much. I suspect it's a pride issue as well – I know that's the case with Albert. Speaking of which, I told him I'll spend the day there on Monday and help him clean out his shed.' The lights were still there – even though I'd adjusted my speed, they'd remained the same distance behind.

Robbie chuckled. 'Rather you than me. Anyway, you must almost be home; I'll drop around tomorrow sometime for the poo bag – and then pay Iris another visit.'

'Okay. Night Robbie.'

'Sleep well, Philly.'

I pulled over to park in front of my house and watched as the dark-coloured four-wheel drive slowed briefly before speeding off. It was probably nothing, but while I remembered, I entered the registration plates into the notes on my phone. Just in case.

Chapter Eight

Despite giving myself a good talking to about coincidences and the number of dark-coloured four-wheel-drive vehicles on the roads, the sign of those headlights following me home last night stayed with me even after I shut my eyes. As a result, sleep, when it came, was fitful, every slight noise waking me with a start.

'You're looking tired this morning,' Bell drawled. Clad, as usual, in black she was perched on the end of Ambrose's desk, her long legs stretched out in front of her, the ubiquitous ballet flats on her feet, a vintage black cloche on her head, her straight black hair falling down her back like a shiny waterfall. Today's shawl was charcoal grey, bold red lips providing her only colour. If her wardrobe was a commentary on the weather, it was an apt one – it had been raining steadily, and it was that sort of February day when staying indoors was the only viable option. Other than the bus trade we had booked in – Ginny had managed to get us booked in as one of the regular stops on a York-based shopping tour – unless the outlook improved markedly, I doubted we'd be inundated with customers.

I placed the tray of mugs I'd been carrying on the desk; Ginny followed with a plate of parkin, which Simon and Eugene almost fell on.

'You do look a bit peaky,' commented Ginny, her face, normally so sunny, full of concern. 'Not sleeping well?'

'It's not this new case, is it?' asked Ambrose, rising from his chair to pour some milk into one of the mugs of tea.

'You're not doing anything dangerous again, are you, Philly?' Eugene added, passing the sugar bowl across to his brother.

The traders of Chipwell Barn Antiques – other than the Proctors, who wouldn't be back for another week or so – had all gathered in the Ashton's shop. It's something we tried to do at least once a week, sometimes more often. We'd chat through what we'd bought and sold, what was coming up for auction, anything we'd come across that might be of interest to one of the others; as far as possible, we tried not to encroach on each other's turf.

'No, it's nothing like that,' I said, firmly pushing away the image of the vehicle slowing outside my house last night, almost as if it wanted me to know it knew where I lived. 'It's early days, though, and nothing seems to fit yet.' I contemplated telling them about the previous evening and the intruder at Albert's, but that was something else that seemed to be, on the surface at least, unconnected, but which instinct was telling me was anything but.

Taking a seat in one of the chairs Simon had dragged in for our gathering, I changed the subject. 'I was out at Albert Horsley's after work yesterday and asked him about the Mouseman ashtray.' News had spread fast through the barn about the oak ashtray, and everyone nodded eagerly. 'Well, it happens that he has some more pieces – a lovely refectory-style table and a kitchen dresser.'

Simon's eyes widened, and he uncrossed his gangly legs and leant forward in his chair. 'Were you able to date them?'

'No. The table was in a shed, and it was quite dark. But I thought maybe thirties – it's an early piece. It all came from his uncle's place when he died. He thought Thompson had paid him in furniture and some smaller pieces instead of cash, so it must've been when he was starting out.' I heard again the clatter of what I now knew to be a paint can against stone and determinedly pushed the memory aside. 'I told him you'd be keen to look at it,' I said to Simon, who nodded emphatically. 'I said you'd give him a fair price.'

'If it's as old as you say, depending on the condition, of course, he'd probably be better off taking it to auction – I certainly can't give him the price that sort of item deserves, but I can help him make sure he does do well.' He excitedly pulled his phone from the top pocket of his flannel shirt and reached for the chain that held his glasses on, brushing parkin crumbs from the front of his Deep Purple T-shirt to the floor as he did so. Bally, who always sat beside Simon during these gatherings, was right onto it. Consulting his phone, he said, 'When did you say I'd go out there? I can move a few things around if I need to.'

Not even trying to hide my smile at his boyish enthusiasm, I said. 'I'm there all day on Monday if you want to come out then. I told Albert I'd help him clean out his shed and sort through it.'

'You know that means you'll be doing all the work, don't you?' Bell had a derisive grin on her face. 'Although knowing you, you'll enjoy that.'

She knew me too well, and I couldn't stop grinning back at her.

'Well,' said Ginny, 'I think it's a lovely thought. And now, I'd love to stay and chat, but it's a bus day today, so I need to bake extra scones.' And with a cheery wave, she collected the empty mugs and left us to it.

'How did you go with Lady Cunningham yesterday?' I asked.

While Bell pretended to the world to be droll and, as we used to term it, 'too cool for school', we all knew it to be a mask, and at my question, her face lit up. 'Lady C and I had the best time. There are some gorgeous items in there – a couple of evening dresses, reticules and the sweetest pair of silk evening slippers that belonged to Sir Antony's grandmother. They're in fantastic condition when you consider their age; I told Lady C they belonged in a museum, and I think she's going to reach out to the V & A about that.' The Victoria and Albert Museum in London had the world's largest fashion collection. 'Then there's plenty from the twenties, thirties and forties that I'll easily be able to sell. Such a treasure trove and Lady C is so chic she can fit into most of it. We really did have the best time trying things on.'

I turned away, hoping she wouldn't hear my laugh of astonishment at the thought of the stiff and upright Lady Cunningham playing dress-ups with Bell.

'Well, may you scoff, Philomena Barker, but Lady C is lovely once you get to know her. Besides, having one's only son arrested for burglary and grievous bodily harm tends to bring one down off one's high horse ...' Her perfectly arched eyebrows rose towards her cloche.

'Lady C,' snorted Ambrose. 'Does Sir Antony know you refer to her as that?'

Sir Antony Cunningham, an avid collector of militaria, had been a customer of the Ashton's for several years, and despite his request for us to 'call me Tony' and his habit of calling into the shop straight after completing a messy animal-related job on the estate, Ambrose still insisted on the respect his baronetcy entitled him to.

'Of course he does,' said Bell, a teasing tone in her voice. 'He calls her that now too.'

Ambrose could never keep up the pretence of being stern with Bell for long and chuckled at the thought. 'Away with you, lass.'

After discussing what each of us had on over the next week or so – aside from a general auction at Young and

Johnsons, it was fairly quiet – we scattered to our respective shops and opened up for the day.

Robbie called by at around two to collect the paint can, grinning at Ginny's gentle jibe about how he always managed to turn up when food was on the go. 'I've got a portion of tomato and lentil soup I can do you,' she offered. 'And there's one sausage roll left.'

'If you're sure you won't be selling it,' he protested half-heartedly, shrugging out of his wet anorak, the drips leaving a puddle where he stood.

'In this weather? Hardly. We had a rush while the bus group was here, but I doubt we'll see anyone else this afternoon, so you'll be doing me a favour.'

'Well, in that case ...' I almost laughed out loud at the almost spaniel-like expression on his craggy face.

Ginny was still chuckling as she headed back to the café.

'How did you go at Iris's?' I asked once we'd both settled into seats, Robbie viewing the peacock upholstered chair with suspicion. 'I know,' I sighed, 'but it's not white so it can't get mucky.'

'It was as Albert had told you – noises after dark, a broken light or two. Nothing malicious, but enough to unsettle her – even though she put a brave face on it when she was telling me.' He pulled his notebook from the top pocket of his shirt and thumbed through the pages. 'She said it started about two weeks ago, and I don't think she would've said a word to us if Albert hadn't told you.' He shook his head in exasperation. 'Pride, I suppose.'

I shrugged lightly, remembering my fitful night. 'I'd be the same. Living on your own, you're vulnerable, but it must be hard to admit that – especially if you're under pressure to sell up and move out to a retirement village.'

'True,' he conceded. 'But I've told her that if it happens again, she needs to ring me.'

'Do you think she will?' I picked up a pen and tapped it against the top of my laptop.

He shook his head, a wry smile curving around his lips. 'No, but I think she'll ring you. Now, go through everything that happened last night – including the part you haven't told me.'

I met his stare briefly, dropping my eyes first. How did he know?

As if I'd asked the question out loud, he said, 'I know you, Philly. You look tired, which tells me that something kept you awake last night, which means there's more to the story than what you told me last night, which means whatever it is, happened between you leaving Albert's and you coming in here this morning.' He tapped the side of his nose. 'I might be retiring soon, but I am still an alright detective.'

It had been a long time since anyone had read me as well as Robbie was beginning to read me and rather than feeling uncomfortable, I felt ... safe? Seen? Pushing aside the feeling for now I tapped the pen some more, inhaled.

'It's probably nothing ...'

'Let me be the judge of that.'

I drew in another breath. 'Last night, when I turned out of Albert's lane, another vehicle pulled out behind me.' He raised his eyebrows, indicating for me to continue. 'I couldn't be sure whether I pulled out in front of it or whether it was stationary and pulled out behind me – if you know what I mean. Anyway, it stayed there, the same distance away from me the entire way home. If I sped up, so did it; if I slowed down, so did it. It was probably a coincidence, but ...' I shrugged; a chill danced across my neck at the memory. 'And then when I pulled up out the front of my place, it slowed down and drove past quite slowly before speeding up again.'

Robbie's eyes had narrowed, the furrows on his brow deep. 'You should have phoned me back. Are you alright?' Without waiting for an answer he continued. 'It obviously worried you enough to keep you awake.' When I lifted a shoulder, he seemed to know I didn't want to dwell on the what-ifs that had been playing through my brain last night. 'What sort of car was it?'

'A dark-coloured four-wheel drive. I can't be sure, but I think it was a Range Rover or a Land Rover. I did get the registration plates, though ... just in case it wasn't all a coincidence.'

A nod of approval was all he gave. 'Do you think it was the same car the intruder at Albert's left in?'

I shrugged again. 'It had crossed my mind.'

'Right. Well, text me through the plate details, and I'll run them through the system while I'm getting this can checked for prints.'

Ginny chose that moment to come in with Robbie's lunch and his expression brightened so instantly I could almost have imagined the concern there just a few seconds ago.

'That smells amazing, Ginny.' He sniffed the soup appreciatively. 'Richard's a lucky man.'

'It'll warm the cockles of your poor overworked copper's heart.' Ginny's dimples formed deep holes in her soft-pink-flushed cheeks. 'I'll leave you two to it.'

While he took the first couple of sips of steaming soup, I ran through exactly what had taken place last night. 'So there you have it. I thought it was probably kids, but if I'm not imagining it and that car was the same one the intruder jumped into and it was the same one that followed me home, maybe it wasn't kids. Besides, what kids drive a Range Rover … if, indeed, it was a Range Rover.' I placed the pen back on the desk and ran my hands over my face. 'Maybe I'm making something of nothing; maybe it's just my imagination and none of it is connected.'

'Maybe,' he conceded slowly.

'But you don't think so.'

'No, Philly, I don't think so. I agree with you. I think it's all connected; we just don't know how yet.' He took the last mouthful of soup, running his spoon around the edge of the bowl to get the dregs. 'What have you got planned this weekend?'

'It's Ryan's birthday on Monday, so Jordan's doing a birthday dinner for him tomorrow evening.' My son Ryan, his husband Jordan and their four-year-old twins – Ada and Alfie – lived in York. 'Then, of course, we're both out at Wych Tree Farm on Sunday afternoon.' There was comfort in knowing the weekend would be full of people; last night must have shaken me more than I was prepared to admit. 'What are you up to? If you're not doing anything, do you want to come by for lunch on Sunday?'

Robbie wiped some flaky sausage roll crumbs from his top lip. 'I'll spend a few hours tomorrow at the allotment; spring will be here before we know it and I need to get some beds ready. Lunch on Sunday would be grand, though – if you're sure.'

'I didn't know you had an allotment; you've never mentioned it before.' Even though we'd been spending time together over the last couple of months, there was still so much I didn't know about Robbie.

'Aye. I'd been on the waiting list for some time and only took it on in November. It had been neglected, though, so I've had a devil of a time getting it right. I haven't planted anything yet, but when I do, I know where to bring my surplus vegetables.' He finished his sausage roll and stood to go. 'I'd better be off back to the nick. I'll let you know about the fingerprints and the licence.' He shrugged into his coat, putting the paint tin in its poo bag into one of the pockets. Picking his used plates up, he said, 'I'll drop these in at Ginny's on the way.' At the door, he turned. 'Mind how you go, Philly. I'll see you on Sunday.'

'So tell me, what's this latest case you're working on?' Jordan and I were cleaning up the kitchen after dinner. 'You and Robbie are becoming quite the crime-solving team.'

Dinner had been a casual affair; we'd filled the table with platters and let everyone help themselves. I'd bought a tray of what the kids called Grandma Goulash (and what Ryan and Chloe had also called Grandma's Goulash – given that it was my mother's recipe – when they were growing up) and another of grown-up goulash. Jordan had made a lasagne and some salads, and Alison had brought along a massive platter of cold meats and cheeses that was almost too pretty to eat.

We'd cut the cake (Ryan's favourite red velvet cake) and sung happy birthday and, with the kids (and Bally) all upstairs jumping around to the Wiggles DVDs I'd bought them for Christmas (if the vibrations coming through the ceiling were any indication), I'd excused myself to begin stacking the dishwasher and washing pans, Jordan joining me.

'Who says I'm working on a case?' The steam from the sink explained any heat in my cheeks. 'Besides, there was only that one case before Christmas, which was accidental.'

'Stewart told Ryan you were consulting with Robbie on some stolen antiques.'

I grimaced; Ryan hadn't been comfortable with my involvement with the last investigation, and I couldn't imagine he'd be any more approving this time either.

Jordan chuckled and wiped the saucepan dry. 'You weren't going to tell him, were you?'

I wrinkled my nose and rubbed it with the back of my gloved hand. 'There's not really anything to tell. Robbie was investigating a robbery, and it just happened that I'd been out at the house and knew exactly what had been stolen so could help him with identification.' I glanced across at Jordan, who was wearing a broad grin. 'In the process, we might've stumbled over a few more, but that's all.' If my hands hadn't been in rubber gloves in hot soapy water, I would've crossed my fingers behind my back.

'If you say so.' Jordan didn't even pretend to believe me.

'What's this about a new case?' Alison joined us, filling her empty glass with cold water from the jug in the fridge. 'What can I do to help with the clean-up?'

'I think we're almost done.' I wiped down the sink and pulled off the gloves.

'She's investigating a chain of antique robberies.' Jordan had a mischievous twinkle in his brown eyes and hung the tea towel from the oven door.

I grabbed the tea towel back and flicked it at his legs. 'It's not a chain; it's just a few which might or might not be connected and I'm not investigating, I'm consulting ... there's a difference.'

'Stewart was saying they don't have a lot of hope of identifying the perpetrators, so there's very little danger that Philly can come to.' Alison's smile was meant to be reassuring, but it didn't match the patronising tone in her voice. I gritted my teeth and counted to ten. Alison continued, 'He thinks it's just someone taking a chance on farmers who don't lock their doors and it's not as if there's anything of great worth being taken.'

'Perhaps it isn't to him,' I bit out. 'But some of these things have been in families for generations and have sentimental value. Then there's the psychological impact – Stewart can't discount that.'

'What can't I discount?' The man himself walked in.

'I was just telling Alison that even though the goods might have sentimental value only, the perpetrator is stealing something more precious from some of these people – their independence.' Ryan appeared behind his father, grinning at the sight of my hands on my hips and my chin pushed forward in battle, and pushed past Stewart to take his place beside his husband. 'Can you imagine how it is for a single older woman used to living on her own to suddenly feel unsafe in her own home?'

'I don't think it's that extreme,' Stewart scoffed his dismissal.

'You don't?' My voice was rising so I deliberately

lowered my volume. 'That's because you've never been in that situation. Take Iris Metcalfe, for example. She's lived on that farm her whole life and is now under pressure from family members to sell up and move into a retirement home away from everything she's ever known …'

'Maybe if she's not fit enough to be self-sufficient, that's what she should be thinking about. Or maybe she should've locked her doors.' Stewart glanced across to Alison, seeking her approval of his statement. On finding no support there, he turned his attention to Ryan. 'Don't you think?'

Ryan held his hands up. 'Don't involve me in this, Dad,' he said with a slightly nervous laugh.

'But that's my point,' I said through clenched teeth. 'She *can* look after herself – and her friends rely on her to help them out, too. There is no reason why she can't stay where she is for several years yet.'

'As we know, though,' Alison said with a conciliatory tone, 'many older people are one fall away from needing help.'

'True,' I conceded, 'but does that mean that as soon as you get to a certain age, you should check yourself into a retirement village, just in case?' I bristled at the generalisation.

Alison shook her head. 'No, of course not. I know I'd prefer my mother to stay in her home as long as possible. All I'm saying is that their family members worry about them, that's all.'

The fact that Alison's mother wasn't much older than me made me inwardly grimace. 'My point is, Iris, Eddie, Jane and Delwyn – and for that matter anyone else we don't yet know about—'

'That's a bit of a reach, isn't it?' Stewart said scornfully. 'To assume there are others out there who've also been targeted?'

Biting the inside of my lip, I paused for a beat before continuing, refusing to rise to his bait and show my anger. 'As I was saying, each of these people live alone and have been doing so successfully – until this person comes along and not only steals their belongings but has them no longer completely trusting in their ability to care for themselves. Something they've always taken for granted has been taken away – their security. So yes, Stewart, while it might just seem to you and that new inspector of yours that a few chocolate boxes filled with seemingly worthless silver and other trinkets have been stolen, to Iris and the others, what's been taken is a lot more valuable than that. The idea that they can be driven from their homes because they're frightened … It doesn't bear thinking about.'

When I finished my spiel, my chest heaved with each breath, the others silent and staring at me as if they were seeing something they hadn't seen before. In the back of my mind, a bell was softly ringing. What was it I wasn't seeing?

'These people really matter to you, don't they, Mum?' Ryan reached out to hug me briefly.

'They do,' I admitted softly. 'They really do.'

'Is that because you believe the perpetrator to be an antique dealer who's making the rest of you look bad or because you're afraid that one day that might be you – alone and afraid of shadows?'

'Dad!'

'Stewart!'

Alison and Ryan spoke at the same time, their voices raised in disbelief.

I held up a hand to let them know I didn't need their support and inhaled. 'Perhaps you're right, Stewart, on both counts. The idea that there's an unscrupulous dealer out there making the rest of us who are doing the right thing look bad makes me furious. And maybe, subconsciously, I do wonder whether that might be me some day – what was it you said? Alone and afraid of shadows?' At my raised brows, he gave a little nod, his eyes dropping quickly from mine. 'And if it is, I hope there's someone who will be as angry for me and prepared to fight in my corner as I am for them.'

'I'm sorry,' Stewart said meekly. 'I was out of line.'

My eyes widened, and I managed to bite back the retort of surprise that Stewart, the man who, during our marriage, refused to apologise for anything, was now able to freely offer an apology – and without a trace of a sulk.

'It mightn't be a big glamourous case, but I'm glad you and Robbie care enough to pursue it.' Alison really had worked wonders with him.

'Even though the likelihood of catching the perpetrators is slim?' My grin was teasing and designed to break the tension I'd unwittingly caused with my speech. Alison let out a snort of laughter.

'Even then,' conceded Stewart with a fond glance towards his wife. 'Just stay out of trouble this time, eh?'

'I'll certainly do my best.'

Bally and I left soon after, and driving home in the dark, I tried to grasp the idea lurking in the back of my mind, the piece of this puzzle I was overlooking. But as the drizzle turned to rain and Libby's wipers struggled to cope, I pushed it away and concentrated on what I could see illuminated on the narrow road ahead – even as I couldn't help but continually check the rear-vision mirror.

Chapter Nine

'Well,' said Robbie, leaning back in his chair and rubbing his belly, 'that was a grand Sunday roast. I haven't had Yorkshire puddings like that since my mother passed.'

A warmth spread across my cheeks at his praise, although the fact he'd been back for more puddings – which he'd proceeded to fill with gravy – had been praise enough. 'I'm glad. It was nice to have someone to cook for.' Aside from when Ryan and Jordan and the kids came for a Sunday roast, I rarely used my dining room. It was lovely to have someone sitting across from me at the large wooden table and to have a reason to light the fire.

Twenty years ago, Stewart and I had immediately fallen in love with this house. After years of living in the outskirts of London, Stewart's transfer to York had seemed like a fresh new start for us both. 'You've always wanted to live in a village, and it's close enough to commute,' Stewart had said.

Even though we'd both fallen for Chipwell and this house, it was this room – the dining room – that had been the defining factor. I'd seen past the faux-brick cladding that had lined the walls and the heavy floral curtains and imagined how it could be ... the heart of a family home. Together, we'd pulled back the ugly brown and gold carpet and polished the floorboards underneath, stripped and painted the walls, restored the fireplace, added a timber mantel, and bought a large timber table with refectory-style bench seats that had been the scene of many happy family dinners and, towards the end, some not-so-happy arguments.

I'd redecorated the room after Stewart left – painting the walls in a deep sage and hanging some oatmeal plaid curtains from the windows – but the centre of it was still this table and the meals we'd all shared around it. Its emptiness in the years since the kids had gone had been, at times, symbolic of the fact that now it was just Bally and me rattling around in a home meant for a family, so as much as I recoiled from the idea, I sometimes wondered whether it was time to downsize.

Now though, with flames flickering in the hearth softly providing the room with more light than the wintry sun outside and Robbie sitting across from me replete after a good meal, I knew this was still my home and where I wanted to be. To cover the embarrassment of emotion I suddenly felt, I said inanely, 'The butcher in Malton always does a nice bit of beef. There's more if you want it ...'

'No, thank you, though; I'm all full up.'

'Too full for a slice of steamed pudding with custard?'

His eyes lit up. 'A proper syrup pudding?'

I nodded, a smirk pulling at my lips. 'Golden syrup and a touch of lemon.'

He grinned, the action taking twenty years from his craggy face. 'Happens that maybe I can squeeze a small slice in then.'

Once the pudding had been eaten, the dishes tidied and the kitchen benches wiped, I made us both a coffee, and we sat on stools at the wood-topped kitchen island.

By mutual agreement, we'd left any discussion about the case until after lunch, but now I was keen to know what Robbie had discovered. 'So tell me, did they find any prints on that paint can?'

He took a sip of his coffee, the small espresso cup incongruously small in his large hand. 'No, none. Not even on the cap or the nozzle.'

My eyes widened. 'So they wiped it clean?'

He shook his head. 'No, and that's the strange thing. There's no signs of smudging and traces of latex on the can, so whoever it was, wore gloves.'

I leant forward, my fingers steepled against my lips. 'Kids tend not to wear gloves when they're spray painting a wall.'

'No.' He placed his cup back on its saucer. 'They don't.' He tapped at his top lip with his knuckle. 'I know Albert thinks it was kids skylarking, but'—he shook his head—'I don't think it was.'

'No. Nor do I. Kids don't escape in upmarket four-by-fours either. Assuming that the one that followed me – if it was following me – was the same car our would-be artist scuppered away in.'

'Which, according to the plates, was a Land Rover and stolen from the railway station in Leeds a few weeks back.' Robbie dropped this information in almost as an afterthought.

The nerves on the back of my neck prickled as though someone had strolled over my grave. 'So, we have a graffiti artist who has decided that Albert Horsely's barn in Dunthrop would be a great place for a spot of painting and he just happens to be driving a stolen Land Rover and has remembered to pack his gloves for the exercise.'

'If the vehicle that followed you was the same dark-coloured vehicle our artist left Albert's place in ...'

'And if it was actually following me ...'

Robbie inclined his head, his lips pursed. 'Happens I don't like coincidences. And there have been too many of them in this case.'

'And yet none of them seem to fit.' Last night's bell was back in my head; it rang faint but insistent. 'Maybe it's not supposed to fit.'

'What do you mean by that?'

'Just that maybe the thefts and the criminal damage are unrelated and it's a coincidence that it's all happening at the same time.'

'To the same people?' Robbie's raised eyebrows conveyed his scepticism.

'Yeah, you're right … That doesn't make sense either.'

My mobile rang. Robbie's frown mirrored mine when he saw the name of the caller. 'Iris, is everything alright?'

'Sorry to disturb you, Philly, but I thought you'd like to know Eileen Taylor – she lives up the lane a bit from Esme – was robbed.'

I flicked the phone onto speaker and met Robbie's eyes. 'Iris, I've got Robbie here with me now … You say that Esme's neighbour has been robbed? When did this happen?'

'Robbie's there, is he?'

Robbie smiled wryly at the speculative tone in her voice. 'Yes, he came for lunch.'

As I justified Robbie's presence in my house, I grimaced.

'Oh, aye?'

'Iris,' Robbie said evenly, 'has Eileen reported the theft?'

'No, pet. I told her I'd tell you myself. The thing is, she doesn't know when it happened, but it's sometime over the last week.'

Robbie rubbed at his forehead, but any exasperation he might've felt didn't come through in his tone. 'When did she last see the items that were taken?'

'She had them out for cleaning on Tuesday – Eileen keeps a clean house, she does; you'd never find a speck of dust anywhere. And she noticed them missing yesterday.

And before you ask, pet, she'd had a visit from that Ron Jackson fella.'

I glanced at my watch before meeting Robbie's eyes – we had time to call in on Eileen on our way out to Wych Tree Farm – but he was already ahead of me. 'Philly and I have somewhere we need to be later this afternoon, and it happens to be out your way. If you text Philly the address, we can drop by.'

'That would be grand. Thanks, pet.' Iris sounded relieved. 'It would put her mind at rest – what with the other shenanigans.'

'What other shenanigans would those be?' I asked slowly, already suspecting the answer.

'Just kids laikin' about,' said Iris. 'Nowt worth worrying you about.'

'The same sort of "laikin"' about that kids have been doing at your place?' I suppressed a cynical smile as Robbie shook his head in exasperation. 'Why didn't you mention it to Robbie? And don't tell me you didn't mention it because he hadn't asked ...'

'Happens I didn't know Eileen had been having the same problems until she told me about the theft.' I pictured Iris drawing herself up to her full five feet and not many inches in indignation.

'Okay,' I said soothingly. 'We can talk more when we get there. Speaking of which, we'd better get moving.' I was about to hang up when I had another thought. 'Iris, would you happen to know if Eileen had also received a visit from our real estate friend?'

'She didn't mention it.' There was a spark of interest in Iris's voice. 'Are you thinking he might be connected too?'

Robbie shot me an indecipherable look. 'No,' I said quickly. 'Probably not, but it's best to have all the details.'

Iris and Esme were already at Eileen Taylor's when we arrived, Iris having appointed herself as Eileen's spokeswoman until Robbie reminded her he needed Eileen to provide a statement in her own words.

The story was, however, the same as all the others. Ron Jackson knocked at the door, apologising for the intrusion but wanting to purchase any bits and pieces that might be lurking around the house being of no use to anybody.

'When he asked, though, it was as if he already knew what my answer would be,' Eileen said. 'Then he apologised again and said he'd been sent out by his boss, who was a proper cow, so had no choice but to ask.'

Robbie and I exchanged glances; this was a new fact.

'Did he mention who he worked for?' Robbie asked.

'No, but it would be on his business card, wouldn't it? The name of the place he worked? Now, I'm sure I put it on this counter … but it's not here now.'

As with every other case, he'd requested a glass of water and, once inside, had begun chatting.

'I might've mentioned that Wednesday was my day for

lunch with the girls – that's Irene and Sheila.' I suppressed a smile at the thought of three seventy-somethings referring to themselves as 'the girls'. 'We go to that pub in Old Malton – sandwiches and a mug of soup, with proper bread and butter pudding for afters. Have you ever been?'

I shook my head and said I hadn't.

'What about you, Inspector?'

Robbie said that he hadn't either.

'You should go. They do proper portions there. Some of these new pubs have forgotten about that. What do they call them? "Gastro pubs?" There was a time when gastro meant something else!'

Esme cackled, and, as Iris was about to step in with her opinion, Robbie gently but firmly brought Eileen back on track. 'I'll bear it in mind. So you told Ron Jackson that you're usually out for lunch on Wednesdays?'

'Aye. Do you think that's when he came back? When I was at lunch?'

'I think it's likely. Do you lock the door when you leave the house?' Even as he asked, his resigned expression said he already knew the answer.

'Nay, pet. There's no need for that around here.'

'Maybe there is now,' I suggested gently. 'Just when you go out and at night.'

'Aye,' said Iris. 'It's best to be safe. It's not like it was when we were girls.' Again I suppressed a grin – this was such a turnaround from Iris's attitude just a few days ago.

'Tell them about the kids and their skylarking. You don't want to leave anything out, you know, Eileen – just because they haven't asked you about it.'

'It's probably nowt,' Eileen scoffed, turning away to wipe down her already clean kitchen bench. 'As Iris said, just kids clattering around.'

'At night?' I prompted.

Without turning to face us, she nodded. 'Aye. They've broken the light – the one just outside the kitchen door – and have been clattering about in the woodshed – moving things and the like. I nearly tripped over a shovel left lying on the floor.'

Robbie was out of his seat and to the kitchen door, examining the light that, if working, would've illuminated the step out of the house and the gravel courtyard that ran between the house and the shed. He took a photo with his phone and then made a call.

'Do you keep a torch in here, Eileen? I wouldn't want you missing that step in the dark and falling.' While she was comfortably padded, a fall like that could result in a bad break – or worse, result in her being out there unable to raise help in the dark and cold.

'Aye.' She finally turned to meet my eyes. 'It's a bad thing when you can't feel right in your own home. Maybe it's time I did what our Lou has been wanting me to do – sell up and go into one of them places in Malton.'

'That's enough of that talk,' said Iris. 'Philly and the

inspector will find out what's going on, won't you, pet?'

'We'll certainly try.' Even as I urged reassurance into my voice, we were no closer to doing that than where we'd been when we first began looking into Iris's burglary.

'In the meantime,' said Robbie, 'someone will be out tomorrow to fix that light for you. I can have him fit some cameras at the same time.'

'What would I be doing with those?' You'd think from Eileen's frown that Robbie had suggested around-the-clock security guards.

'They can be a deterrent—' Robbie began.

Eileen was shaking her head. 'No, I won't be doing with that. It's bad enough I have to lock my doors, but I won't be living in a fortress.'

'It's hardly that—'

Eileen cut me off, her chin tilted determinedly. 'There's no need for all that carry on. I'll thank you for fixing the light, but I won't be needing any of them cameras.'

Robbie raised his hands in a calming gesture. 'Alright, that's a no to the cameras, but at least allow us to add a motion detector to the light.'

'So it can turn on any time a fox runs through?' Eileen wasn't impressed by this idea either.

'Perhaps, but it might also deter anyone wanting to cause trouble.' Robbie's tone was even and patient.

Eileen's shoulders relaxed. 'Aye,' she nodded. 'Alright then.'

He turned to Iris and Esme. 'I'll have him do a check of your outside lights too and fit motion sensors.'

'It's better to be safe than sorry,' Esme finished.

'Exactly.' Robbie flipped his notebook shut and glanced at his watch. 'And now we'd better be on our way. Call me if there's any more trouble.'

Iris's mouth quirked slightly at his emphasis on 'call me'. 'You mean as opposed to phoning Philly? I would've phoned you today but must've misplaced your card,' she said artlessly. 'And it being a Sunday and all. It was lucky you were there with Philly.'

Even Robbie couldn't ignore the speculative gleam in her eye and chuckled, shaking his head. 'Right you are.'

Iris turned to me. 'Albert said you'll be around in the morning. We might see you there.'

'I'll look forward to it,' I replied.

'Yes, well, mind how you go then.'

Chapter Ten

'You found us alright then.' Gordon Willoughby strode out of what I assumed was the estate office to meet us, his brown dealer boots crunching on the gravel. Dressed in jeans and a navy and red checked shirt, if it hadn't been for his stomach straining against the confines of the zipped navy gilet, he could've stepped straight from the pages of a country gentlemen's outfitters.

After shaking hands with Robbie and giving me a hello kiss that lingered just a tad too close to my mouth and prompted a double eyebrow raise from Robbie, Gordon said, 'Marlene's in the stables, so I'll grab a jacket and give you the tour while we're out here.' Shrugging into a tweed shooting-style jacket, he led the way down the drive.

'How long have you lived here?' Robbie's hands were shoved deep in the pockets of his brown padded wax jacket, shoulders hunched against the cold.

'It would be going on for ten years,' Gordon said. 'Marlene grew up here and took it over when her father passed away.'

'What did you do before that?' I was slightly breathless as my much shorter legs hurried to keep up with Gordon's brisk pace.

'Real estate.' He smiled ruefully. 'I'd never had anything to do with horses until I met Marlene. I've learnt to ride – I couldn't be married to her and not know how to ride, but I'm more suited to the business side than the saddle.'

'What exactly do you do here?' Robbie was having no problems keeping up with Gordon, their strides matching.

'Well, there's the riding stables, of course – and while we keep our own riding school horses, students also have lessons on their own horses. We also have a dressage arena and showjumping course. Then there's the livery—'

'Livery?' I asked.

'Yes, we stable or paddock horses here.' Reaching the end of the drive, he turned and led us through a brick archway. 'Some people take full livery, which means we take complete care of the animals – box, bedding, feeding, mucking out, exercising – the works. Others just pay for the box and the bedding and will look after the rest themselves. Some horses we have just for holidays and others have been here for years.'

We emerged into a large quadrangle lined on three sides with stables. Marlene appeared from one of them, bolting the door firmly behind her and stroking the neck of the horse whose head appeared over the top of the gate.

'You came!' Marlene greeted us with double air kisses and more enthusiasm than our short acquaintance deserved. Outfitted for light stable work in close-fitting jeans, a printed shirt under a quilted jacket and leather yard boots, Marlene seemed more in her element than she had in the pub the other night. On that occasion, she'd blended into the space in a way that diminished her. Here, though, she was clearly visible. 'Has Gordon given you the grand tour?'

'We've not long arrived,' said Robbie, sweeping his arm around the yard. 'But what we've seen so far is impressive.'

'Gordon was just telling us about what you do here.' The sound of a horse whinnying echoed around the quadrangle. 'It must keep you busy.'

Marlene's smile was one of unmistakable pride. 'It does, but I love it.' She walked back across to the stall she'd just been in and stroked the neck of the chestnut horse watching our every move. 'This place is my life. Do you like horses?'

Robbie held his hands up and eyed the heads appearing over stall doors. 'I haven't had very much to do with them.'

Marlene's smile was understanding. 'Their size can be quite daunting when you're not used to them. What about you, Philly?'

I moved to the grey horse watching me from the stall closest and reached out a hand to stroke the soft neck, the horse nuzzling into my shoulder. 'I love them and used to ride a lot as a kid. My best friend in primary school kept polo ponies, and she and I used to take off on horseback for the day – a sandwich and a fruit juice in our saddlebags.' I inhaled the warm, musty scent of the animal. 'She went off to boarding school in Sydney and my family moved back to Sydney, so I haven't ridden in years; I've probably forgotten how to.'

'You should come out one day and go for a hack. It'll come back to you quickly – just like riding a bike.'

Marlene's offer seemed genuine, so I smiled gratefully. 'I'd like that, thank you.'

'Did Gordon tell you we also school horses here?' Marlene led us back through the arch and up the drive towards the house.

'School?' Robbie looked puzzled and dropped back to keep pace with Marlene and me. Gordon was ahead and fiddling with his phone.

'It's not just riders who need training,' she said. 'Sometimes the horses need to know what to do too, so we teach them: dressage, showjumping, general eventing.' She giggled almost girlishly. 'It's where my passion lies; in fact, if I had my way, that's all I'd do! That and finishing horses for sale.'

Gordon must've heard that remark and guffawed, slowing his pace until we caught up with him. 'Marlene knows how to bring them into peak condition, and we have the facilities here to show them at their best for sale. Sadly for her, though, schooling or finishing doesn't pay the bills.'

'What does pay the bills?' Robbie asked. 'Lessons?'

Gordon shook his head. 'No. The livery is a more reliable source of income. We've begun taking racehorses for their spell periods, but I'd like to bring in more.' He paused and glanced mournfully at his wife. 'Unfortunately, when we took over the stables, we also took over the debts Marlene's father left. It's been a battle, but we're keeping our heads above water now … just.'

'Dad loved the horses as much as I do, but Gordon's right; he left the business in terrible shape. But'—a quick look at Gordon—'I promised him we'd do what we needed to keep it afloat. Gordon ran his own business before this. Did he tell you?'

I nodded. 'Real estate, he said.'

'Yes. So he knows how to market, and he suggested we get into spelling racehorses, and it was also his idea to convert a couple of the barns on the estate into short-term rentals. I wasn't sure to begin with,' Marlene continued, 'but Gordon said the future was in barn conversions and he's been right. They're rarely vacant, and the income is really helping.' We'd arrived at the end of the drive and were back where we'd started. The sun had given up on the day, and I wound my scarf tighter around my neck, regretting leaving my gloves in the car.

'Here we are,' announced Marlene with a sweep of her hand. 'Wych Tree Farm.'

Before us stood a long limestone farmhouse that had

probably been built sometime in the eighteenth century and then added to over the years.

'I've been meaning to ask,' said Robbie. 'What does Wych Tree mean?'

Gordon led us through into a hall, a bench seat along one soft-pink wall, a rose and soft-sage-hued Turkish rug protecting the parquetry floor and horse-themed oils hanging on either side of a Georgian mahogany console table. My practiced eye judged the paintings as British school, probably late nineteenth century – one of which was the painting she'd bought from me – nice but not exceptionally valuable.

'For a start, it has nothing to do with witches.' Gordon chuckled. 'The wych tree is a type of elm. Apparently, witches avoided elm trees because they were associated with death. They used to make coffins out of elm, you know; the wood's quite pliant, so no good for building houses. There's a rather old one in the garden, and I think that's what the farm is named for.' He put his arm around Marlene. 'That's right, isn't it, darling?'

Marlene nodded. 'Yes, the tree is older than the house. My mother also used to say elm was good for things like arthritis and diarrhoea, but I don't know how true that was … an old wives' tale, perhaps. Anyway'—she let out another of those uncomfortable girlish giggles—'hang your coats here if you like. We'll have a drink in the drawing room, and I can show you my antiques.'

The relative simplicity of the entrance was continued in the drawing room. Walls in a soft sage highlighted the white painted details in the windowpanes, ceilings, cornices and skirtings. A cream two-seater lounge was given interest and colour with red botanical printed cushions – the same red used as a print on the cream curtains and in the two plaid armchairs. A fire was burning in the grate, above which sat a Victorian mantel clock; my eyes were immediately drawn to it.

'Now,' said Gordon, standing by an Edwardian drinks trolley, 'what can I get you? You look like a G & T type of woman, Philly. Am I right?'

Good God, had he winked at me? I didn't dare look at Robbie – any amusement on his face would've brought me undone. 'Thank you, that would be lovely.'

'And you, Robbie? Can I tempt you with a Scotch?'

'Thank you, just a small one.' He used his thumb and forefinger to demonstrate. 'I'm driving.'

As Gordon fixed the drinks in one corner of the room, Marlene directed me towards a display cabinet in the opposite corner. 'As you can tell, I'm partial to equine-themed pieces.'

The annoying girlish giggle was gone and, in its place, a shy smile – almost as if she was anxious for my approval. 'You have a lovely collection. May I?' I pointed to the lock on the cabinet door.

'Of course. Please do have a closer look.'

When Marlene had said she had a passion for horse-themed pieces, she hadn't been joking. Inside the display case was the usual range of Beswick ceramic figurines – including a couple of rarer pieces – and everything from vesta cases to hat pins, silver spoons, brooches, and china cups, but all with some sort of equine reference.

I picked up a silver-plated match holder in the shape of riding boots. 'This is sweet. I don't think I've seen one like this before. Oh … this flask is rather lovely.' Pulling my loupe from my jacket pocket, I held it against my eye to examine the maker's mark on a silver-topped hunting flask. 'There's the anchor, so this was made in Birmingham … early twentieth century … very nice. I don't think I've seen one in such nice condition.' I set it back in the cabinet and locked the door again.

'Thank you. It was my father's. In fact, most of what's in here has come from my parents; my father used to buy a Beswick figurine for my mother for her birthday each year.' A shadow passed across her face at the memory.

'When did you lose your mother?' I asked gently.

Marlene blinked twice and smiled a half-forced smile. 'When I was fifteen.'

I reached out and touched her arm lightly. 'I'm sorry. It's lovely to have these memories of her, though.'

'Thank you for saying that. It is.' She smiled again, this time with warmth. 'Here, take your drink and tell me what you think of the paintings.'

Clinking my glass against hers, I took a sip, raising my eyebrows involuntarily at the gin's strength.

'I should've warned you,' she said with a good-natured shrug, 'Gordon can be a tad heavy-handed with his pours.'

As Marlene and I wandered out of the room, I vaguely registered Robbie and Gordon talking about the fortunes of (what I assumed) was the local rugby club.

'Is there anything in the cabinet that's worth something?' Marlene asked as I examined the paintings in the hall.

I turned back from the painting, her question taking me by surprise. 'You have some nice things in there – I particularly like the flask and the match holder – and there are a couple of hat pins that would appeal to collectors, as would that pair of brass door stops. If you're interested in monetary value, though, the mantel clock would be my pick.' Running my hand over the patina of the console table, I said, 'I didn't think you were interested in selling anything.'

'I'm not,' she said hastily. 'At least I'm not at the moment. It's always good to know, though … don't you think?'

Standing beside me, she stared up at the painting she'd purchased from me, her eyes running over every brushstroke as if she hadn't seen it before. 'I think it's always best to know as much as possible about the value of one's … assets. Don't you?'

As her eyes met mine, I got the impression she wasn't talking about the painting. 'True,' I acknowledged. 'But I also think some things need to be appreciated for their beauty or the pleasure they bring you regardless of their monetary value.'

Her smile was faint, and I wondered if my answer had disappointed her somehow. What was it she was trying to tell me?

She reached out her hand and gripped my arm, the pressure stronger than I would've imagined for such a slight woman. 'I'd appreciate it if you didn't mention any values to Gordon,' she said. 'I don't want to give him another reason to push me to sell any of my parent's collection.' When I nodded, unable to think of a suitable response, she released my arm and let out another of those half giggles. 'We'd better be getting back in there before Gordon sends out a search party.'

The men were still talking about rugby when we came back into the room.

'So, Philly, what do you think? Any treasures?' Gordon's voice boomed with good humour. He patted the seat beside him, but I pretended not to see and sat in the armchair opposite Robbie – whose wry grin I was trying hard not to dwell on.

'There are some nice pieces to be sure – a couple of good paintings and some very collectible items, although Marlene assures me she's not intending to sell any. Besides, it's not so much what the item is worth as what it's worth to you.' I rubbed at where Marlene had gripped my arm.

Robbie's eyes met mine for an instant, his brows raised in a silent question.

Gordon let out a laugh and clapped his hands together. 'Very diplomatically said.' He stood and poured himself a refill, holding the bottle up in a silent question to Robbie, who shook his head. Marlene held her glass out for a refill, but I'd barely touched mine. 'Drink up, Philly, and tell me, how did you get into antiques?'

'The long way around.' I sipped at my drink, the strength of the gin hitting me afresh. 'I was all set to study fine arts at university in Australia but came here for a holiday and never quite went home.'

'Let me guess,' chuckled Gordon. 'A man?'

'Yes, my ex-husband. So I joined the police force instead'—Marlene's eyes widened—'and didn't get around to doing the degree until after I came here and left the force. My kids were teenagers by then.'

'How many children do you have?' Marlene asked.

'Two – Ryan, my eldest, is an accountant in York. He has two children, and Chloe is married too and living on the Sunshine Coast in Australia.'

'From the police force to antiques is quite the leap, though,' said Gordon with a laugh that sounded forced.

I wasn't sure whether Marlene's frown was at the mention of me being in the police or puzzlement regarding how I got from there to here. 'Perhaps, although there were some years in the middle where I worked at an auction house in York – it was that which helped me fall in love with the trade. Besides, I do use some of the investigation skills I'd learnt over the years in what I do today.' I laughed, but Marlene's frown didn't soften. 'To track down the provenance of a piece – where it's come from, who owned it, I mean.'

'It's hard to see you as a policewoman,' said Gordon. 'And Robbie, what do you do?'

'I'm a detective with the police force.' Robbie's expression was impassive. 'Although I am retiring in a couple of weeks.'

For a second, neither of them seemed to know what to say. The beginning of a small smile played around Robbie's lips.

'Well,' said Marlene eventually. 'That's a surprise.'

Gordon recovered more quickly. 'So, how did you two meet?'

'Oh, we're not together—' I began.

'But I thought—' Marlene said.

'On a case, actually,' said Robbie. 'I needed Philly's help with some fake ceramics, and she's also helping me on my current case.'

'It's not all business though, is it?' Gordon asked with another wink, this time in Robbie's direction. 'After all, you were out together the other night.'

'No, it's not all business.' Robbie sent me a look I couldn't decipher. What did he mean by that? It was almost as if he wanted to imply there was more to our relationship.

'I thought as much.' This time, the wink was in my direction and I understood why Robbie had implied what he did.

'Can I get you another drink, Philly?' Marlene had stood to refresh her glass.

'Thanks, but a small one, please.' My head was feeling fuzzy after the first gin.

'You mentioned you're working on a case right now.' Marlene busied herself at the drinks trolley. 'What's that about?'

'We've had reports of a few burglaries in the region.' Robbie placed his empty glass on the table beside his chair, shaking his head at Gordon when he offered him a refill. 'Mostly older victims and mostly household antiques, but enough of a pattern that we're concerned. Philly's helping me with identification, mostly.' He shot me a quick grin. 'She has a photographic memory when it comes to antiques.'

'How interesting.' Marlene leant forward in her chair. 'Do you have any leads?'

'Just the one,' Robbie said. 'In fact, you might be able to help us there. A person of interest—'

'You mean a suspect?' Marlene's expression was avid.

'A person of interest,' Robbie repeated with a straight face, 'has been seen at The White Horse … It's a long shot'—he looked first at Marlene and then Gordon—'but do you know someone by the name of Ron Jackson? He's an antique dealer.'

Marlene shook her head immediately, but Gordon was slower to react, his eyes narrowing.

'An antique dealer, hey ...' Gordon spoke slowly. 'As it happens, I came across an antique dealer the other day in The White Horse but I can't say it's the same person you want to speak to "in relation to your enquiries".' He laughed at his joke, but seeing we didn't laugh with him, he sobered and frowned as if trying to recall the occasion. 'We got talking, and he offered to come by and give me a quote if I ever wanted to sell. I told him I wasn't in the market to sell, but if Marlene here is going to buy more, I might need to off-load some just so we have room in the display cabinet.' This time his grin seemed forced. 'Now, what was his name?' Gordon tilted his head to one side and pulled at his earlobe. 'Let me think... It could've been Ron Jackson. I asked him for a business card in case I needed to get in touch with him.' He opened his wallet and rummaged around. I held my breath. 'No, it's not in here.' He held a finger in the air as if that would help him remember. 'I put it in the pocket of the jacket I was wearing that day. I'll have a look shortly.'

Hoping my disappointment didn't show on my face, I said, 'Was he midfifties, average build, grey hair, cut short at the front, longer at the back ...'

'That sounds like him.' Gordon gaffawed. 'It sounds as though you're putting together a witness description.'

Hoping the embarrassed flush in my cheeks would be put down to sitting too close to the fire, I forced a smile. 'Sorry, I'm used to classifying antiques: Regency period, Sheffield hallmark ... You probably do the same with horses.'

Another guffaw. 'You've got me there – chestnut gelding, three-year-old, lightly raced ... I'll see if I can find that business card.' Gordon sprang from his chair and disappeared towards the hall, returning a few seconds later brandishing a card. 'Here it is.'

'Thanks.' Robbie accepted the card, glanced at it quickly, and slid it into the breast pocket of his shirt. If I hadn't seen the tiniest involuntary tic at the side of his mouth, I would've assumed the card had told him nothing.

'When you were talking to the dealer,' Robbie began, 'did you happen to mention where you lived?'

The beaming smile that Gordon had worn for most of our visit slipped. 'Is this Robbie asking or the detective asking?'

'The latter, I'm afraid.'

'Aaaah, I see.' Gordon rubbed at his clean-shaven head. 'Probably. I tend to throw in a mention of the farm whenever I'm meeting someone new.'

'Do you or Marlene have any designated days where you are both away from the farm?'

Robbie made the question sound casual, but the way Gordon's shoulders tightened, I knew he wasn't fooled. 'That I also might've mentioned?'

Robbie nodded.

Gordon frowned as he recollected the conversation. 'The day I met him, I'd stopped in for a pint or two on my way back from York – I'd been in town looking for an anniversary present for Marlene – it's our tenth wedding anniversary on Tuesday.' At my start of surprise, he added, 'It's the second time around for both of us. Two divorces but no kids between us.' The joking line sounded practiced. He tilted his head to one side. 'Come to think on it, I might've mentioned I was taking her out for dinner on Tuesday night …'

'To the restaurant where we had our first date,' Marlene interjected.

'Other than that, I'm usually in the office and Marlene at the stables … except for once a week when you go to Leeds …' The smile he bestowed on his wife was loving. 'Marlene has a school friend there who's not well – she visits her most weeks. I didn't mention any of that to him, though.'

'Okay,' said Robbie solemnly. 'You don't really fit the profile, and I'm sure you lock up securely—'

'We do,' Marlene said quickly.

'I wouldn't worry about it then,' said Robbie.

'Well, if we do have trouble, at least we have our own policeman on speed dial now.'

Robbie returned Gordon's chuckle and when I asked Marlene to tell me how they'd met, the conversation moved away from the burglaries and onto safer ground.

Soon after this, we took our leave.

'I'll call in and see you during the week, Philly – I'm interested in looking at the vesta case and painting you mentioned the other night,' Marlene said as they saw us out. 'And I meant it when I said you should come out for a ride.'

'I'll look forward to it.' I opened the car door. 'Actually, I've come across something else recently too – a Mouseman ashtray with a horseshoe and a racing slipper embedded in the top. I think it might've had something to do with York Racing Club. It's an unusual piece and would be perfect for your collection.'

'It sounds like it would be. Thanks for coming by, and I hope you find your burglars, Robbie.'

'I'm sure I will,' said Robbie. 'Happy anniversary.'

I waited until we'd turned out of the entrance gates before exhaling audibly. 'What was with Gordon and the winks?'

Robbie chuckled. 'I think he fancies you, Philly.'

So that was wht Robbie had implied we were more than friends – to deter Gordon. I pushed aside the slight feeling of disappointment that came with that knowledge. 'Too funny. Something tells me he's all talk and no walk.'

'You could be right. Marlene certainly didn't seem upset by it.'

'No, she didn't, did she?' I thought some more on it. 'She was neither surprised nor upset by it. Maybe he has history?' I paused for a beat. 'Not that it's any of our business, I suppose. Now, what was on that card that had you so concerned?'

One hand still on the steering wheel, he reached into his shirt pocket and handed me the business card Ron Jackson had left with Gordon. Using the phone light, I read it, my breath hitching in my throat. 'This makes no sense … It says that Ron Jackson works for Young and Johnsons Auctions … but Catherine …?' I couldn't finish my sentence. The very idea that Catherine could be behind a scheme to cheat elderly residents out of their precious treasures was unfathomable. While I knew plenty of shady characters in the antique world, I could never believe that Catherine would be one of them. 'There must be another explanation,' I finally said.

Robbie glanced across at me so quickly I couldn't read his expression. 'Maybe.' He turned onto the Chipwell road. 'We might be jumping to conclusions – we still don't know that Ron Jackson has anything to do with this. It could be completely legitimate.'

'Hmmm.' Neither of us believed there was anything legitimate about Ron Jackson's visits.

'He might be acting on his own initiative and using Catherine as a cover. There's no use you tying yourself up in knots until you ask her what she knows about him.'

My mind was racing, but Robbie's tone was even, and in the dark, I couldn't make out his expression, but surely he must've been as shocked as I was when I read the name on the card.

'I can't believe Catherine has anything to do with this.'

Robbie's hands tightened on the steering wheel. 'We still don't know for sure —'

'That Ron Jackson is involved? I know, but even if he isn't, why is he cold calling farmhouses looking for stock? That's not Catherine's style either.' I'd known Catherine for years – both as an employer and a friend. She got me started in the industry and taught me almost everything I know. While she was a canny businesswoman, I refused to believe she – or the auction house that bore her name – could be involved in anything nefarious. 'That business card is the only real clue we have regarding Ron Jackson's whereabouts. And now it seems Catherine's part of it too.'

We'd pulled up outside my house, and he smiled at me in a way that should've made me feel reassured but just made me more wretched. 'I'll talk to her – it's best if you stay out of it. On a more positive side, at least I have his phone number. Try not to worry; it could be something of nothing.'

'Summat of nowt, as they say around here?'

His smile was as forced as mine. 'Aye. Sleep well and I'll call you tomorrow.'

I nodded and let myself into the house, but sleep was a long time coming – and when it arrived, there was nothing peaceful about my dreams.

Chapter Eleven

After a disturbed night, I gave up on any attempt to sleep at around six and got up for the day, taking advantage of the early morning to whip up a quick lemon tray cake and some sandwiches from the leftovers of yesterday's roast beef to take to Albert's.

When the sun finally decided to show itself, the day was crisp and blue, and Bally and I did our favourite no-work Monday thing and took an extra-long walk. While the frost on the path was crunchy under my boots, clumps of snowdrops were here and there, beside the hedgerows, under trees, growing up through the frozen ground and leaf litter – the first sign that spring was coming. If I looked closely, the faintest of faint green smudges on the bare branches of the trees and hedges showed. I breathed out a little 'ha' and watched my breath turn white. Yes, spring might be coming, but it was still a way away.

Albert and Jess were happy to see Bally and me, and the first few hours flew by. Although Albert's barn – like many others in this part of the country – appeared to be a daunting task, I soon worked out a system, and it wasn't long before we had some designated piles: throw, donate, keep and sell. While there was little of real value, we had unearthed the missing chairs for the Mouseman table, and there were a few boxes (including an unusual Victorian candle box), some smaller Mouseman items and some kitchenalia that would sell well. The mahogany table crank was matched with a Victorian dining table which had been languishing under yet another tarpaulin. Most importantly, by the time we were finished, the barn (at least) would no longer be a tripping hazard.

Iris and Esme arrived midmorning, the former with a batch of fresh teacakes and a willingness to get stuck in to help (and order me around), the latter happy to keep the tea coming and to provide gossip.

Simon turned up, as Simon was apt to do, right as we were about to start lunch, making me glad I'd packed extra sandwiches and the cake. He was pleased with the mahogany extension table, delighted with the Mouseman furniture, surprised at the condition the pieces were in and promised to do some phoning around of his contacts for a possible buyer.

'We'll make sure these go to a good home for you,' he assured Albert, wiping the lenses of his glasses with the end of the (Black Sabbath) T-shirt he wore under a heavy checked flannelette jacket. 'The tarpaulin has kept them safe, and they should come up nicely. If you're prepared to part with the kitchen dresser as well, we can market them as a set.'

'Aye, do that. Happens that dresser's always been too big for the kitchen.'

'I remember our mum complaining about the size,' said Esme. 'If it belongs with the table, though …'

'I think by the time we've finished with the kitchen, Albert, there'll be plenty of room for your plates and things in the other cupboard. Or we can bring in the one we found in the barn – it's not nearly as big, so you'll still have somewhere to keep your papers and such.'

He patted the hand I'd placed lightly on his arm. 'Aye, you're probably right, pet. Let's do that.'

Simon named a price that left everyone speechless and then, misunderstanding the silence, added, 'But to the right buyer, we might even get more.' Albert's mouth hung open.

'That'll set us up alright, love,' he said to Esme, his eyes suspiciously moist. 'I've never felt right that our dad left the house and farm to me.'

Esme, however, had no words.

'Right, well—' Simon shifted his feet, awkward at the sibling's show of emotion. 'I'm away for the next few days on a buying trip down south so will come back later in the week to measure up and take photos if that's okay.' To me, he said, 'There's no point cleaning out the dresser until we have a buyer.'

Albert agreed, and Simon was soon on his way with

one of Iris's buttered teacakes and a slice of lemon cake wrapped in paper napkins.

The activity, for the most part, kept my mind from fixating on the business card Gordon had given us yesterday and what it potentially meant, but at various points during the day, my mind wandered in that direction, wondered whether Robbie had spoken to Catherine yet. As certain as I was that she wasn't involved – couldn't be involved – with the robberies, according to that business card we'd been given, Ronald Jackson worked for her. Yet, I leant back against the barn wall, cradling yet another cup of hot tea, absently watching the steam spiral skywards. I'd never met him at the auction house or, indeed, at any of the sales. And given I was at Young and Johnsons most weeks, I thought I knew everyone who worked there as well as all the regulars who attended the sales. Perhaps he was new and trying to make an impression. I let out an involuntary snort that made Iris lift her head. If that was the case, he wasn't going the right way about it.

'Penny for them, pet.' Iris walked over from where she, Esme and Albert had been sitting in the sun.

This part of the courtyard caught the afternoon sun and the three of them had been making the most of the late winter warmth. 'My thoughts aren't worth a penny.' I chuckled at my attempted humour.

'No closer to finding that bugger who's been causing us trouble, then.'

I sipped at my tea and shook my head. 'Not yet. To be honest, Iris, I can't see how it all fits together.'

'What? The robberies and the trouble?' At my nod, she looked thoughtful, her forefinger tapping against her lower lip. 'Why would he rob us and then come back to break lights, paint barns and meddle with wood piles?'

There was something to what she said that rang a faint bell. 'Esme's had no trouble yet, has she?'

Iris looked back at Esme, happily sitting in the weak winter sun with Jess on one side and Bally on the other. 'No ...' She paused thoughtfully. 'Although there was her fall – she said she'd heard noises just before it happened and swears she hadn't left that ladder where it was. It was probably nowt, and I don't think she could cope with knowing someone had been lurking about.'

'What do you mean by that?'

She sighed once as if choosing her words. 'She's not like me; Esme's not comfortable on her own ... it wouldn't take much for her to sell up and move into a retirement village.'

'Would that be such a bad thing? For her, I mean.' I took another mouthful of my tea.

'Maybe not,' she conceded. 'But ...'

Iris didn't need to finish the sentence. Nor did she need to tell me she'd miss Esme if she moved away – as would Albert.

'Let's hope it doesn't come to that then.' I tossed the dregs of my tea onto the gravel. 'Right, well. I think that's all we can do out here. I'll help you take these plates inside and—'

My phone started ringing. Pulling it from the back pocket of my jeans, I stared at the caller's name for a few seconds, unable to answer at first, my heart skipping a beat. 'Catherine, hi … what can I do for you?'

'I think I've found your firefly cage.' Her voice was full of excitement. 'And, possibly, some of your missing silver.'

My mouth dropped open, and for a second or two, I couldn't speak.

'Philly?'

'Let me call Robbie … We'll be right there.' I hung up on Catherine and immediately called Robbie.

'Hiya, Philly, how's the clean-up going?'

'Really well … Have you had a chance to speak to Catherine yet?' My heart was in my mouth as I waited for his answer. If Robbie had spoken to Catherine about Ron Jackson, maybe she'd called me in response – to prove her innocence.

'No, not yet. To be honest, I'd been putting it off,' he said sheepishly. 'I hope you haven't been worrying about it all day.'

'She's got the firefly cage,' I said without further preamble. 'Catherine's got the firefly cage – and what she thinks is probably some of the missing silver.'

There was a brief second of silence before Robbie responded. 'Flippin' 'eck'—he slipped into Yorkshire vernacular—'I wasn't expecting that!'

'Me neither. What do you think it means? Surely it must mean she has nothing to do with it … doesn't it?' I knew I was grasping at every possible reason to believe Catherine knew nothing about what Ron Jackson had been doing.

'Perhaps.' Robbie's tone was noncommittal. 'Can you meet me at Young and Johnsons … in, say, thirty minutes?'

I glanced at my watch. 'Yes, I can make that. Bally and I will see you there.'

While I'd been on the phone, I'd forgotten I had an audience, but now Iris said, 'Have you found my firefly cage?'

I hesitated briefly, debating whether to prevaricate, but her steely gaze warned me not to. 'You know, Iris, I think we might have.'

'You certainly didn't waste any time,' Catherine exclaimed when we appeared in her doorway not half an hour after receiving her phone call. With an arch look, she added, 'You seem to be becoming a fixture with Philly, Inspector Dawkins.' Robbie smiled one of his wry half-smiles but gave no other explanation. 'You'll be wanting to see the goods?'

At our nod, she shrugged into a black wool coat, tying the belt tightly around her waist and led us out of the office past her assistant Becky's desk – where we left Bally – and into the cavernous warehouse behind the office and showroom. I wound my scarf more tightly around my neck, hoping to ward off the chill.

'Here it is.'

On the table was indeed Iris Metcalfe's firefly cage, along with the silver I recognised as being from her house. Beside it all sat the Terry's of York drawer chocolate box Iris had told us about, and beside that, another in the shape of a treasure chest. I exchanged a glance with Robbie – the second box matched the description of the one Eddie had given us – as did the Victorian jewellery and Eddie's father's medals.

'Where did this all come from?' Robbie asked, and I held my breath as we waited for her to answer.

'Do I need to tell you that?' Her red-painted lips curled into a resigned grimace. 'Don't answer that; of course I do. It was a private consignment – apparently a deceased estate. I'll get you the details later. I probably wouldn't have thought too much about it if it wasn't for the firefly cage. There's nothing out of the ordinary about the rest of it.' She exhaled heavily, her shoulders slumping. 'I don't suppose there's any doubt?'

I reached for the firefly cage, but Robbie tapped my arm lightly to stop me and pulled a packet of silicon gloves from his overcoat pocket. 'You'll be needing these.'

Nodding my understanding, I opened the packet and pulled the gloves on before examining the firefly cage. 'No,' I said, placing the firefly cage back on the table and picking up an enamelled ring. 'There's no doubt – or at least not unless there are two of these in Yorkshire which, given that up to the other day I'd never seen one in real life, makes that scenario unlikely indeed. Plus'—I pulled my loupe out of my handbag and raised it to my eyes, squinting at the inscription on the gold band of the ring—'this is definitely the ring that was reported stolen from the same house, and I've seen this other silver too – it all came from inside the chocolate box, didn't it?'

Catherine nodded, the action making her black-rimmed glasses slip from the bridge of her nose. She pushed them back in place.

Robbie stepped forward, his notebook open and wordlessly began marking items off against his list. 'We have reason to believe all of this is stolen, Catherine.' He snapped his notebook shut. 'I'll need to take it back to the station for identification.'

Tilting her head slightly to the side, her eyes narrowed. 'All of it? Are you telling me these things are stolen too?' Her hand waved towards the treasure chest and the items on the table beside it. When Robbie didn't immediately answer, she turned her attention to me. 'Well?'

'We have reason to believe that these items have been stolen,' Robbie said again, his hazel eyes unflinching.

'Right. Okay, well, do what you need to do, I suppose. You can use the boxes they came in – that's them under the table – and I'll get one of the warehouse boys to help you box it up.'

But Robbie was already pulling another pair of gloves

from his pocket. 'No need, Philly and I will take care of it.'

Catherine watched their every movement. 'You can't be thinking of getting fingerprints from any of that.'

Robbie's lips curled into a tight smile. 'You never know. We'll also be needing to take the fingerprints of your staff—'

Catherine's eyes widened, her groomed eyebrows rising to hide under her steel-grey fringe. 'Do you suspect someone on my team?'

'For elimination purposes,' he added, his jaw firm, his mouth tight.

Catherine held his stare another few seconds before letting hers drop. 'We have nothing to hide,' she finally said.

Robbie nodded briskly. 'I'll send someone by.'

I laid a gloved hand on Catherine's arm. 'Sorry to ask, but we need to know where you got this from.'

'It came in yesterday.' Her eyes rested wistfully on the firefly cage as I placed it carefully into the box. 'I wasn't here at the time, so I'd need Becky to check the records, but Ashley took the goods – he's the new porter and salesroom assistant. If you need a description, he'd be the one to ask.' She lingered for a short while longer. 'I'll fetch Ashley, shall I?'

'Please,' said Robbie. 'And if you can get the contact details of the seller as well …'

'You didn't ask her about Ron Jackson,' I commented once she'd left the room.

'Let's see what information she has first,' Robbie

replied cryptically.

I searched his face for additional meaning, but his expression was neutral. 'You're waiting to see whether she'll give us his name,' I guessed. 'You can't honestly still believe she has anything to do with this. Why would she call and tell us she had the firefly cage if she was involved? You saw the way she was looking at it – she'd like nothing more than to sell one of these.'

Under my stare, his expression softened slightly. 'I don't want to believe it, Philly, but we have to follow procedure and keep an open mind – you know how it works.'

Recognising his words as a gentle scolding, I nodded slightly. He was, of course, right.

Catherine was soon back, and with her, a younger, stockily built man. 'Inspector Dawkins, Philly, this is Ashley Poole. Inspector Dawkins is investigating a break-in and believes this could be stolen property, and Philly is a dealer at Chipwell Barn Antiques and is … What exactly are you doing with the inspector, Philly?'

'She's assisting the police.' Robbie effectively closed off future questions.

Ashley held his hand out to shake ours. 'Catherine tells me you'd like a description of the man who brought these boxes in?'

'Yes, please.' Robbie pulled his notebook from his pocket. 'What he said, what he was wearing – in as much detail as you can remember.'

'Right, well ...' Ashley pushed his hands into the pockets of his jeans. 'He came in late – must've been around four-ish, I'd say. Told me he was in York to clean out his mother's house after she'd passed away. He said she'd been quite the collector of silver and that he couldn't be bothered packing it all up to take back home with him.'

'Did he mention where he was from?' Robbie's pen was poised.

Ashley tipped his head back to gaze at the warehouse rafters and wrinkled his nose. 'No, sorry.'

'What did he look like?'

Ashley looked up, surprised the question had come from me rather than Robbie. 'He was an old bloke – probably about fifty, maybe sixty?' I exchanged a quick rueful glance with Catherine – old indeed. 'About average height, I'd say, grey hair, sort of spiky on top.' He patted his own crew cut. 'Like mine, but a bit longer at the back.' Frowning, he cupped his chin with his thumb and forefinger, tracing the path of his beard. 'But clean-shaven.' He lifted a shoulder. 'Sorry, that's all I noticed.'

'Thank you.' Robbie looked up from his notebook. 'That's a big help. Did you see what he was driving?'

'No, sorry. I didn't catch his name either. I sent him in to see Becky to complete the paperwork.' His eyes flicked between Robbie and me. 'Is that all?'

Robbie nodded. 'Aye, if you think of anything else, here's my card.'

Ashley took it and held it for a few seconds before nodding abruptly and shoving it into his pocket. 'Aye, well, if you don't need me anymore, I'll be getting back to work.'

He addressed his last comment to Catherine, who nodded. 'Thank you, Ashley.' To us, she said, 'I've got his details here – name, number, address …' She handed the paper across to Robbie who, other than a slight raising of his eyebrows, gave nothing away.

'Have you heard the name Ron Jackson?' Robbie asked.

She shook her head. 'No.' Then, after a beat, 'Is there a reason I would have?'

'If he comes back, please let us know,' he said.

Catherine held his stare for long enough to let him know she hadn't missed his deliberate avoidance of her question. 'What do I say if he calls wanting to know about the auction?'

'When were these due to go to auction?' I asked.

'We're cataloguing now for the last week in February,' she said.

'I don't think you'll hear from him before then,' said Robbie. 'But if you do, tell him you forgot to get him to sign a purchase order – or something else to get him back in here. Whatever you do, don't let him know you've contacted us.'

Becky was in the process of sneaking Bally a treat when we approached.

'No wonder he loves coming here,' I said as Bally shot me one of his nothing-to-see-here looks.

'He asked so nicely for it.' Becky held out another little piece of dried beef from the stash that she kept in her drawer for visiting pooches. 'You were asking about the man who brought in those boxes last night?' At my nod, she continued. 'Well, I don't know if it will help, but I saw him getting into a dark-coloured Land Rover when he left. It was either black or grey – I wasn't really paying attention, and I'm sorry, I didn't get the plates.'

'That's a great help, thank you,' I said. 'A really great help.'

Robbie didn't show me what had been written on the paper Catherine had handed to him until we were back in the car. As I read it, I let out a gasp of disbelief. 'Ron Jackson? What the hell is going on here, Robbie? Why would Catherine say she'd never heard of him when his name is on one of her business cards?'

'The most obvious reason is because she's telling the truth. But I'll take this back to the station for logging and see if the fingerprint guys can get anything useful from it. It's getting late, but tomorrow I'll pay Mr Jackson from Leeds a visit.' He opened the car door for Bally to bound in while I leant against the closed driver's door.

'Another dark-coloured Land Rover – do you think it's the same as the stolen vehicle that followed me home?'

He shrugged one shoulder. 'It's possible, and if it was,

that means it was Ron Jackson who was out at Albert's that night.'

Was the Land Rover the link we'd been looking for? 'It couldn't have been him with the spray can, though. That person ran away quickly and all the descriptions we've so far had of Ron haven't led me to think he could be the running away quickly type.'

Robbie's half smile was rueful. 'Perhaps ... but he might have an accomplice.'

While waiting for my response, he arched his eyebrows. 'And he's just the getaway driver? Yes, that could make sense ...' What was it Iris had said earlier? 'Maybe we're trying too hard to make it all fit.' As he would have said something, I held my hand up. 'I've been going through it all over and over, and I can't understand why Ron would rob the houses and then come back to cause criminal damage. Why not do it at the same time? And then there's the type of damage that's being done.' I shook my head and opened the door. 'It doesn't make sense.' My words came out with an exasperated sigh. 'Maybe we're trying to make sense of something that isn't meant to make sense.'

Robbie gripped the top of the door as I slid into the driver's seat and fastened the seatbelt. 'You could be right. I'll check in tomorrow after I visit this address.'

'You don't think Catherine is involved, do you?' I guessed.

'No, Philly, I don't. I think the business cards he was

using were fake. He could've picked any auction house.' He chuckled sardonically. 'So much for the chief super giving me something to keep me amused while ticking down the days to retirement … Don't look at me like that, Philly. I know that's why I'm on this case – it's low profile and keeps me from sticking my nose in while Whitely finds his feet; nobody expects I'll solve it.'

I grinned up at him. 'Which is why you'll do your best to do just that.'

'Aye. Tea at the pub tomorrow? I'll catch you up on what I find out.'

'Sounds good. Let's go to The White Horse again.'

'Do you think he's likely to come back there?'

'Who knows?' I lifted a shoulder. 'But I rather fancy that mushroom pasta on the menu.'

'Mind how you go, Philly.' He chuckled as he shut the door.

When I looked in the rear-view mirror as I drove away, he was still standing there, his hands in his coat pocket, his shoulders hunched against the cold.

Chapter Twelve

Yesterday's clear weather continued and with the sun came passing traffic to Chipwell Antiques Barn – enough to keep us steadily busy throughout the day.

Marlene called by midafternoon to look at the items I'd spoken to her about and went into raptures over the Mouseman ashtray. 'I've never seen anything like this. Where did you say it came from?'

'A farm out near Dunthrop. We're not entirely sure of the provenance, but I believe a family member used to do some work for the York Racecourse.'

'Well, however they came by it, I must have it for my collection. And this little vesta case is sweet too. I'll tell Gordon it's an anniversary present.' The girlish giggle was back. While it was annoying, it also seemed self-conscious. 'Now, where's that painting you were telling me about?'

I led her across the room to the wall I liked to hang my oils from. 'It's British school, but not by anyone remarkable – just, I think, a nice example of the type. I've done some research on the artist and, while he's not well known, he was from Yorkshire.'

'Would you be able to get it off the wall so I can look more closely at it?'

'Absolutely.' I dragged my stepladder out from the storeroom and climbed up, steadying myself by placing a hand on the adjacent bookshelf as I reached for the picture. 'Here.' I passed it to her while I climbed down. Propping the picture against the wall, I dusted my hands down my jeans. 'What do you think?'

'I love it.' Marlene stepped closer, studying it intently. 'I really love it. I don't suppose you could hold it – and the ashtray – for me for a couple of days? I'm expecting some money to come through, and you know …' Her cheeks coloured and she ducked her head, a silvery curtain of hair falling about her face.

I hastened to put her at ease. 'Of course. I'll mark them as sold, and you take your time – no pressure. If you want, we can even do an instalment program.'

She lifted her head and tucked her hair back behind her ears. 'Thank you, that would be a help.' Glancing around, and with no customers in sight, she said, 'I don't suppose you'd have time for a coffee. I spied some lovely looking apple scones in the café's cabinet.'

I glanced at my watch. 'As it happens, yes I do, but let me buy you a coffee – to say thank you for your hospitality on Sunday.'

She blushed again, and I wondered whether she had

many friends unconnected with the horse world. 'That would be lovely, thank you.'

In the café, I introduced Marlene to Ginny. 'I adore that jumper,' Marlene said shyly. Ginny was today resplendent in a hot pink jumper with bright red cherries on the front that made me think of spring. 'I could never wear anything so bright.'

Ginny beamed at the compliment. 'Whereas I would love to be able to wear neutrals as well as you do. Now, what can I get you? I've still got a few scones left … or if that doesn't appeal, I always have some parkin …'

We both opted for the scones, and Ginny left us to it. 'It's your anniversary today, isn't it? Happy anniversary.'

Marlene's smile was bright. 'That's sweet of you to remember, thank you.'

'Are you looking forward to your night out?'

'I am. Gordon's taking me for dinner at the pub where we had our first date. Back then, it was nothing special, but now it's one of those gastropubs. It will be such a treat for it to be just us.' Her smile slipped slightly, but she caught it so quickly I almost thought I'd imagined it.

'But it was just you two at The White Horse the other night …' I started.

'Oh yes, it begins that way, but Gordon always finds someone to talk to, or there's always calls coming through.' This time when her smile slipped, she didn't attempt to stop it. 'He's always doing some business deal or another …

He tells me not to worry about it, but I sometimes wonder what he's got himself involved in, and I can't help but remember the trouble he had, although I suppose deals are better than other women ...' She gave herself a little shake as if she realised she was telling me too much. 'Don't listen to me; I'm just prattling on. I think all marriages end up like that, don't they? With each person living their own lives. Besides, I'm tied up with the stables so much I don't really have time to wonder what Gordon is up to – and I'm sure it's all above board these days.'

Despite wanting to react, I kept my expression impassive, making a mental note to share her comments with Robbie later.

'I'm sorry if I assumed too much about you and Robbie,' she continued, pale pink flushing her cheeks again.

'That's okay. It's a simple mistake to make.'

'And he's a policeman – that was a surprise. You mentioned you have children from a previous relationship ...'

'Yes, and before you ask, my ex-husband was a policeman too.' I smiled to soften the words. 'And you? Gordon mentioned it was the second time around for each of you. How did you meet?'

As she was about to answer, Ginny placed our scones on the table, and when she'd left, Marlene took so long splitting and buttering her scone with the apple and sage butter Ginny served with it that I thought she'd forgotten my question.

'We met through my brother-in-law, Charlie. He was in real estate too, you see, and had been doing some business with Gordon.'

'Your brother-in-law?' I knew my surprise probably showed on my face.

'Yes, I was separated from my husband by then.' She paused as if wondering whether to tell me more. 'My ex wasn't a very nice man,' she finally said. 'He was also in real estate, but he'd been involved in some shady deals. Also, he was …'—her head lowered so I couldn't see her expression—'not nice to me sometimes.'

'He was abusive?' No wonder Marlene sometimes seemed unsure of herself, as if she could blend into the background and disappear.

'Not physically, but it doesn't need to be, does it? A tight smile crept across her face. 'There are other ways of making you feel like you don't matter.' She took a sip of her coffee and looked me straight in the eyes. 'Thankfully, Charlie helped me see that and helped me make the break … not that there was anything like that between us,' she rushed to add, 'even though at the time I might've wanted there to be.' She let out one of those girlish giggles that still sounded surprising in a grown woman. 'In any case, I vowed I'd never let anyone do that to me again, and Gordon has certainly never treated me in that way – tried to control and own me. Sometimes I think it's completely the opposite and he doesn't see me at all. I could be invisible.' Her voice was wistful, her eyes unfocused and far away, as if I wasn't there. 'Charlie warned me that when a man marries his lover, it leaves a job vacancy. Perhaps he was right.'

'Gordon was married when you met?'

She nodded. 'Yes. He'd told me it was over between him and Brenda, but'—she shrugged—'I wonder ...' She took a mouthful of her scone. 'This is a wonderful scone ... and I've never tasted anything like this butter.'

Her abrupt change of subject silenced me for a second. 'Ginny's certainly a fabulous baker; we're very fortunate to have her on the team.' I waited for a beat. 'I'm sorry you went through that, but glad you've found happiness the second time around.' When she didn't immediately agree, I added, 'You *are* happy, aren't you?'

Another of those little shakes that were almost as disconcerting as the girlish giggles. 'Of course I'm happy. We muddle along nicely, but no relationship is perfect; I'm sure I don't have to tell you that.'

'No, you don't.'

'Besides, I have the stables now and the horses. I'm exactly where I want to be, and no matter what Gordon does, it's where I'll be staying.' Before I could think too hard about what a strange statement that was to make, she'd plastered a bright smile on her face and was asking me about my marriage. 'And your ex-husband. Was he nice to you?'

'Mostly,' I said, suddenly unwilling to share too much. 'We had a good run – over twenty years – and raised a couple of great kids. It ended badly, to be sure, and he's remarried, but we get on well these days.'

'And is he still in the force?' She busied herself, buttering the other half of her scone.

'Yes, he is.'

'And he's okay with you helping Robbie on his investigations?'

A ripple of unease at the direction of her question ran through me, yet her expression was open as if she was just trying to get to know me better. Maybe she was; maybe I was imagining an undercurrent that wasn't there. 'He's fine with it. Anyway, I'm not involved as such, just advising on stolen antiques.' I forced a chuckle. 'I seem to have a photographic memory when it comes to antiques.'

Marlene nodded. 'That's what Robbie said.' She hesitated. 'And that's what I'm counting on.'

My brows raised in silent question as I waited for her to continue.

'You see, I think some of mine are missing – from my cabinet.' My mouth opened in surprise, but no words came out. 'They were there on Sunday when you visited, and I'm sure they were there yesterday morning, but this morning they were gone.'

'What was taken?'

'That's the thing; I'm not sure. There are no spaces

where things that were there aren't anymore, but I can tell some pieces are missing and everything else has been moved around so that I wouldn't notice. I know for sure the little flask is gone and that matchstick holder.' Marlene pulled her phone out of her bag and flipped through the screens until she found what she was after. 'Here's a photo of the cabinet – I took it this morning.' She handed the phone over, her eyes meeting mine. 'What do you think?'

Using my fingers, I zoomed in on the cabinet shelves. 'I see what you mean,' I finally said. 'Things look to have been moved, but I can't tell from this what might have been taken. I'm happy to come out and have a look, though. What does Gordon say?'

She picked up her coffee mug, cradling it in both hands, and shook her head. 'I haven't told him.' She took a sip and swallowed, placing the mug carefully back on the table. 'I didn't want to until I was sure. Do you think it's connected to the other robberies you're looking into?'

I considered my answer carefully. 'We don't know for sure anything has been taken yet, and it seems to be a different pattern ...' There was something in the way she was looking at me as if there was a message she wanted to give me without actually saying the words. 'Is there any sign of a break-in?'

'No,' she said, holding my eyes. 'But then there wouldn't be, would there?'

'What do you mean by that?' I knew the answer before

she said it and needed her to say it aloud.

'If Gordon was the one who took the pieces from the cabinet ….' Her chin firmed, almost daring me to argue with her, to tell her she must be mistaken, that there was no way her husband would've taken things from her cabinet and then attempted to cover up his actions. 'After all, it wouldn't be the first time.' My eyes widened, and she shook her head. 'I don't know why I said that; pay no attention to me. It's just … no, it doesn't matter. In fact, I'm probably imagining it all and everything is still in the cabinet where I left it.'

'Are you sure you don't want to talk to me about whatever is bothering you?'

'I'm sure.' There was a determined tilt to her chin. She drained her coffee and stood. 'It's been lovely to catch up, Philly, but I'd best be getting back. I have another couple of things to do before we go out tonight.' She gripped my arm, and again, I was astounded by her strength. 'I meant it the other day about coming for a ride. How does Friday morning suit you? We'll go early so you can still be back to open up and there's nothing like breathing the early morning air on horseback – the fields are at their best. Shall we say seven-thirty?'

'That sounds lovely, although, as I said, it's been many years since I last was on a horse.' My heart skipped a little at the thought of falling off and hurting myself, but I determinedly pushed the fear away and plastered a brave smile.

'You'll be fine. It will surprise you how quickly you remember. I have some boots and a helmet you can borrow, so just be sure to rug up – and be prepared to be a little sore afterward.' Releasing my arm, she gave me a little hug. 'See you then.'

'I'll look forward to it.' And as she left, I realised I meant it. Despite that self-conscious girlish giggle, there was something about Marlene that was growing on me … and the idea of an early morning ride? That was growing on me, too.

Chapter Thirteen

Albert, Esme and Iris were sitting around the same table as the last time we'd eaten at The White Horse. With their heads together, a half-empty pint glass in front of Albert, and small wine glasses on the table for the two women, they looked like they were busy plotting something.

'You three look as though you're up to no good.' My words startled them so much that Esme spilt her wine.

'Hello, pet,' she said beatifically. 'And there's that nice inspector too.'

'So was it my firefly cage?' Iris straightened; her defensive pose and the fact that Albert's eyes were furtively darting around the room rather than meeting mine told me I hadn't imagined the huddle they'd been in when we arrived.

'Yes, we have,' said Robbie, a glint in his eyes. He had the same suspicions I did – these three were up to something. 'We need to hold on to it for a while longer, though, I'm afraid.'

'For evidence, I suppose,' said Esme with all the knowledge that watching TV police procedurals brings.

'They'll need to check it for fingerprints and the like, I expect.'

Robbie suppressed a smile. 'I'll need you to come down to the station and identify the other items too when you're able. I can come and get you if you like.'

'Oooh, Iris, you need to go to the nick,' teased Esme. 'Do you need our statements too, Inspector?'

I swallowed my chuckle. That was probably not the first glass of wine Esme had consumed tonight.

'I don't know, Esme … Is there anything you need to tell me?'

I almost laughed out loud at Robbie's wicked grin and the wash of guilty colour that immediately spread across first Esme's and then her brother's face.

'And how are you, Albert?' I grinned as the older man's eyes were forced to meet mine.

'Fair t'middlin',' he said gruffly, his focus again shifting past me to the door.

'You three wouldn't happen to be waiting for someone, would you?' I asked.

'We thought maybe Ron Jacks … ow! Why did you have to go and kick me like that, Iris? That were my good leg too.' Esme rubbed at her leg through her trousers. Iris, rather than being contrite, glared at her friend.

'You thought Ron Jackson might come back, is that right?' Robbie asked slowly, his gaze lingering on each in turn. Esme and Albert both looked away under his stare, but Iris met it.

'And why not?' Again Iris drew herself to her full height in her chair. You buggers aren't getting any closer to finding him—'

'And they always return to the scene of the crime,' finished Esme, her sore leg now forgotten.

'Except that this wasn't a crime scene,' I pointed out. 'Rather somewhere he stopped for a drink.'

'And who's to say he won't stop here again?' Iris's shoulders were squared for battle.

'Fair point,' conceded Robbie. 'Although, mind you, let me know if he does happen to be back.' This time Iris dropped her eyes first.

'Now that you and Philly are here, you can take over the surveillance,' said Albert, draining the remainder of his beer. 'It's well past tea time for Jess and me.' At the sound of her name, Jess's tail thumped hard on the floor, Bally's tail joining in just in case he was involved as well.

'It doesn't look as though he's coming tonight anyway.' Esme finished her wine and reached behind to pull her walker closer. 'So we might as well let you continue the stake-out.'

'What time would it suit you for me to come to the station tomorrow?' Iris got to her feet, her head held high.

'Any time after nine will be fine.' The corner of Robbie's lips twitched.

Iris nodded once in acknowledgement.

'Would you like me to pick you up and take you in?' I asked. 'I'm absolutely happy to.'

'No, thank you, pet.' Iris's shoulders softened. 'I can get there under my own steam.'

It wasn't until the three of them and Jess had shuffled out that I let out the laugh I'd been keeping in during our conversation. 'What are they like?'

Robbie scratched at his brow and shook his head in amused exasperation. 'I think they fancy playing the detective. I don't suppose there's any harm in it, though.'

Bally settled on the opposite side of the fire to an ageing labrador who had lifted his head in a brief greeting while Robbie and me, drinks in hand, found ourselves at the same table we'd been at the other night.

'Tell me about Leeds.' By unspoken mutual agreement, neither of us had spoken about the case during the short drive here.

Robbie frowned into his pint glass, took a long swallow, and wiped his top lip with the back of his hand. 'It was a complete dead end.'

'He didn't live there?'

Robbie shook his head. 'No. It was one of those terraces built in the fifties; you know the ones – postwar rendered brick, two up, two down.' I knew the type – quickly and cheaply constructed; most had a kitchen and living room downstairs and two bedrooms upstairs. 'This one had babies playthings out the front, but the occupant

– Chelsea Beattie, her name was – a young woman with a bairn – said they were renting and had never heard of him.'

'Did you believe her?'

'The house was a mess – sink full of unwashed dishes and piles of clothes and toys everywhere – but I didn't see any sign that a man could be spending time there.' His nose had wrinkled, and I imagined the scene inside the terrace. 'I called in at the real estate, though, and they've never heard the name either. The landlord has a few of these properties – and by the looks of the one I saw, barely maintains them – and he's also not heard of Ron Jackson.' He took another mouthful of beer and rubbed behind the back of his neck wearily. 'As I said, a dead end. Iris is right; we're getting nowhere with this case.'

'I don't know ...' I said slowly. 'Marlene Willoughby called in today, and we had a very interesting conversation.' I tapped my nails against the stem of my wineglass. 'The more I think on it, the more convinced I am that she was trying to tell me something without actually telling me.'

His eyes narrowed. 'Go on ... actually, no, hold that thought. Let's order first, and then you can tell me. It's been so long since I ate that my stomach is beginning to think my throat is cut.'

'I doubt you'll fade away.' I chuckled and he patted his well-fed belly and grinned.

'And before you argue – after that cracking roast you cooked on Sunday, it's my shout tonight. What do you fancy?'

He picked the menu up and began reading it.

'I'll go for the mushroom pasta, but I don't know why you bother reading the menu – we both know you'll be ordering the gammon, egg and chips.' His rumbly laugh followed him all the way to the bar.

Once back, and with fresh drinks, I told him about Marlene's visit. 'I got the feeling she was pointing me in Gordon's direction … when she said he was always taking calls and she wasn't sure what business he was into at any point in time. Then she made reference to him having troubles in the past, and I got the impression he'd gotten into trouble over money.'

Robbie took his notebook from his top pocket, his lips pursed. 'Sounds like it might be worth looking into Gordon Willoughby.'

'I think so. She also mentioned that she thinks some items from her collection have gone missing.'

'Since we were there on Sunday?'

'Yes.'

'Have they had a break-in?' Robbie's brow was furrowed, his finger curled against his top lip.

'She said there's no sign of forced entry and she's not even sure anything is missing but thinks they've been moved around in the cabinet to look like nothing is. Because you told them I had a photographic memory as far as antiques were concerned, she's asked me to go and have a look.' I hesitated slightly before continuing. 'She thinks that if anything is missing, Gordon has taken it.'

'He's taken things from the house before?'

'Apparently. She said it wouldn't be the first time, but when I asked her what she'd meant, she clammed up and wouldn't say anything more, so I don't know for sure.'

Robbie made another note in his book. 'If you were so inclined, what would you take from that cabinet?'

I screwed my nose up as my brain drifted back. 'It's mostly porcelain; of that, only a few pieces would be worth more than a few hundred, five hundred tops. Some lovely silver, to be sure, and those things I pointed out on Sunday – the boot-shaped match holder and hunting flask would definitely do well at sale.' I cast my eyes to the ceiling. 'There was some jewellery too – mostly Victorian and Edwardian. I remember seeing a brooch with a horseshoe and crop on it – I think that would have been nine carat gold, but I didn't look that closely – and another horseshoe pin in pearl and enamel, also on gold that you'd get maybe a hundred for. Those, plus a painted ceramic brooch – another hunting scene – would be the stand-outs from that lot. I'd be more interested in what else was in the room. There was a lovely clock on the mantel that I'd target – high Victorian, inlaid black marble – that would fetch between a thousand to fifteen hundred at auction. There's also a sweet pair of Victorian horse brass door stops that are quite unusual, and the drinks trolley he served us from was lovely, and did you notice that tantalus? French, I think

– not that I got a good look at it. But in the cabinet? I'm not sure I'd bother with a piece here and there.'

'Tantalus? That sounds dangerous.'

I laughed at his bemusement. 'Not at all … although, maybe. It's a contraption you put your spirit decanters in – lockable so the servants can't sneak a sip here and there. One was on the shelf of the drinks trolley disguised as a pile of books. I would've loved to see inside that; if it still had its original decanters and glasses – it would probably have come with four glasses and a spirit measure – you could be looking at a thousand, maybe more.'

Robbie's eyes widened. 'That much?'

'Depending on the condition. As I said, I didn't get a chance for a close look. If they're having financial problems, that's what I'd sell first, but when she took me into the other rooms to see the art, Marlene told me that most of the furniture and art had been in the house since her grandparent's day. I got the impression they'd had the money, her father lost most of it, and now she and Gordon are doing their best to keep things running. She's devoted to the stables – doesn't care so much for the racing side of it – and I suspect she's more comfortable in the company of horses than people.'

'You could be right. Did you tell her how much those things were worth?'

'Some of it, yes. She'd asked me not to mention it to Gordon – which I found strange at the time, but then she'd laughed and said he'd try and convince her to sell some of it. Then she giggled that weird giggle and I thought it might've been an in-joke between them so hadn't thought about it again. Maybe it wasn't such an in-joke.'

The conversation paused while the server placed our meals in front of us. 'Robbie,' I began, pausing for a beat while my brain put my thoughts in order. 'What if Gordon Willoughby knows Ron Jackson? What if they're in this together and when they were here in the pub the other day, it wasn't a chance meeting but rather a, well, meeting?'

Chewing thoughtfully on his gammon, Robbie pondered the question. 'Why would he have Ron Jackson's business card if that was the case?'

My shoulders slumped. 'You're right; there's no reason for that. In fact, it was a ridiculous idea … Forget I said anything.'

'No, Philly, it's not ridiculous. At this point, any suggestion is worth considering. Maybe Gordon volunteered the business card because he'd heard we'd been looking for Ron Jackson and knew the Leeds angle would be a dead end.'

'But who would he hear that from?'

Robbie ran a chip through the egg yolk. 'I don't know. Perhaps he'd heard Iris, Albert and Esme talking the other night and when he saw us talking to them …'

'But why would Ron make sure the business card was removed from each of the robberies if Gordon was simply going to hand it to us?' Even as the theory was beginning to make some sort of sense, so much of it made no sense at all.

'Because we already had the name and had connected Ron Jackson with the robberies.'

'Thanks to Iris's attention to detail.'

'Aye. Once Gordon heard the name mentioned, he must've realised it would draw our attention away from him if he offered the business card up first.'

'Especially if he'd heard we knew he'd met with Ron Jackson.'

'Aye.'

I wound creamy fettuccine onto my fork as I went back through the conversation we'd had that night. 'Ron Jackson's name was mentioned, as were stolen antiques – and Iris pointed you out to Esme as being the policeman on the case. While he seemed surprised the other day to find out you were a policeman, he didn't seem *that* surprised.' My fork poised in the air as I made another connection. 'He was at the bar when this conversation was happening, so he might've heard. Did you hear us?'

Robbie's eyes shifted to the ceiling where the collection of brass hanging from the beams was gleaming from the fire. Then he nodded slowly. 'Aye, not all of it, but definitely some of the conversation. If I'd wanted to listen, I might've heard more.'

'Like if you'd heard the name Ron Jackson and then actively listened for more.'

'Aye.'

We fell silent as we ate, although thoughts and possibilities were whirling through my head. Glancing across at Robbie, who seemed preoccupied with his plate, I guessed he was doing the same. 'I have to say, though, I'm relieved Catherine's got nothing to do with it.'

'Your instincts were right there—' He broke off as his phone rang. Frowning at the name on the screen, he held up a hand in apology and answered. 'When did this happen?' He looked at his watch. 'I'm not far away, Gordon'—my eyebrows rose at the name—'I have Philly with me. We can be there in fifteen minutes.'

'Gordon Willoughby?' I asked.

'Aye. He and Marlene have just arrived home to find they've been broken into.'

'Maybe we're wrong about Gordon,' I suggested slowly.

Robbie shook his head. 'Maybe,' he conceded. 'But I don't think so.'

'You think he's staged this?' The idea seemed extreme. 'Had Ron Jackson break into his own home?'

'Perhaps. It's certainly a way of covering up any theft from Marlene's cabinet and deflecting any suspicions we might have.'

'Except that he doesn't know what Marlene has told me,' I reminded him.

'Hmmm. No, he doesn't – and that puts a different spin on things.'

•

The lights were all on as we drove up to Wych Tree Farm. Parking on the drive, a dishevelled Gordon came out to meet us. Far from the confident man we'd met on Sunday, tonight he appeared flustered, his cheeks red, and when he spoke, he repeatedly rubbed at his head as if trying to make sense of what had happened.

'Sorry to call you out at this time, but a spot of luck you were nearby. I was going to call the station, but then I remembered you'd given me your card. Maybe I should've called the station … I didn't think … I'm not thinking straight … Sorry.'

Robbie smiled briefly and automatically reached for his notebook and glasses. 'It's alright; I've phoned it in. How did they gain entry?'

'I think through the back door – it appears to be forced.'

'And your alarm wasn't triggered?' Robbie had moved into policeman mode, his methodical questioning forcing Gordon to begin to calm down and think.

'I'm sure I armed it before we left.' He rubbed his head some more. 'Yes, I'm sure I armed it. Maybe I didn't?' Gordon appeared genuinely perplexed; were we wrong about him?

'We can check in with the alarm provider to check whether it was armed, but how about you show me where entry was forced.'

'I'll take you around this way.' He held a torch and indicated for Robbie to follow him towards the back of the house. 'Philly, you go through. Marlene is in the drawing room – she'll be glad to see a friendly face.'

Leaving Bally in the car with instructions to be a good dog, the window wound down for air, I made my way into the house.

Marlene was standing in the centre of the drawing room when I walked in. Her arms were wrapped around herself, making her seem smaller and more vulnerable, the expression on her face one of someone who has no idea what's happened and what they should be doing about it.

At the sight of me, she burst into silent tears. I drew her in for a hug. After a few seconds, she stepped back and, taking a tissue from the pocket of her black pants, dabbed delicately at her eyes and blew her nose. 'Who would do this, Philly?' When I raised my eyebrows, she added, 'I don't blame you for wondering. I virtually accused my husband this afternoon of taking some of my collectibles to sell, but this…' She swept her arm wide. 'He couldn't have done this. Besides, he was with me.' She paused. 'Do you think it's related to the other robberies you've had?'

I shook my head and a shoulder lifted. 'I don't know. It's too soon to tell.' I didn't mention that force hadn't been required to enter the premises in the other robberies, so this didn't fit that pattern. Although there was the fact that Gordon had mentioned to Ron Jackson that they'd be out for their anniversary … Were we right back where we started? With a mental shake, I switched gears and focused on providing practical help. 'Let's leave the speculation to Robbie, but I can help you identify what's missing.'

She sniffed again, but the tears appeared to have stopped for now. 'The clock's gone,' she said mournfully, 'and the door stops.'

My practiced eye swept around the room, noting the clock's and brass's absence. The tantalus was still on the drinks trolley where I'd last seen it. There was, however, a lot missing from the cabinet.

'I should be grateful, I suppose, that more of my figurines weren't smashed,' Marlene said dolefully, picking up the remnants of what used to be a Beswick goldfinch.

'Yes,' I said absently, my brain automatically beginning to list the items I'd remembered seeing in there. 'China is harder to get out in one piece and tends not to be worth the effort unless it's rare – and even then, your average robber isn't going to have time to treat the items with the care they need to get to a salesroom in one piece.' I turned back to Marlene. 'Your robber certainly knew what they were taking.' Before she could reply, I added, 'Do you have a notepaper and a pen so I can write this list while it's fresh in my mind?'

By the time Marlene was back with the requested stationery items, Robbie and Gordon had returned. And judging by the flashing blue lights on the driveway, the local constabulary had also arrived.

Gordon appeared somewhat calmer – there was no more of that anguished head-rubbing – but there was something in the way his gaze bounced around the room and the deep furrows in his brow that gave him a truly confused expression and one I didn't think was contrived. No matter what our suspicions had been, and regardless of his possible involvement with Ron Jackson, I was positive Gordon had nothing to do with this robbery. But if he didn't, where did that leave us? Robbie's eyes met mine, and with the slightest shake of his head, he indicated he'd update me later.

We left the Willoughbys soon after – Marlene running out to the car to remind me about our scheduled ride on Friday morning.

'Do you still want to do that?'

She smiled a smile that seemed forced and a little watery. 'Yes, please … I … it's not just the ride, I … well, I need a friend at the moment.'

I nodded and hugged her. 'See you on Friday, then.'

Before we left, Robbie instructed the attending officers which surfaces needed to be dusted for prints; although he confided to me in the car on the way home, he didn't believe they'd find any. 'If we have graffiti artists wearing gloves these days, I doubt our burglar will be any different.'

'Do you think they're connected? That's a very long bow to draw.'

'I have no idea, Philly,' he sighed wearily. 'I really have

no idea. What I am sure about is that Gordon Willoughby didn't arrange the break-in of his own home.'

'No.' I shook my head in the darkness. 'I don't think he did either. But that doesn't mean he isn't involved with Ron Jackson.' I hesitated before adding, 'It feels as though they're connected – the robberies, this break-in, and the other trouble Iris and Albert have had – but I don't know how.'

'I agree. There's a link.' Robbie glanced at me briefly, his mouth slanted into a wry smile before returning his attention to the road. 'We just need to find it … and something tells me we're getting closer to that. Now, what's this about you going riding on Friday morning?'

'That's right, bright and early.' I chuckled. 'I'm a tad scared about getting on the back of a horse again after so many years, but it might be fun. Besides, I think Marlene wants to confide in me about something, and I suspect she'll find that easier to do on horseback.'

'Aye, you could be right.'

Chapter Fourteen

Over tea and parkin the following morning, I filled Ambrose, Eugene, Bell and Ginny in on what had been happening. While Ginny's normally sunny disposition had turned cloudy as I relayed what had occurred last night, Ambrose was more vocal about it.

'I don't like the idea of you getting involved in this, lass. You know what happened last time.'

'Antique duelling pistols at the OK Corral.' Eugene attempted to bring a little lightheartedness into the situation by drawing a parallel with the legendary Western movie, *Gunfight at the O.K. Corral.*

'Not to mention an angry Rochester getting his claws out,' drawled Bell, today bedecked in a purple velvet stole, a matching cloche stamped firmly on her head. 'Seriously though, Philly, with forced entry, it's beginning to sound more serious than just a few random robberies of unlocked premises in broad daylight.'

'We don't know that it's connected yet, though—' I traced the bluebell pattern on my Shelley cup.

'Of course it's connected,' said Ginny. 'I know you haven't told us everything about the investigation, but you've said enough to tell us *you* believe it is ... which means it probably is.' She finished with a smile that was meant to be reassuring but convinced no one.

Glancing around at the little band of dealers gathered in Bell's shop – Bell relaxed in a William Morris upholstered wing-backed chair embroidering the cuff of a velvet jacket, with Bally curled up on a patchwork cushion by her feet, Ambrose and Eugene wearing contrasting shades of tweed (Ambrose in heather, Eugene in olive) but both with matching expressions of concern and Ginny in a bright blue knitted jumper full of stars – I realised it was unfair to cause them any worry. While they were all interested in the investigation, there were some elements of it I'd keep to myself. Even Bell, who always appeared (and sounded) so nonchalant, hadn't attempted a stitch in minutes.

'Anyway, enough with all of that. Bell, have you heard how Simon's shopping trip is going?'

Bell raised one arched eyebrow but accepted my change of subject and, needle moving easily again, began telling us of the furniture he'd be bringing back to Chipwell. 'He did mention he might have someone interested in Albert's Mouseman table, chairs and dresser and wondered if you'd be able to measure up the items for him.' She directed the question to me. 'No rush, but Simon probably won't be back now until Tuesday.' She ducked her head but not before a very un-Bell-like flush stained her cheeks. 'I'm thinking I might go down after work on Saturday and join him for a couple of days.'

'Why don't you go down on Saturday morning? I can watch the shop for you,' I suggested.

'And I'll watch yours tomorrow so you can get those measurements for Simon.' Her almost-bright smile was also very un-Bell-like. While we all knew there was a heart of gold under that sardonic cat-like exterior, for reasons she'd never expanded on, she guarded that organ carefully. Bell, it seemed, was falling in love, and I couldn't be happier for her.

Back in my shop, I called Albert and arranged to be at the farm the following morning and was preparing to open for the day when my phone buzzed. I only needed to see the caller's name to know how the conversation would likely go.

'What's this I hear about you being at the scene of a break and enter last night?'

'Good morning to you too, Stewart.' I injected a breezy note into my voice even as my body tensed. 'And you know very well what I was doing there.'

A sound that could have been a harrumph came down the line. 'I know what you were doing there – Dawkins said you'd been out with him when the call came in.'

'If you know all that, then why ask me?' I tucked the phone into my neck and straightened a pile of books.

'I agreed to you helping Dawkins out with this matter on the proviso that there was no danger, but again, it seems you've found it.'

It was hard not to laugh out loud at his suggestion I'd deliberately gone looking for trouble. 'Thank you for caring, Stewart, but I'm in no danger, and all I did last night was work with the owner to collate a list of items that had been stolen.'

'Dawkins said you know them personally. He mentioned you were both out there on Sunday afternoon.' His tone was now accusatory and my nerves bristled in response.

'Yes, we've met them socially, but only the once. They're acquaintances more than friends; I'm sure Robbie told you that.' I paused for a beat. 'What is it that you're annoyed about? That we've socialised or that we've socialised with someone who's turned out to be a suspect?'

After a brief silence, he said, 'Don't you mean a victim?'

Heat rose on my face; I squeezed my eyes shut, annoyed at letting Stewart rile me. 'Possibly both. We think Gordon Willoughby might have something to do with these other thefts Robbie's been investigating – it was something his wife said to me. Robbie said he'd run him through the system today.'

'But you don't think he had anything to do with last night's robbery?'

'No, we don't, so therefore, I'm in no danger at all.' I softened my voice. 'You know Robbie wouldn't let me get into anything dangerous.'

He snorted a laugh. 'You and I both know Robbie has very little ability to stop you from getting into anything you decide to get into.' Another pause. 'Maybe I should hand this over to Whitely, let him finish it off.'

My heart jumped into my throat at the thought of what that would mean to Robbie. 'Please don't, Stewart. Not now. This new inspector of yours will have plenty of opportunities to impress once Robbie's gone; let Robbie head into retirement with the dignity he deserves. Besides, he thinks we're nearly there.'

'I'll talk to him this morning, but if he thinks he's close to a resolution, I might as well leave it as is. He only has another week or so, and it's not like I have anything I want him to get into in the meantime.' Another pause. 'Well, mind how you go, Philly, and don't stick your nose into anything without letting Dawkins know about it.'

'Promise.'

When he hung up, I uncrossed my fingers.

Robbie dropped by early in the afternoon – just late enough for it not to be obvious he'd timed his arrival for lunch, but also early enough that when Ginny asked the inevitable 'Have you eaten?' he could answer in the negative.

'Excellent, I don't think Philly has either, and I've still got some potato and leek soup left that should warm you through – you're looking right nithered!' Ginny grinned conspiratorially at him. 'I can pop one of my sausage rolls on the side for you. Philly, you sit yourself down too – I'll let you know if anyone comes through for the shop.'

'Thanks, Ginny.' He shrugged out of his coat and hung it over the back of the chair. 'It's raw out there today. I wouldn't be surprised if we have some snow tonight.'

'How did you go with Iris this morning?' I asked once we were both settled. Robbie chuckled in response. 'That good?'

'She's quite the character; she identified the pieces you'd marked as hers and had something to say about the other pieces and the condition of the chocolate boxes. Then when she'd finished with that and given the constable a lecture on how to make a proper brew – the poor boy has only just moved north – she informed me she'd woken up this morning to find that someone had smashed her outside light again during the night.'

'You'd installed the CCTV, though, hadn't you?' Despite originally being against the idea, Iris had asked the technician who was installing the movement sensors to also add cameras … by then, however, it had become her idea.

'Yes, we had, so then she insisted on watching that as well – and this is where it gets interesting. While she couldn't identify the face as the perp was wearing a hoodie and had been careful to keep his face away from the camera, she was positive the build was the same as the real estate agent who'd called on her. Plus, and you'll like this, Philly, we can see the tail end of a dark-coloured four-wheeled drive.'

A rush of butterflies flew from my stomach to my throat; finally, we had a connection to the real estate agent.

'I know,' he said. 'It's not an absolute identification, but it's the link we've been waiting for.'

As quickly as the excitement rose, it deflated. 'But still no connection between Ron Jackson and the estate agent.'

'No, we still can't connect them.' He paused while Ginny placed steaming bowls of soup in front of us. 'This smells good … You spoil me.' He grinned at Ginny, the action relaxing his features, smoothing out the craggy bits.

'Away with you,' she said, laughing at him and his attempted flirtation.

I shook my head. 'You do know she's attached, don't you?'

He tilted his head back and laughed from his belly – a lovely rumbly sound that made me laugh too, half from embarrassment, half from enjoyment at seeing him relax so much in my company … in our company.

When the laughter died down, it felt like we'd reached a tipping point in our friendship and moved to another level – still friends, but more relaxed. I hid my smile, and the warmth in my face, by leaning forward to smell the soup.

'Did you get around to completing a search on Gordon Willoughby?' I asked after we'd each taken a sip of Ginny's excellent soup.

He nodded, suddenly sober. 'Aye. I'll be heading out there after here.' He grimaced at the thought of the awkward conversation ahead. 'Gordon has form. Back in Leeds, there was a complaint from a'—he consulted his notebook—'Brenda Willoughby about a robbery.'

'Gordon's first wife?'

'I think so. No sign of a break-in but some antiques went missing – silver, collectibles, that sort of thing.'

'That sounds almost exactly like what Marlene had said.'

He nodded. 'I thought so too. The complaint was withdrawn, but there's a note on file that the complainant's brother, Ron Jackson – who also has form ... petty con jobs and scams mostly, a few short stretches inside – provided Gordon with an alibi on the night the items were stolen.'

'So what you're telling me is that Ron Jackson is Gordon Willoughby's brother-in-law?' While pieces of information were sliding into place, it raised more questions. 'Why then would he volunteer his business card?'

Robbie shrugged. 'Who knows? There might be no love lost. Either way, I intend to ask him ...' He tilted his head to the side. 'I don't suppose you can get away this afternoon?'

'And join you?' At his nod, I said, 'Let me check with others if they can keep an eye on Bally and the shop, but yes, I'm in!'

•

We found Gordon in the estate office, his shoulders hunched, his head in his hands, a laptop open on the table, a half cup of coffee that, judging by the skin forming on the milk, had been hot some time ago.

At the sound of the door, his head jerked up, a practiced smile forming on his face, but when he saw it was us, the smile slipped away. 'I take it this isn't a social call.' Far from the garrulous man we'd met just a week ago, Gordon Willoughby now sounded completely defeated.

'I'm afraid not.' Robbie was all business as he reached for his notebook and flipped it open. 'I need to ask you about your association with Ron Jackson.'

'Ron?' Hearing the name, Gordon's eyebrows furrowed in surprise. 'What's he done now?'

'Why don't you tell us?'

Gordon's eyes flicked between Robbie and me. 'I have no idea what you're talking about. Ron is … was … my brother-in-law, but until I saw him the other day at The White Horse, I hadn't seen him in years.'

'You're saying you've had no contact with Ron Jackson recently?' Robbie's head was tilted slightly, his tone even but his gaze unflinching.

'That's exactly what I'm saying. I thought I'd seen the last of him ten years ago when …'

'When he gave you an alibi for a complaint your ex-wife

made regarding some missing antiques,' Robbie finished.

'Yes, that.' Gordon squirmed slightly in his seat. 'Is that what this is about? Do you think I stole some of Marlene's antiques and then staged a robbery to cover it up?' His eyes turned to me, and I dropped mine, suddenly uncomfortable. 'I know what Marlene told you,' he said. 'She all but accused me of the same thing. I didn't take Brenda's things back then and haven't touched Marlene's now, and I certainly didn't arrange for the break-in of my own home.' When Robbie remained silent, Gordon exhaled heavily. 'I wasn't, however, entirely honest back then. On the night Brenda's things were taken, Ron said I was with him, but I wasn't, I was with another woman – not Marlene, but I was with someone else.'

'Marlene told me you'd met her while you were still married, but it was over between you and your wife.'

A flush of red stained his cheeks. 'I mightn't have been completely honest with Marlene back then ... or completely exclusive ... at the time.' He grimaced and continued. 'It wasn't until long after that I realised that in giving me an alibi, Ron had been giving himself one too. I often wondered whether he'd been the one to take Brenda's silver and put the blame on me. He'd always been in and out of trouble that one – looking for the next quick payday, losing everything on a sure-fire win and coming to Brenda for a bail-out.'

'And you haven't seen or heard from him since?' I

asked. If what Gordon was saying was true, it blew all our theories out of the water.

He shook his head. 'Not at all. While I was surprised to see him last week, I wasn't surprised to hear he'd fallen on hard times again. Now though, he was living with his daughter down Leeds way who, from what I can understand, is a chip off the old block.'

Robbie's eyes narrowed. 'Do you know her name?'

'Aye. Chelsea ... Beattie, I think. As far as I can recall, Ron never married her mother – I'm not sure he had much to do with Chelsea in those days ... That must've changed if he's moved in with her.'

Robbie's eyes met mine.

'You've met her then?' Gordon asked.

Robbie's lips were pursed, his nod slow and deliberate.

'And she denied all knowledge of him?'

'Something like that,' conceded Robbie.

Gordon nodded slowly. 'She must know he's up to no good. Do you think he's involved in these robberies you're investigating?'

'Let's say he's a person we'd like to speak to,' Robbie said carefully, his facial expression showing none of the frustration he must be feeling.

'Hang on ... do you think I had something to do with these robberies?' Gordon's face flushed a dark red, and he pushed against the desk as if ready to stand and face off against Robbie.

Robbie held out a hand and gestured for him to stay where he was. 'The thought had crossed my mind – especially since you lied to us on Sunday when we asked if you knew him.' He paused for long enough for Gordon to absorb that. 'Can you tell me how you came to meet Ron the other day?'

'It really is best if you tell us everything,' I said in a calm voice, trying to convey my empathy for his situation.

'Sure.' Gordon's expression was still wary, his eyes flicking between Robbie and me. 'How is it you're involved again, Philly?'

'I'm just here to help with the antiques.' I shrugged, hoping to encourage him to keep talking.

'Right.' He inhaled deeply. 'You're probably not going to believe me, but I called in at The White Horse after I'd been out to buy Marlene an anniversary present in York – a lot of good that did me given she thinks I organised the break-in of our home.' He shook his head and let out a sigh. 'I should never have told her about the accusations Brenda had made, but it was early days with Marlene, and I needed to give her a reason why the divorce was so messy.'

'You mean other than repeated infidelity?' I failed to hide my judgement; it was evident in the tone of my voice.

'Something like that. Anyway, Ron was there having a pint when I arrived. I was surprised to see him and thought he was surprised to see me, but now I'm not sure. He must've found out where I lived, and I've always liked a pint at that time of the afternoon, so perhaps it wasn't a surprise to him. I asked him what brought him to Dunthrop, and he said he'd moved into the antique game – acquisition and sales he called it. He handed me his business card in case, as he said, I was ever in the market.'

'What did you think he meant by that?' Robbie busily scribbled in his trusty notepad.

Gordon hesitated for a moment. 'I assumed he was into something dodgy, and I didn't want to know. It's why I lied to you about knowing him – and why I gave you his card. I heard you talking to those older people and heard his name mentioned. I didn't hear much more of the conversation but enough to hear his name in the same sentence as the word robbery. If he was involved, I didn't want there to be any reason you might suspect me of being involved with him.'

'Is that why you befriended us?' I asked. 'To find out more about what we might know?'

He bent his head and rubbed his temples. 'Yes, to begin with, but I could tell that Marlene took a shine to you and, well, she doesn't have many friends who aren't associated with horses, so ...' He shrugged.

'I see.' Robbie tapped at his bottom lip with his finger.

'I've told you everything I know,' Gordon said, desperation sneaking into his voice. 'You've got to believe me.'

'Do you think he had anything to do with your break-in?' asked Robbie.

Gordon shrugged again. 'I don't know … maybe … it's not really his style, but I did tell him where we lived and mentioned I was taking Marlene out for the night, so maybe he was involved … but if he was, it's not because I asked him to be or arranged for him to be. I set the alarm and took every precaution.'

'Okay/' Robbie flipped the notebook shut and tapped at his chin with his finger, his eyes focused on the bookcase behind where Gordon sat.

'You believe me, don't you?'

Rather than answering him directly, Robbie said, 'If you hear from him again, please let me know immediately.'

'Absolutely. Immediately.' Gordon's nod was jerky.

As we settled back in the car, I turned to Robbie. 'Do you believe him?'

Robbie nodded once. 'Aye, I'm inclined to. You?'

'Yeah, me too. Where does that leave us, though?'

Robbie's reply was blunt. 'Needing to find Ron Jackson.'

Chapter Fifteen

The ground had a light dusting of snow when Bally and I headed out for our walk the following morning. It wasn't enough to blanket the fields around Chipwell in white, but it was enough to make the path slippery where it had frozen. Glancing at the leaden skies, I predicted there'd be more before the day was out.

Whistling for Bally to leave the scent of rabbit, fox, or whatever else it was that had left a message worth sniffing, we headed for home.

I quickly whipped up a batch of scones to take out to Albert and arrived at the farm just past nine. Bally took off immediately as he always did. This time, though, there was no Jess to meet him. Albert must still be holed up inside by the fire – I couldn't blame him for that.

Zipping my coat up, I called for Bally, and when he didn't immediately come, followed his furious barking and headed towards the back of the barn. Frowning when I noticed the door to the barn open, I ducked my head inside, expecting to see Albert's white head bent over the workbench, Jess at his heels, but it was empty. Although the tarpaulin was still protecting the Mouseman table, something was off, as though things had been disturbed, the energy of that disturbance still in the space. Shivering involuntarily, I hunched my shoulders and rubbed my gloved hands together.

Bally's bark had become more insistent, so with my heart racing, I cautiously made my way around to where only a few nights ago, we'd surprised a would-be graffiti artist. Upon hearing me approach, Bally's head lifted from the snow-dusted mound on the gravel he'd been sniffing at and barked once more.

At my whistle, Bally retreated, his attention not on me but on the lump. Pulling my green woollen beanie down over my ears, I tightened the scarf around my neck, drew in a deep breath and stepped close enough to ascertain that the lump on the ground was indeed a man – a man who, judging from the rusty stain on the snow around his head and gaping wound in the middle of his forehead hadn't died by accident.

Letting out a breath I hadn't realised I'd been holding, with fingers shaking I reached into my pocket for my phone and tapped in Robbie's number.

'Robbie? It's me, Philly. I'm at Albert Horsley's place.' I paused, getting my thoughts in order. 'There's been a murder.' Before he could jump to the wrong conclusion, I leapt in with, 'It's not Albert; I've never seen this man before, but I know blunt force trauma when I see it.'

'Okay, first things first. Are you safe?' There was an urgent edge to Robbie's voice.

I nodded, my attention on the stranger's wound. There was something about the shape of the wound in his forehead ...

'Philly?'

'Sorry, I'm nodding. I'm safe, I don't think there's anyone here. Mine is the only vehicle here and Bally's been barking fit to drive anyone away.' My laugh was forced, high-pitched and nervous. 'Oh god, Robbie, I thought it was Albert.' My words came out in a half sob – relief that the snow-covered mound wasn't my friend, but also fear ... Where was Albert and where was Jess?

'Have you touched the body?' Before I could reply, Robbie answered his own question. 'Of course you haven't; are you sure he's dead?'

'Yes, and judging by the snow on the body, he's been lying here most of the night.' I cast another fearful glance at the body before retracing my steps, Bally pushed close into my leg. 'There doesn't appear to be any tyre tracks or footprints – other than my own – but they could have been covered by the snow too.'

'What I need you to do is go back to the car and stay there until I arrive.' When I didn't immediately respond, he said, 'Do you understand, Philly?'

'Yes, but I need to find Albert. He must be here somewhere.' I looked around wildly as if Albert would suddenly materialise from within the barn or walk out of the house with an 'Ow do, Philly?'

He exhaled loudly. 'Even if I warn you not to, you're going into that house, aren't you?'

'I'm sorry, Robbie, and I know you're worried about me, but I'm concerned about Albert and Jess. I'll be careful, but I honestly don't think whoever did this is still here.' As much as my heart was pounding outside my chest and my every instinct was to do as Robbie said and wait in the car with Bally until he got here, I couldn't do that, not while Albert could be lying injured – or worse – inside the farmhouse.

'Okay,' he said, a resigned tone to his voice. 'Mind how you go, Philly; I'll be there as soon as I can.'

When he rang off, for reasons I couldn't explain, old habits from when I was on the force, perhaps, I gingerly approached the body again and, being careful not to disturb anything about the scene, used my phone to take photos. There was something about that wound ... I zoomed in on the photo I'd just taken. Yes, the shape looked familiar ...

Bally heard it before I did, his head lifting, his ears forward. The low siren-like wail, a mournful sound that hung in the cold air. Jess! The realisation hit us simultaneously, and we bolted towards the farmhouse.

As I knew it would be, the door to the boot room was unlocked and swung open easily. Motioning for Bally to stay beside me, I stood still for a second, maybe two, listening for any noise that didn't belong. At the sound of the door opening, Jess's low howl turned into a bark, and Bally ignored my command and bounded through the door into the kitchen. Following more slowly, pausing between every step to listen for sounds of movement, a creak perhaps from the floorboards upstairs, the soft tread of a boot on the stairs, I approached the entrance to the kitchen to find Albert lying motionless on the floor, Jess nestled in beside him in sphinx position, her head up, her ears pricked, her breath coming fast. All intentions of stealth gone, I rushed to Albert's side and, crouching beside him on the cold stone floor, reached out to place my fingers on his neck, Bally snuffling around his feet. The breath I'd been holding left my body in a relieved sigh at the fluttering of a faint but steady pulse.

Jumping to my feet, I rang for an ambulance before taking my jacket off and wrapping it over him. The fire had long gone out, and the room was freezing; Albert's skin had been cool to the touch.

'How long has he been lying here, Jess?' The dog, now her person was being cared for, had dropped her head to her paws, but her ears were still pricked, and she was watching my every move. Bally had settled down beside her as if to offer some doggy comfort.

'Help's coming soon, lass,' I soothed. 'He'll be alright.' As if she understood, her tail thumped twice on the floor. 'Now, where will I find a blanket I wonder?' I unfolded a thin throw-rug that was hanging over the back of one of the chairs but as I was about to leave the room in search of something warmer, Jess whined again. 'It's okay, I'll be back.'

In the boot room, I found a couple of Albert's coats and draped them over him. In the living room, I grabbed a blanket that had been tossed over the sofa and added that too. 'There,' I told the dogs. 'That will keep him comfortable until help arrives.'

My phone rang, the sound startling in the silence. Robbie.

'Have you found him?'

'Yes. He's unconscious but alive – appears to have banged his head quite badly. I've not moved him so can't tell if he's broken anything, but I've called the ambulance. I was going to call you too but needed to make him a little more comfortable before I did.' I shrugged my jacket back on, zipping it up against the cold. 'The only reason he's not frozen is that Jess has been lying beside him keeping him warm.' I choked up at the thought of the dog snuggling into her master all night.

Hearing my voice break, Robbie's tone was gentle. 'I'm only a few minutes away, so hang in there.'

I nodded and then, remembering he couldn't see me, said, 'It's Albert I'm worried about.'

'I know you are, but you've done all you can for now – the ambulance isn't far away.'

Once he'd rung off, I turned my attention back to Albert, checking his pulse again, adjusting the coats and the blanket. I contemplated putting something under his head but was loathed to move him in case I caused more injury. Rubbing my hands together against the cold, but knowing I couldn't disturb things further by lighting a fire, I sat on a kitchen chair and settled down with the dogs to wait for help to arrive.

The ambulance and the police arrived simultaneously, Robbie, just a couple of minutes later, and a few minutes after that, another car with Robbie's sergeant, Lewis Stanley, and another more snappily dressed younger man, who I assumed was the new inspector. I pointed them towards the body and stood back as the two paramedics tended to Albert.

'Is he going to be okay?' I asked, even though it was too early for an answer.

'Too early to tell,' replied the taller of the two. 'It's good that you found him when you did, though. Are you his daughter?'

His question shocked me back into action; I hadn't alerted anyone about Albert's injuries. 'I'm just a friend … his daughter doesn't know.'

'Do you have her details?'

I shook my head. 'No, but I can reach his sister. She'll know how to get in touch with his daughter.'

Robbie sidled up beside me just as I opened my mouth

to ask if I could go to the hospital with Albert. 'I'm sorry, Philly, but we need you to stay here for now.'

Nodding numbly, I said, 'Can I call Iris first? I don't have Esme's number, and she'll need to know about Albert – and how to contact his daughter.'

'Yes, do that – Iris will know how to break the news to Esme as well.' Glancing across to where both dogs were milling around the ambulance and the police cars, he added, 'It might be an idea to restrain the dogs. I'm not sure Whitely is much of a dog person –especially not when he thinks they might be contaminating his crime scene.'

Iris was phoned, and she accepted the news with her typical practicality and promised to contact Esme and head straight to the hospital. Once the dogs were shut away safely in Libby (with the windows open, of course), I made my way over to where Robbie was talking with Inspector Whitely and Sergeant Lewis Stanley.

'It's nice to see you, Philly … but perhaps not in these circumstances.'

At the sergeant's greeting, I forced a tight smile and turned my attention to the new inspector and the introduction Robbie was making. 'Philly Barker … DI Whitely.'

'Mrs Barker.' Placing the inspector somewhere in his midthirties, I silently agreed with Robbie – Inspector Whitely was one of the new breed.

Before he could say anything else, another car pulled up. This time it was Stewart who slammed the door and stalked over to us.

'Sir.' DI Whitely greeted him.

Stewart ignored him, his glare intended for me. 'Philly, what's this about you being the one to call this in?'

Out of the side of my eye, I caught DI Whitely's eyebrows rise. He mouthed 'Barker?' to Stanley, who nodded and mouthed back, 'ex-wife.'

'Good morning to you too, Stewart. And yes, I was here to see Albert about some Mouseman furniture, but Bally found the … the body.'

'Bally?' asked the inspector.

'Her dog, sir,' replied Lewis.

'And before you ask, I haven't touched anything.' I glanced towards the mound that forensics were now gathered around. 'Bally sniffed at it, but that's it.'

'Then how did you know he was dead?' The question came from the new inspector.

I cast him a look of pity. 'When I arrived, he had a layer of snow on him, and his eyes were wide open. Then, of course, there's the gaping wound in his head.' What was it about that wound?

As the inspector would've opened his mouth again, Stewart turned to him. 'To save your speculation, Philly is my ex-wife and was on the force for about twenty years. It's not the first dead body she's seen, and I'd hope she's remembered how to conduct herself on a crime scene.'

Ignoring Robbie's slight grin, I continued. 'When I

arrived, the barn door was wide open – Albert never leaves it like that – and I think someone had been in there.'

'How do you know?' Whitely asked.

I shrugged. 'I just do. Again I didn't touch anything in there – although, so you know, I was here on Monday cleaning out the barn, so my fingerprints will be on everything in there.'

'Do you know the victim?'

I pulled my beanie down further over my ears and huddled into my jacket. 'No, Inspector, I've never seen him before.'

'Are you sure about that?' His eyes narrowed as if he didn't believe my story.

'Absolutely sure.' DI Whitely's attitude was making me bristle. I drew in a depth breath. 'As I said, I found him lying there and called Robbie. Then I heard Jess – that's Albert's dog – howling in the farmhouse, so I went in to find Albert. All I did for him was check his pulse and keep him warm … I didn't disturb anything in there either.'

'No one is saying you did, Philly.' Stewart gave the younger man a warning glance. 'So you can push that chin back where it belongs.' I swallowed a retort. He straightened his back. 'You mentioned the barn was unlocked … What about the house?'

I nodded, mollified slightly. 'It was unlocked too – Albert rarely locks up, but I've been telling him he needs to lock up at night at least. He does, however, keep the barn door shut – especially after the trouble he's been having.'

'What sort of trouble would that be?'

'The sort that if reported to you, DI Whitely, you'd probably ignore as being below your notice.'

'Philly …' warned Stewart.

'Sorry, but that happens to be the truth. Albert's had what he thought were kids causing trouble – knocking down his firewood, breaking lights. The other night I was out here, and we surprised someone about to spray paint the barn. None of it serious enough to warrant the attention of a big-shot detective from the south trying to make a name for himself, but serious enough to have someone like Albert …' I didn't finish what I was about to say, which was, as a pattern it was enough for the right person to come along at the right time and convince someone like Albert who'd been spooked just enough that maybe they should be selling up. No pressure, just the right place at the right time. Was that what this was about? Robbie had noticed how I broke off my sentence and raised an eyebrow before nodding – the movement slight but enough to tell me he was thinking along the same lines as I was.

'That's the case you've been working on, Dawkins?'

'That's right, sir. We believed it was somehow connected with the antique robberies Philly has been consulting on for us.'

'And have you found a connection?' Stewart's question was directed at both Robbie and me.

'Not quite, sir, but we have a couple of theories'—a snort of disbelief from DI Whitely—'and believe the perpetrator of the robberies to be a Ron Jackson.'

'I see …' Stewart gripped his chin between his forefinger and thumb.

'Unless it's escaped your notice, Dawkins, we're no longer playing with the burglary of some old dude who can't lock his back door. This is murder.' I wanted to slap the smugness from Whitely's face. 'I think Sergeant Stanley and I should take this one on now, sir. It's a big case for someone who's retiring next week.'

As I was drawing myself up to my full five foot three to argue on behalf of Robbie, the forensic examiner, still in her scene of crime suit, joined us. A trim, capable woman in her early sixties, Penny Chan had been with the department for decades; there had been many a Christmas party in the days when I was still married to Stewart where we'd be found in a corner trading gossip or on the dance floor dancing like no one was watching.

'Philly! It's been a while … You called this one in?'

'I did—'

'What have you got for us, Pen?' Stewart asked, shaking his head in my direction.

'I won't be able to give you a definitive cause until I get him on the table, but I'd say our victim has been dead for at least twelve hours. And before you ask, we're looking for a heavy—'

'Let me guess,' drawled DI Whitely. 'A heavy blunt instrument?'

'Actually, no … not this time.' Ignoring Whitely, Pen addressed Robbie. 'What you're looking for is a heavy object, but with quite a distinctive shape on the end.'

The bells ringing faintly at the sight of the wound began pealing. 'Something like a table crank,' I said.

Five pairs of eyes turned in my direction. 'A what?' asked Penny.

'A crank that you use to wind extension tables in and out. I told you something was missing from the barn, and that's what it was.'

'Philly has a photographic memory where antiques are concerned,' said Robbie.

'And other matters too,' commented Stewart, just loud enough for me to hear. 'What does it look like?'

Pulling my phone out, I swiped through my photos. 'Like this …' I held up the picture I'd taken on Monday as part of the cataloguing process. 'It has a mahogany handle and a metal arm with a hexagon at the end that fits into the winding mechanism on the table. And before you ask, my fingerprints will be on that too.'

Penny looked closely at it and nodded. 'I won't be able to tell for certain until it's found, but I'd say it's likely that this'—she indicated the crank—'could've done that.' She inclined her head towards the body on the ground.

'Any idea who our victim is?' asked Stewart.

Saying nothing, she handed Robbie a wallet in a plastic evidence bag. He slid on his gloves before opening it, pulled out a driver's licence and looked across at me. 'It appears we've found Ron Jackson.'

Chapter Sixteen

Although DI Whitely had insisted he'd be better placed to handle the investigation, Stewart had waved his words away. 'You stay and finish up here. Robbie – you and Philly can fill me in on what you know about the victim.' He glanced at his watch. 'Chipwell Barn is close; we'll talk there.'

The dogs and I were the first back at the barn, and once I'd made them comfortable in my shop, I checked in on Ginny, who assured me business had been slow. 'Who wants to come out in this?'

I filled her in on what had occurred, and she'd listened, her eyes wide and mouth open. 'That poor man!' she exclaimed when I'd finished the telling.

'Which one, Albert or Ron?'

'Both, I suppose, but especially Albert. And Jess – she must've laid beside him all night.' Ginny's eyes moistened at the thought of the faithful sheepdog helpless to do anything but add comfort to her master.

'I know – and she's quite anxious, so I've brought her here with me. She and Bally get on, so I think she'll be fine.

Robbie and Stewart will be here soon, though … Is there any chance of getting something to eat?'

'I'm on it,' she said. Then touched my arm gently. 'Are you alright? That must've been quite the shock.'

A lump rose into my throat at her kindness, and suddenly, I couldn't get the words past it, so instead, I nodded jerkily. It had been a shock and a rollercoaster of emotions. There was that time when I'd thought it was Albert lying dead in a heap under the snow, with Jess somewhere else in the same condition, and then the relief at finding him alive, followed so closely by those interminably long minutes while I waited for help. My heart sped up again as I relived it.

'Yes,' I said finally, my smile faint and tight. 'It was quite the shock.'

Robbie and Stewart arrived soon after and, after finding enough chairs for everyone, sat around my desk with tea and teacakes, none of us speaking until the fragrant brew had warmed us through and the teacakes had performed their restorative magic.

'Robbie, tell me what you know about this character.' Stewart carefully placed his cup back on its saucer.

Robbie pushed his plate away and reached for his notebook. 'A man fitting Ron Jackson's description presented himself at least five houses where robberies later occurred. On each occasion, he presented a business card introducing himself as Ron Jackson, an antique dealer working for Young and Johnsons.'

At the mention of the auction house, Stewart turned to me, his brows knitted together. 'You didn't mention Catherine was involved,' he said accusingly.

'Because she's not. He might have her name on his business card, but she's never heard of him. We haven't interviewed all the staff there, but unless he has links to one of her staff members, I suspect he's chosen the name at random to give him some legitimacy.' As I spoke, I ran my brain back through when we were last at Catherine's. Who was it we'd spoken to? The porter ... I made a mental note to speak to Robbie about him.

'I'm satisfied Catherine isn't involved,' Robbie said. 'Although we will speak to her employees in more detail now.' He made a note in his book.

'Right,' Stewart said. 'So this Ron Jackson shows up at the farms with a fake business card saying he's what? Wanting to buy antiques?' I nodded. 'And then he gets inside somehow—'

'Usually by asking for a glass of water,' I said.

'And then scopes out the house and its security – or lack thereof.'

'That's right, sir. During the conversation with the occupants, he learns enough about their habits to know when to return – which he does a few days later when he knows the occupants will be out. He's able to obtain access without force – to the extent that most of the victims didn't realise they'd been burgled until some days later.' After pausing to sip at his tea, he continued. 'Other than Iris Metcalfe's firefly cage – which was his only mistake – everything that's been stolen is the sort of silver or jewellery that is difficult to identify and can be easily sold at auction. He's also careful to remove his business card from the premises.'

'If he's so careful to remove them, how did you get your hands on one?' Stewart had settled back in his chair, his legs stretched out and crossed at the ankle, his hands clasped and resting on his stomach.

'Iris Metcalfe was the perfect witness,' I said. 'If it wasn't for her, we wouldn't have a name … or a case. But it was Albert who told us he'd seen someone fitting Ron Jackson's description talking to Gordon Willoughby at The White Horse – and it was Gordon who offered up his business card.'

Stewart nodded slightly, indicating for Robbie to continue.

'We thought we had enough circumstantial evidence to place Ron Jackson at the scene of each of the robberies we were investigating, but then Catherine alerted us to the fact that someone with his name had brought in a firefly cage and silver that matched descriptions given by Iris and some of the other victims. Philly was able to identify Iris's items as well from when she'd been to the farm the week before.' He paused and tapped at his open notebook. 'If it wasn't for that cage, it all would've gone to auction and no one would have been any the wiser.'

'Do you think he's done this before?' Stewart asked. 'It certainly sounds as though he has a pattern of behaviour.'

'That's a good point, sir, and one we haven't looked into.' Robbie turned to me, his expression thughtful. 'Philly, do you know any other auctioneers in the area? Perhaps he's used another one in the past to sell goods through.'.

'I can check.' I made a note on my phone and added another to find out who Ashley Poole had worked for before Catherine.

'He's either very confident of not getting caught or very stupid to leave his name in the contact details,' Stewart mused.

'A bit of both, I think, sir.' Robbie consulted his notebook. 'The address Ron provided Youngs was in Leeds. I called there and spoke to a young woman who purported not to know him but have since found out that she is his daughter, and he's been staying there with her.'

'And you know that how?' Stewart's eyes narrowed. I knew the expression of old; it was his putting-all-the-pieces-together look.

'Philly and I spoke to Gordon Willoughby—'

'He's the one whose house you attended on Tuesday?' I nodded again. 'Do you think he's involved?'

Robbie tilted his head, indicating for me to speak. 'It was something his wife said to me. She'd thought some valuable items were missing from her display case and hinted that she thought Gordon had taken them and that it wasn't the first time he'd done something like that. When we looked into it, we discovered Gordon used to be married to Ron Jackson's sister and that she'd accused him – Gordon, that is – of something similar. This led us to believe that Gordon was somehow involved with whatever Ron's been doing.'

'And you thought he engineered the break-in at his own house to cover up the theft of his wife's antiques?'

'That thought had crossed our mind,' Robbie said, a wry half smile on his lips. 'We suspected Gordon had offered up the business card to deflect suspicion from himself.'

'But now you don't think so?' Stewart phrased the question slowly, carefully watching Robbie's reaction.

'No, sir, we don't.'

Stewart sat back in his chair, stippling his fingers under his chin. 'What am I missing?'

'The same thing we are, I suspect,' I said. 'There are two other things that have been happening – all of the properties that have been burgled have also received a visit from a real estate agent wanting to know if they'd be interested in selling up.'

'You said two things.' Stewart was beginning to sound impatient.

'I'm getting to that.' At my raised eyebrow, he shrugged a shoulder and settled back to listen. 'The farms are all owned by elderly residents, and they've also been subjected to'—I cast my eyes to the ceiling as I searched for the right words—'troubles. As I mentioned to DI Whitely, it's nothing worth reporting: broken lights, petty vandalism, things going bump in the night. A broken outside light in an uneven cobblestoned courtyard or a ladder or garden tool lying where it isn't supposed to be can very quickly, for someone of that age, become a tripping hazard – as Esme could attest to. And given they're all coming under pressure from family members to sell up and move to aged living, what might seem like petty incidents to you can be enough for them that the next time this guy turns up offering to take the property off their hands for a good price without any hassle, they could just say yes.'

'And you believe the two things are connected – Ron Jackson's robberies and whoever it is, that's, for want of a better word, terrorising these elderly farmers.' Stewart might have sounded sceptical, but he was leaning forward slightly in his chair, eyes trained keenly on me.

'Yes, we do. We haven't found the link, but I suspect once we do, we'll also find the murderer.' I held my breath as I waited for Stewart to answer; had I said enough to convince him that Robbie (and by default, me) deserved to see this case through to the end?

Finally, he nodded slowly. 'I think so too. It might all be a series of coincidences, but I tend not to believe in coincidences.' His snort was sardonic. 'As long as you stay out of trouble, Philly, you can continue to help, but Robbie, this is your case. It's up to you if you want DS Stanley for the legwork, but leave me to deal with DI Whitely.'

'Thank you, sir.' He turned to me. 'I'd understand if you wanted out, Philly, but if Bell is happy to look after the shop for you, I'd like to have you onboard.'

'I'll check with her, but yes, I'd like to stay involved.'

'Right, well if that's settled, I'll be off back to the nick.' Stewart stood to leave, retrieving his coat from the stand and shrugging it on.

'Good luck dealing with DI Whitely,' I said.

He turned back and grinned. 'Thanks.' His lips twisted. 'He reminds me a bit of how I was at his age.'

'That's what I mean.' I managed to keep a straight face, but a laugh burst out of Stewart, and as it did, the years slipped away, and I realised that we'd finally moved far enough past the divorce to be comfortable enough in each other's presence for me to tease him and for him to laugh like that.

After Stewart left, I checked in on Bell. While Bally was happy to continue dozing on his cushion, as soon as I moved, so had Jess. I reached down to ruffle her head. 'It'll be alright, lass,' I said. 'But you're going to need to stay with Bally and me for a bit.' The sheepdog's tail wagged weakly, but she'd been through a lot and was going to need company for the next few days at least – or until Albert came home –

and I wasn't going to be able to take either her or Bally out with Robbie and me today.

After I explained the situation, Bell readily agreed to mind the shop – and the dogs – for me, tempting Jess over for a pat with one of the tasty treats she thought I didn't know she kept in her top drawer. 'Just don't go telling anyone about this,' she whispered to the dog with a side smile at me. 'This secret is between you, me and Bally – everyone else can continue to think my heart is hardened.'

'I hope she'll be okay,' I said as Jess circled three times before settling on a cushion beside Bell's wing-backed chair.

'Don't worry about her,' Bell said. 'We're going to get along just fine.' When Bally trotted in a few seconds later, he received his treat with a much more enthusiastic wag and flopped onto the scarlet cushion on the other side of Bell's chair, his ears splayed against the red velvet.

'You go off and catch killers in the cold,' she said with a fond look at both dogs. 'We'll stay here where it's warm.'

Chapter Seventeen

'One of the local boys has broken the news to Chelsea Beattie,' Robbie told me in the car on the way back out to Wych Tree Farm. 'She said her mother will drive her up here – either can identify the body.'

'She must've known some of what he was up to when she lied to you about knowing him,' I said.

'Unless she's used to him being up to no good and lies for him out of habit.' Robbie's lips had a quirk to them. 'Did you ring the hospital?'

'Yes, I spoke with Iris. She and Esme are there – Jenny and Jim are on their way. Iris said he's still touch and go, but they're staying positive.' It was snowing again, flakes falling softly against the windscreen. 'There's something she's not telling me, though, and I suspect it's to do with whatever they were plotting the other night in the pub. It didn't seem the right time to be pressing her on that, though.'

'You think they might've drawn Ron to Albert's with the hope of catching him in the act?'

'I wouldn't put it past them. They were definitely

planning something they didn't want us to know about.'
I glanced at Robbie. 'I can't think why else Ron would be
out at Albert's – unless he's also the one committing the
vandalism.'

'There's something – or someone – linking this all
together: the robberies, the real estate, the vandalism, the
murder. It's all linked; I know it is.' He hit the steering wheel
in frustration. 'There's something we're not seeing, Philly.'

'And you think Gordon Willoughby can cast some
light on that?'

He shrugged. 'Maybe. It's a start. There was another
angle you thought of too – something to do with Catherine
…?' He flicked his eyes briefly in my direction and grinned.
'I'm getting to know your "bells are ringing in my head"
expression.'

'Really?' I laughed. 'Well, as it happens, you're right.
It's something about that porter of Catherine's. He's new –
well, I've never met him, and I know everyone who works
there. I wondered whether he and Ron had worked together
in the past and if the places he'd worked at before Young
and Johnsons had also received goods for sale from Ron
Jackson. The only thing is, he did offer up a description …'

'He didn't have a lot of choice in that,' Robbie said
ruefully as we pulled up outside the estate office. 'Right,
let's see where Gordon was last night and if his attitude to
Ron Jackson changes when I tell him he's been murdered.'

•

Gordon Willoughby's rough few days were showing on his drawn face. 'Dead, you say? How? Was it a car accident or something?' Gordon was attempting to meet our eyes, to portray a posture of transparency; his finger, however, was tapping on the table.

'I'm afraid your friend was murdered.' Robbie placed the slightest emphasis on the word 'friend'.

'He was no friend of mine,' Gordon rushed to say. 'As I said the other day, it had been ten years since I last saw him, and I hoped it would be at least another ten before I saw him again.'

'It seems then that you have your wish – you won't be seeing Ron Jackson again.'

Gordon scratched at the side of his neck and sighed in resignation. 'You'd better sit down,' he said grudgingly. 'How was he … Where was he …?'

'How was he killed?' Robbie finished the sentence for him. 'I can't disclose those details, but it was murder.'

Gordon covered his face with his hands. When he removed them, his eyes were bleak. 'You're here because I'm a suspect.'

'You're a person of interest,' Robbie clarified. 'And to rule you out, we need to know where you were between eight and ten o'clock last night.'

'An alibi?' With his elbow on the desk, Gordon rested

his cheek against the back of his fist and looked away towards the paddock where a chestnut horse was grazing.

'Were you here – with Marlene?'

Turning his gaze back to Robbie, he finally said, 'No, but I can't tell you where I was.'

'Can't or won't?' Robbie asked.

Gordon proceeded to look even more wretched. 'You can't tell us where you were because you were with another woman,' I guessed. 'Where does Marlene think you were?'

'At a business meeting,' he replied miserably, his hand dropping back to the desk.

Robbie leant towards him. 'You know you're going to need to give us her details,' he hesitated briefly, his stare unflinching. 'At the moment, you're the only person we can link to Ron Jackson ...'

'And that makes me a prime suspect.' Thoughts flickered across his face. 'Will you be discreet? You see she's ... um ...'

'Married?' I finished the sentence.

He slumped back in his chair. 'Does Marlene need to know? She'll divorce me if she does and I don't want to leave here.' He waved his arm towards the paddock where now two majestically built horses were grazing. 'And yes, I know I should've thought about that earlier ...'

Neither Robbie nor I commented, and Gordon wrote some details on a notepad, ripped the page off and passed it across to Robbie before again placing his hands over his face.

Robbie picked up the paper and wrote the details in his notebook. 'Who knows the code to your alarm?'

Uncovering his face, Gordon frowned. 'Who else knows the alarm code? Just Marlene and me.' The penny dropped, and a panicked look came over his face. 'You're saying the alarm was disarmed so I must've given the code to someone? Someone like Ron Jackson?' He shook his head vehemently. 'No, I didn't do that. I didn't ask Ron Jackson to break into our home, and I certainly did not kill him!'

While Gordon's voice rose, Robbie's remained even. 'What about Marlene? We'll need to talk to her as well.'

The panicked expression was replaced by confusion. 'No, there'd be no reason for her to do that – after all, it was her things that were stolen. No, they must've come about it some other way – a tradesman perhaps, or one of the house sitters we've had in from time to time to look after the horses when we've gone away. Can't the clever robbers work out the code from, I don't know, knowing your birthday or something? Or from fingerprints?' His hands emphasised the wildness of his thoughts. 'I've seen TV shows where that's happened.'

'Is your code aligned to a birthday?' I asked.

'Yes, Marlene's.' His face brightened. 'That means anyone who knows Marlene might be able to guess the code!'

'Where is Marlene now?' I asked softly.

'Leeds. It's her day to go there – she has a friend from school she visits. She's having cancer treatment, and she has no one else, so Marlene is her support person.'

Robbie nodded to me, and we stood to leave. 'One more question before we go,' began Robbie. 'Did Marlene know about your other woman?'

He shook his head miserably. 'No, I'm sure she didn't. I was careful.' He smiled ruefully. 'I've had plenty of practice … Am I going to need a lawyer?'

Robbie paused in the door, his expression inscrutable. 'That's up to you. At this point you're helping us with our enquiries. We'll see ourselves out.'

As we left Gordon lowered his head to the table.

Our next stop was the hospital to check in on Albert, where we found Iris and Esme in the waiting room nursing styrofoam cups of tea. Both seemed to have aged overnight, even Iris appearing to have shrunk into her lilac woollen jumper.

'How's Albert looking?' I asked after greeting both with a kiss.

'He's broken a wrist but other than that, they think he'll recover,' Esme said, her voice quivering. 'Jenny and Jim are on their way; they'll be here soon.'

Robbie lightly touched her arm in reassurance. 'I'll go get us a brew.'

Smiling my thanks, I sat down beside the two older women. 'Now,' I started, keeping my voice soft, 'What is it you two aren't telling me?'

Esme's shoulders slumped, her pale blue eyes moist.

'It's all our fault, Philly. What happened to Albert and that poor, poor man.'

'How is it your fault?' Esme looked at Iris, so I did too. 'Iris?'

Iris took a deep breath. 'You know how we mentioned Ron Jackson had called in on Esme?'

'Actually, no, I don't believe you did mention that.' Exasperated, I slipped into the same tone I used on the kids – mainly Chloe – when they were teenagers.

Iris's eyes dropped, faint pink coming to her cheeks. 'I know we should've told you. It was Tuesday – the day we saw you at the pub.' I nodded for her to continue. 'We'd agreed amongst ourselves that if he ever did come to Esme's – and we thought he probably would – she was to let him know that on Wednesday evenings, she went to The White Horse for tea.'

'The idea, presumably, being that you'd all, instead, be at Esme's waiting for him,' I guessed. 'That's what you were talking about when we saw you?'

Iris nodded. 'We kept to the plan and went to Esme's …'

'Iris brought a proper beef stew with her, and I did some puddings,' offered Esme.

'But he didn't turn up, so at about eight, Albert and Jess went home,' Iris finished.

I thought through what they'd said. 'Did you specifically tell Ron Jackson that all three of you went to the pub?'

Esme considered the question. 'No. I just had to tell him that on Wednesdays, I went to the pub for tea.'

'And you didn't mention Iris or Albert?'

She shook her head emphatically.

I reached across and put my hand over hers. 'None of this was your fault. I don't know why Ron Jackson was at Albert's, but we don't know that he assaulted Albert.'

'So Ron Jackson was murdered?' Iris had straightened with the knowledge that Ron Jackson probably wasn't there because of their plotting. 'Do you think he was the one who hurt Albert?' She hesitated. 'You're surely not thinking Albert did for him.'

'As to the first, we don't know … and regarding the second question, I think it's unlikely.' Another thought occurred to me. 'Iris, I know how much attention you pay to everything. Can you think back to Tuesday night in the pub?'

Quick on the uptake, she said, 'You want to know if anyone was sitting close to us who might've heard what we were talking about.' When I nodded, she added, 'Someone like Ron Jackson or Gordon Willoughby, you mean?' Not wanting to put the suggestion to her, I remained silent. 'Neither of them were there, but Ron's car was.'

My stomach flipped. Robbie chose that moment to return with our teas. 'Iris was just telling us that even though Ron Jackson wasn't in the pub on Tuesday night when they were, his car was – the dark grey Land Rover.'

'I saw it when we came out,' she said, 'but didn't think

anything of it because we hadn't seen him inside.' Robbie raised his eyebrows as a sign for Iris to continue. 'Now, let me see …' Her eyes were to the ceiling; she was back in the bar, working around the room. A light came into her eyes and a smile came to her mouth. 'Neither Ron Jackson nor Gordon Willoughby were there, but that real estate agent was. He was at the bar when we got there … Why didn't I notice that before? If I had and he had anything to do with it …'

My stomach flopped. Was this the connection we'd been after?

'It's fine,' said Robbie gently. 'We don't know that he had anything to do with what happened to Albert.'

Iris drew herself up to be ramrod straight in her chair. 'I might be old, pet, but I'm not a fool. If that real estate agent has been everywhere Ron Jackson's been, the two are connected, and'—a gleam came into her eyes—'that's what you're trying to find, isn't it, a connection.'

'Can you remember if there was anyone else with him?'

As Robbie asked the question, Iris's brow furrowed. 'Hold your horses, pet; I'm getting to that. There was someone …' She pursed her lips. 'I know there was another man, but I can't get the picture. Mind, it'll come to me.' After a few more seconds, she shook her head. 'I'm sorry, pet, it's gone.'

I patted her hand. 'That's okay, Iris; if it comes to you, give me a call.'

Chapter Eighteen

Becky looked up from her position at the front desk as we walked into Young and Johnsons for the second time this week. 'Hiya, Philly, Inspector Dawkins ... If you're here to see Catherine, you'll find her in the warehouse – and she's not happy.'

'Why? What's happened?' Catherine's temper was slow to rouse but legendary once it was.

'We're a porter down, expecting plenty of deliveries for next week's auction, and the warehouse is in a mess.'

Beside me, Robbie stiffened. In my most casual voice, I asked which porter it was who hadn't shown up.

'The new one – Ashley Poole. And he hadn't just not shown up; he's resigned without notice.' Becky shook her head in exasperation. 'His resume read so well we had high hopes – and the reference from Millers was glowing.'

'Millers in Leeds?' My pulse quickened.

'That's the one. He'd been with them for a few years – knew his silver too. Catherine was hoping to train him up as an auction coordinator.' She paused. 'You know how you asked about Ron Jackson the other day?'

'Aye,' prompted Robbie, notebook at the ready.

'I think Ashley might've known him.' She leant forward confidingly. 'I don't know why it didn't come back to me earlier, but when Ashley went out to help carry in the boxes, I'm sure I saw him shake the man's hand – and they seemed to be talking quite easily.'

'Ashley helped him carry in the boxes?' I knew Robbie would've picked up on that too – Ashley had told us he hadn't seen the vehicle and certainly hadn't mentioned he knew Jackson personally.

'Aye.' She relaxed back in her chair. 'I just thought you should know. Anyway, if you want Catherine …'

Robbie slid the notebook back into his top pocket. 'No, it's fine; we won't bother her; what you've told us has been very helpful.'

'Thanks, Becky,' I said. 'Good luck with Catherine today.'

'Thanks, Philly. You know what she gets like.' She rolled her eyes. 'See you at the auction?'

'Would I miss it?'

Becky's laugh followed us out to the car.

'That car was stolen from outside Leeds Station,' commented Robbie.

'And now Ashley Poole is from there,' I added.

'And our elusive real estate agent drives a similar vehicle.' He turned to look at me. 'I'll get someone looking into the background of Ashley Poole, I think …'

'I'll give Millers a call – I know the auctioneer there, and he'll tell me whether they've had any consignments from Ron Jackson. So,' I said, opening the car door. 'What next?'

As Robbie went to answer, his phone rang. Holding up a finger, he answered and spoke to the caller briefly before ringing off. 'That was DS Stanley … Chelsea Beattie and her mother have arrived. He'll take them to identify the body; we can talk to them after that.'

Chelsea, her mother and her child were waiting in an interview room when Robbie and I arrived at the station. Chelsea, who looked to be in her late twenties or possibly thirty, was that type of woman who used to be pretty – and possibly could be again if only she had some sleep and a reprieve from a constant worry about money. Her blonde hair was once probably her crowning glory but now hung lank and dull around her face, and her blue eyes, which I imagined used to sparkle, now carried their own luggage. Exhaustion and a poor diet had taken the roses from her cheeks and left behind a sullen complexion and a sense that the world had beaten her down. Her mother, Jean, on the other hand, was plump and relatively well maintained, although her eyes were hard.

When Robbie introduced us, Chelsea merely shrugged, and Jean was attempting to restrain the toddler squirming in her arms for release.

'I'm sorry, but we need to ask you a few questions,' Robbie began, earning another shrug.

'Don't be like that, Chels,' said her mother, throwing Robbie an ingratiating smile. 'Inspector Dawkins is just doing his job.'

Robbie smiled his thanks. 'When was the last time you saw your father, Ms Beattie?'

'I don't know … last week maybe.'

'Were you close to your father, Chelsea?' I asked softly, leaning in slightly.

'Not really.'

'He didn't have much to do with us when our Chels was growing up,' Jean said, echoing what Gordon Willoughby had told us. 'He used to send birthday cards and the like, but that was it – at least until our Chels started going around with Ashley.'

'Ashley?' My pulse quickened.

'Aye, Ashley Poole – this bairn's dad. Although he proved himself to be no better than her dad – and his own dad, for that matter. Took off as soon as the bairn came along, he did. It was his father what put her up in that place.'

'Mum!' Chelsea glared at her mother.

'What, love? They're trying to find out who killed your father.'

'Well, it wasn't me, and it wasn't Ash,' she said sulkily, pouting like a teenager.

'Do you know if your father had any business deals

with Ashley Poole?' Robbie asked.

Another shrug. 'Maybe. He was always doing something, and I think he knew Ash's dad from, like, way back.'

'What's Ashley's father's name?' I asked.

'Charles Morrison.' Jean answered, the toddler on her knee now sucking the ear of a toy bunny. 'He was already married when he took up with Ashley's mum.'

'And he's in real estate, you say?' Robbie's tone was overly casual.

'Aye, he owns the place our Chels lives in – and more besides.'

So the real estate agent Robbie had spoken to also lied. 'What vehicle did Ron drive?' I asked Chelsea.

She shook her head. 'None. He didn't own a car. Sometimes he turned up in a Land Rover or something – but that was Ash's dad's car.'

'So they were doing business,' Robbie said.

'Maybe.' She pouted. 'I don't know, do I? I'm not his keeper.'

'So why did you lie about knowing him when I called by on Tuesday?'

Another shrug.

'Can you think of any reason someone would want to kill him?' I asked trying not to lose my patience with her non-commital answers.

'Other than me sometimes?' Chelsea glanced at our

blank faces. 'It was a joke, alright? No, is the answer. I don't know why anyone would want to kill him. I don't know what business he was up to, and I don't want to answer any more questions. And I only lied because I knew he was up to something, but I don't know what. Can I go now?'

Robbie glanced at me, and I shook my head once to indicate I had no more questions. 'Do you know where Ashley is?' he asked.

A cloud settled over her face. 'No, but if you see him, tell him he's behind in maintenance.'

'We have our connection, don't we?' I said once we'd seen them out of the station.

'Aye, we do.'

'Excuse me, sir.' A plain-clothes policeman called Robbie over to his desk.

'Philly, this is DC Park.' I smiled a greeting. 'What do you have for me?'

'You wanted to know the name of the owner of that stolen vehicle?' Robbie nodded. 'It was a Charles Morrison, and ... Does that name mean something to you?'

Robbie let out a short laugh. 'It certainly does.'

'I also took the liberty of obtaining a photo of him – and running him through the system.'

'And?'

DC Park's smile spread across his face. 'He has form, sir, from several years ago. He was the developer in a case where menaces were being applied to some elderly landowners in order to persuade them to sell.'

'What sort of menaces?' Even as I asked, I knew what the answer would be.

'Nuisance value: broken lights, damaged boilers, graffiti ...'

'In other words, the type of activity that would make them feel unsafe in their homes and prompt them to sell?' My heart skipped, we were so close to the answer.

'None of the charges stuck, but his co-conspirator was a real estate agent by the name of Gordon Willoughby.'

'Gordon Willoughby!' Robbie exclaimed, slapping the back of one hand against the other in a gotcha movement. 'Excellent work, thank you. Now, can you take it an extra step and find out whatever you can about both Charles Morrison and Gordon Willoughby? I want to know everything there is to know about them before I pull Willoughby in for formal questioning.' He paused and added, 'And I also need anything you can find on Ashley Poole and ... do me a favour and look at any unsolved robberies in the Leeds area. I'm interested in anything from remote farms involving elderly victims and antique silver and jewellery.'

'On it, sir.'

Robbie smiled his thanks to the constable, glanced at his watch and turned to me. 'I'd better get you back so you can reclaim your dogs. We'll take this up again in the morning.'

In the car on the way back to The Barn, I said, 'I'm scheduled to go riding with Marlene early tomorrow. Should I cancel?'

The furrows in Robbie's brow grew deeper. 'I don't think I like the idea of you being out there alone around Gordon, especially as we know for sure he's connected with this case.'

'But not necessarily the murder,' I pointed out. 'Besides, I won't be alone with him, I'll be with Marlene, and she's the one who put us onto him in the first place. Plus, she did say she wanted to talk to me … What if what she needs to tell me is associated with the case? It could be the piece that ties it all together.'

'I suppose …' he said slowly. 'Just keep me updated and mind how you go.'

Choosing to ignore how displeased he looked at the idea of me being out at Wych Tree tomorrow, I said, 'Don't I always?'

Chapter Nineteen

The sun was still in bed and tucked under the covers when I got out of mine the next morning to take the dogs for a quick walk. Stables were not an appropriate place for a cocker spaniel or a sheepdog, so I gave them each a bone and left them at home. I'd collect them on my way to work after I finished riding.

Donning my stretchiest jeans, Chelsea boots and a woollen jumper over a layer of thermals, I grabbed my anorak and a scarf, climbed into Libby and headed to Wych Tree Farm.

Driving down the lane towards the farm, I had to admit I was looking forward to the morning ride. The day had dawned blue and bright, and as the sun hit, steam rose from the frost on the hedgerows. As I pulled up to the stables, my phone rang, my heart skipping a beat when I saw the caller's name. 'You're early this morning, Iris. Is Albert okay?' I'd phoned her last night to be told he was out of danger and had woken with seemingly no ill effects other than a busted wrist. While he'd told Iris that he'd been hit from behind and hadn't seen his attacker, Robbie was going to see him first thing this morning and get his statement. A call from Iris this early in the morning, though, couldn't be good news.

'He's fine, pet. I wanted to call and let you know I remembered who I'd seen the real estate agent with the other night. It came to me in the middle of the night – you know how that happens? And once I'd remembered, I couldn't go back to sleep.'

My heart skipped again but for an entirely different reason. 'Yes …?'

'There was a younger man, quite stocky, hair cut in that way where it's short but sticks up – a crew cut I think they call it. I'd know him if I saw him again. There was someone else too …'

Marlene was walking out of the stables towards Libby, dressed in taupe riding breeches, tall dark-brown riding boots and a long-sleeved navy thermal with matching quilted gilet. I waved and smiled through the windscreen and motioned to my phone. 'Did you recognise him?'

'That's the thing. It wasn't a him – it was a woman. I didn't see her at first, but noticed her when she left – she's that sort of person, isn't she? I remember thinking the same that night you met them for the first time. I didn't see her that night either until she moved.'

'Who is it?' I knew the answer before Iris said it.

'Gordon Willoughby's wife. She was there … and she was close enough she would've heard us talking.'

I couldn't stop staring at Marlene even though I had to pretend to be talking to someone about the weather – or something else equally ordinary. Her bright smile slipped slightly but was soon back in place.

'Was Gordon there?' I asked.

'No, just her – and she seemed quite familiar with that real estate agent too – if you know what I mean. There was no obvious display but you know, don't you?'

'Yes, you do.' Marlene was knocking on the car window. What had Marlene said? Her brother-in-law was in real estate and had saved her from her ex-husband. I'd wager that those trips to Leeds weren't to visit a sick friend. Gordon Willoughby wasn't the only one playing away from home.

'She didn't stay long though – kept looking at her watch as if she had somewhere she had to be.'

'Yes, on her way out to an anniversary dinner with her husband,' I mused.

'Philly,' said Iris slowly. 'Where are you?'

'At Wych Tree Farm – about to go horse riding with Marlene Willoughby.' I smiled and held up two fingers to Marlene to indicate I'd be off the phone soon.

'You can't! What if she's involved?' Iris sounded horrified.

Heart racing, I plastered a smile, hoping it would fool Marlene into thinking my conversation was about something more mundane than it was. 'I need to go now, Iris, but do me a favour; please phone Robbie and tell him exactly what you've told me – and ask him to find out the name of Marlene's ex-husband.'

'I'm on it.' If the situation wasn't suddenly so serious, I could've laughed at the expression in her voice, but it was so I didn't. Instead, I hung up, but before opening the car door to face the smiling woman, who I now believed to be (at the very least) an accomplice to murder, I hit the record button on my phone and placed it in my jacket pocket.

'Is everything alright?' Marlene asked as I left the warmth of Libby. 'That seemed like a serious phone call for so early in the morning.'

'Sorry.' I shrugged in a 'can't be helped' sort of way and decided to be as close to the truth as possible. 'A close friend of mine was assaulted in his house on Wednesday night, and I've been waiting to hear if he made it through the night. That was the update I'd been waiting for.'

'Oh, dear. That's terrible. Did it happen around here? Will he be alright?' When I first met Marlene in the pub, she seemed petite and vulnerable. Now, though, her stride was long and firm, the tight-fitting breeches showing the strength in her legs and making her seem taller than she was. Even though I was relatively fit, I had to rush to keep up with her.

'He lives on a farm not far from here. He hasn't regained consciousness yet, so it doesn't look good.' I hoped Albert would forgive me for exaggerating the seriousness of his injuries. 'We were hoping he'd be able to identify his attacker, but if he doesn't wake up ...' I shrugged.

'Not far from here? In Dunthrop? How horrible! Do you think it was a robbery like ours? Maybe he walked in on the burglars.' I had to hand it to her, she was a great actress, but two could play that game.

'That's what Robbie thinks, although we're pretty sure the criminal was part of a scheme designed to menace elderly landowners to sell their property below market value.' Was it my imagination or had her step faltered when I said that?

'Oh really?' She seemed distracted as she directed me into what I assumed was the tack room. On two timber-lined walls were rows of wooden 'horses' with saddles of varying shapes and sizes – depending, I supposed, on both the horse and the purpose. Above them, bridles, halters and other ropes and harnesses hung from hooks. In between, on the third wall, were shelves holding helmets, the sizes of which were chalked on the back.

'Yes, it's really quite clever – you see a real estate agent calls by and mentions that he's looking for properties just like this one and is told in no uncertain terms by the occupant that they're quite happy where they are. No problems, he says and goes on his way.' Marlene had her back to me as she walked along the row of saddles. 'Then things begin to happen – outdoor lights getting broken, boilers breaking down, the odd bit of graffiti, things that go bump in the night. Just kids skylarking about, they think.

Then there's a fall – someone trips over a ladder that wasn't there the day before and with the outside light not working, they didn't see. But they're old and forgetful, so maybe they forgot they left the ladder there. Before too long, they're no longer comfortable living on their own, so the next time our friendly real estate agent calls by, he's surprised when he's invited in. The property is bought for below market – saving both parties expensive legal and advertising fees – and the resident moves into an aged care facility. The real estate agent now has a property that's perfect for renovating and on-selling or letting out as a holiday rental.'

'That doesn't sound like it's a crime to me,' Marlene commented, pausing in front of one of the saddles and tracing the line of the burnished leather seat with her finger.

'It mightn't sound like it, but they can be charged with both wilful damage to property and harassment. Unfortunately, though, the person we thought was behind it was murdered.'

Marlene pulled a saddle off its wooden 'horse'. Stiffening briefly, she rested the saddle along one forearm while she reached for a bridle. 'Heavens. Murdered, you say?'

'Yes, at the same farm where my friend was attacked.'

She turned to face me, a bright smile back on her face. 'You can take this.' She held out the saddle and bridle. 'And choose a helmet from the shelf.'

I did as she said, wondering how long I could delay her until Robbie arrived – assuming, that is, that Iris had phoned him.

'The person who was killed,' she said conversationally. 'Who was it?'

'A man by the name of Ron Jackson.'

Again she stiffened, then frowned. 'Oh dear. I was afraid of something like this.'

'Something like what?' I feigned ignorance.

She chewed on her bottom lip as if wrestling with her conscience. 'It's why I wanted to talk to you.' She giggled, that annoying high-pitched giggle. She was nervous. 'You see, Gordon knew Ron Jackson.' She paused, wrinkling her nose before continuing. 'Years ago, before we were married, he paid Ron Jackson to break into his own house. It's why I thought he was behind the break-in at our house – because it was the same pattern as before. He stole some of his wife's things and then staged a burglary to cover up the theft.' She pulled a riding crop off the shelf and snapped it against her booted leg.

'Was he ever charged?' Far from blending into the background, Marlene was in control here, her manner almost one of a dominatrix.

'No, Ron gave him an alibi.' She giggled again. 'Gordon thinks I don't know the whole story, of course, but Charlie told me.' Biting at her bottom lip, she casually examined the leather loop at the end of the crop.

'Charlie?' My eyes were drawn to the crop and I willed myself not to respond – even though my heart felt as though it would beat its way out of my body.

'Yes, my ex-brother-in-law – he's done business with Gordon in the past.' She smiled a secret, knowing smile. 'I do hope Gordon wasn't involved with the death of this Ron Jackson – you probably should talk to him though … You see'—her eyes darted around the room as if checking for eavesdroppers—'Gordon wasn't home on Wednesday night and when he did come home – quite late it was too – he told me he'd been at a business meeting, but I could tell he was lying.' She wrinkled her nose and lifted the crop to play with the leather on the end. 'I've always known when he was lying. He has a "tell", you see. It's his mouth, it quirks a little at the end.' She lifted her eyes to mine. 'Did you always know when your husband was lying?'

'Not always,' I conceded. 'But I don't think he made a habit of it until the end.'

'You're lucky if that's the case. I've always known when Gordon was lying – and he's done an awful lot of it during our marriage … He's always had an eye for an attractive woman. He thinks I don't know, but I always have done … I just pretend not to.' She narrowed her eyes. 'I saw how he flirted with you the other day. Was he with you on Wednesday night?'

Not dignifying that with an answer, I said, 'If you've always known, why have you stayed with him? You must really love him?'

Marlene tipped her head back and laughed – not the

girlish giggle, but something more disbelieving. 'Because of Wych Tree, of course. I told you once that I'd do anything to keep it – and I will … even stay with my husband. I couldn't risk divorcing him and losing it. Besides, the agistment and racehorse spelling he's been doing has brought in enough money to allow me to concentrate on what I love – the riding school. It's the holiday lets that have made the biggest difference, though.'

'You said before that was Gordon's idea?'

'It was, but as Charlie says, Gordon has never really had vision. More holiday lets would ensure Wych Tree was returned to the prosperity it had when my grandparents were alive before my father almost lost it all.' She grimaced. 'He was like Gordon, you see, couldn't resist a pretty face. I never understood why my mother tolerated it, but she once said to me that she'd tolerate anything for the farm. She'd promised her father she'd never risk losing it – the same as I promised her.'

'If you're unhappy and don't want to risk divorcing Gordon, what are your options?' How long had we been in the tack room? With the saddle on my arm I couldn't see my watch, but even though it felt like an age since I hung up on Iris surely it couldn't have been more than fifteen or twenty minutes? I had to somehow keep her talking until help arrived. If help arrived …

She shrugged again. 'If he's in jail for burglary or even murder, I won't need to divorce him.'

'And you'll be free to be with Charlie?' She gave a little start of surprise. 'I assume he's the sick friend you've been visiting in Leeds.' My forearm was beginning to ache from the weight of the saddle.

'Charlie's different to his brother and Gordon – he'd never cheat on me, and he doesn't want my farm.'

My eyes widened in disbelief. 'Isn't he buying the farms you'll be turning into holiday lets, barn conversions and the like?'

'Well, yes, but he'll make sure it's all worked out legally.'

I scoffed at her gullibility. 'Don't kid yourself, Marlene – he wants Gordon out of the picture and your land ... and not necessarily in that order. Mark my words, read any contract he gives you carefully or before the ink is dry, the horses will be sold and the stables ripped down.'

For the first time this morning, uncertainty flooded her face. 'He wouldn't do that to me.' Frowning, she bit at her bottom lip. 'He said he's always been in love with me – that's why he helped me leave.' A little pause and then, 'You know, I don't know that I feel like riding now.' She flicked the crop against her boot again. This time, though, the action felt threatening. I recalled how strong her grip had been on my arm and a shudder ran through my body. 'But what to do with you ...'

Attempting to sound more casual than I felt, I said, 'There's no point doing anything with me – we've already linked Charlie and Ashley with Ron – and Ron's murder.'

'You're lying – you should be investigating Gordon for the murder and the robbery. It's a carbon copy of what he did to Brenda. He's the one with the motive.' Her face flushed a delicate pink, her movements jerky; I'd rattled her.

'That's where you're wrong – Gordon wasn't the one who stole Brenda's things and then staged the robbery.'

'He was – Ron Jackson lied for him, but he admitted to Charlie that Gordon wasn't with him. So there.'

'As I was saying, he wasn't with Ron Jackson that night – he was with another woman, and she's confirmed his alibi.'

Her pout turned to a frown as she absorbed the context of what I'd said. 'He was with someone else even then? But we'd only just started dating!'

Hoping that Gordon would forgive me – although really, he only had himself to blame – I continued. 'We've spoken to Gordon in connection with both the break-in at your house and the murder of Ron Jackson, and we're satisfied he had nothing to do with either of them.'

'You're wrong!' Her voice rose to the point she was almost screaming. 'You need to investigate Gordon. He must be charged. None of this will work if he isn't.'

I forced myself to shrug nonchalantly. 'Sorry, but he has an alibi for Wednesday night – and witnesses.'

'They're lying!' She brought the riding crop down hard on her booted calf. I flinched at the thwacking sound.

With my pulse racing, I slid the saddle across to my right arm and glanced surreptitiously at my watch. If Iris had called Robbie, he should be here by now. I had to keep her talking. 'Was it your idea or Charlie's to set Gordon up for the burglaries?'

'Charlie's, of course. He lost a lot of money once before over Gordon's stupidity. If Gordon hadn't staged that burglary and involved Ron, the police would never have investigated the property acquisitions Charlie was making.'

'The one where he was scaring elderly residents into selling their properties to Charlie?'

'You know about that, do you? I wondered if you'd find out.' She lifted a shoulder as though it didn't matter. 'As soon as Ron's name came up back then, they began looking into everything he was involved with. Charlie lost a lot of money because of that.'

'The same scam he's been building here.'

She smirked as she flicked the leather top of the crop back and forward over her boot, the clicking sounding loud in the otherwise silent room. 'It's a good idea, don't you think? And it's not hurting anyone. After all, when you get to that age, you should be in a home somewhere – Charlie was just helping them see that … with Ron's help.'

'Not Gordon's?'

'Good God no. Gordon had nothing to do with it.' She waved the crop idly in the air, that secret smile back on her face. 'He never did.'

'You know,' I said idly, the weight of the saddle sitting heavy on my arm, the ache running all the way up to my shoulder. I couldn't hold this for much longer. 'We know Ashley Poole is Charlie's son and we've connected Ashley Poole with Ron and the robberies. By now, Robbie will have finished searching Ashley's house, where I'm sure he'll find the items stolen from your house, as well as anything Ron hadn't been able to off-load to local dealers. He will also have found the Land Rover that Charlie reported stolen … Why did he report it stolen?'

Marlene closed her eyes briefly and rubbed at them. 'Because he didn't know Ashley had brought it up here for Ron to use. It was a mistake – Ashley was a mistake … Ashley's always been a mistake.'

'Following me home from Albert's that night and allowing me to see the licence plate was also a mistake – or is that why Charlie had to report it stolen?'

'It's all going wrong,' she wailed. 'And it's all your fault!' She pointed the crop at me, stabbing the air. 'Yours and that idiot son of his.' Stepping forward she prodded my chest with the crop pushing me backwards into an empty saddle "horse". At the sound of my involuntary groan of pain, she stilled, her eyes narrowed on me. 'What am I going to do with you?' she said again. 'You know too much.'

Her stillness was more unnerving than anything else up to that point and an icy chill I couldn't let her see rippled through me. My eyes darted around the tack room, but Marlene stood between me and the only exit. 'You've already killed one person – or was that Charlie?'

Marlene's eyes widened, her chest rising and falling in panic. Pointing the crop again at me her voice rose. 'Don't say that!' I didn't kill anyone.' She prodded again at my chest, forcing me back into the timber "horse". 'That was that stupid son of Charlie's too. He and Ron between them nearly brought the whole thing down – with that robbery scam they had going on the side.' Stepping backwards she seemed to be deliberately tryinging to calm herself down, to control her breathing. The next time she spoke her voice was lower, the tone more even. 'I might've mentioned that to Charlie, but I certainly didn't suggest he kill him.' Her nose wrinkled in a moue of distaste. 'Nor would I kill you … although accidents happen around stables all the time. Horses, you see'—she leant towards me conspiratorially— 'can be so unpredictable.' With her eyes locked on me, she strode the couple of steps to the locked cabinet on the wall and tapped a combination into the lock. 'Take the stallion we have in now. A beautiful creature – seventeen hands of pure muscle, but quite skittish with it, needs careful, trained handling.' Reaching into the cabinet, she pulled out a shotgun; my blood ran cold. 'He's not keen on having people in his space either.' She shook her head. 'I have no idea why you thought entering his stall was a good idea – and it was a great pity you did.' She waved the shotgun towards the stall door. 'Off you go.'

Unable to take my eyes off the shotgun, I struggled to remain outwardly calm. Inhale. Exhale. Inhale. Exhale.

'You won't get away with this – someone is bound to come in … a worker maybe, or Gordon …'

Marlene snickered again, her smirk triumphant 'It's just me this morning, and Gordon won't be up yet, and even when he is, he rarely comes to the stables unless he's showing anyone around. So, Philly, it's just you and me.'

Another shiver ran across the front of my chest; I gulped. Robbie, it seemed, was my only hope – if Iris had gotten through to him. 'What do you want me to do with the saddle?'

'What?' Her nose screwed up in confusion.

'This saddle you gave me and told me to hold on to. Do you still want me to hold it?' The question was ridiculous, but it was all I could think about to delay her. 'Quite frankly, it's getting really heavy, and I'd sooner put it down if it's all the same to you.'

'I'm waving a shotgun in your face and you're worried about a saddle?' Her voice rose again, echoing around the stables.

Out of the corner of my eye, I thought I saw movement outside. Robbie? Had help arrived? A horse whinnied and Marlene's head spun around. 'What was that?' She turned back to me. 'What was that?'

'I don't know.'

Narrowing her eyes, she examined mine. 'Right, no more delaying … move.'

She stood aside and motioned with the gun for me to

move ahead, but a clattering outside had her head spinning back around. I took advantage of the distraction to yell, 'I'm in here!' When Marlene swivelled back to face me, I hurled the saddle with all my strength in her direction. Taken by surprise, she staggered back into one of the saddles on the wall, and as she did, the gun fired. I squeezed my eyes shut and threw myself to the stone floor, expecting any second to feel the pain of pellets tearing into my flesh.

Chapter Twenty

'Philly! Are you alright?'

My eyes fluttered open to the sight of Robbie leaning over me while DS Stanley restrained a struggling Marlene. I nodded and sat up; he held out a hand to help me up. I dusted myself down, rubbing at my knees which had taken the brunt of my dive to the floor. 'I'm fine … I think.'

'Are you sure?'

I didn't know whether it was the concern in his eyes, my relief at seeing him, or the sight of the shotgun that even now was being parcelled up by another officer, but suddenly it hit me, and I began to shake and cry all at the same time. Robbie put his arms around me and pulled me into his chest, saying nothing but holding me until the shaking subsided.

'It's over now,' he said into my hair. 'We've got Ashley Poole and Charles Morrison in custody.'

'Good.' I reluctantly pulled away from him, already missing the comfort and reassurance he offered. 'The gun …? Where did the pellets …?' I seemed unable to string together a sentence.

'When it went off and you hit the ground …' He paled, his hand over his mouth. 'She fired as she fell back, so they hit the wall rather than you.' He pointed in the direction somewhere above where I'd been standing.

Approaching the wall, I peered up. Holes punctured the stone behind the timber cladding; a chill ran through me at just how close I'd come. Wrapping my arms around my body, I turned back to Robbie. 'How did I not know it was Marlene? Looking back, the signs were there, but …'

'I missed it too.' Robbie scratched the back of his head. 'We all did. But when the evidence pointed in her direction, we followed it – you followed it. That's just how it goes, Philly, you know that.' He shook his head, an expression I couldn't quite read floating across his face. 'If Iris hadn't called you when she did … and if she hadn't then called me …'

'It's okay,' I soothed, feeling suddenly awkward in the face of his concern, my hand reaching out to gently rub his arm. 'I'm okay.'

'There you are, pet.' Iris strode into the tack room, greeting me as if I'd simply been in the kitchen popping the kettle on instead of holed up in a tack room with a desparate woman waving a shotgun.

'Are you still in your pyjamas?' The forest-green jumper she wore over a striped shirt was faded and threadbare and she'd tucked the matching man-style pyjamas pants into wellington boots.

'Well, I didn't have time to think about my fashion sense, pet – not when you were in danger. I phoned Robbie, like you said, and then came straight here. I would've called by for Esme, but that would've taken too long and besides, I don't think she'd have been much help. It was all I could do not to come in and try and rescue you myself, but I wouldn't have been much good to you, so I waited for back-up to arrive … but I did record the conversation – as much as I heard anyway.' She held her smartphone in the air.

'She's also the one who threw throw rocks at the stable door when it seemed you were in trouble,' Robbie added, explaining the clattering I'd heard.

Iris nodded seriously. 'It's lucky you all arrived when you did. I don't think I would've been able to take her on my own … but I would've tried.'

I pictured the image of the seventy-six year old Yorkshire farmer dressed in pyjamas and wellington boots tackling Marlene and saving the day and tipped my head back and laughed. 'Oh, Iris, you're a marvel, you are!' The laughter as much a letting go, relief at my escape, as it was amusement at the picture in my mind.

The next to arrive on the scene was Stewart – who had also obviously dressed in a hurry and was still in his post-cycle tracksuit. I steeled myself for a verbal haranguing, but instead, he took me into his arms and held me tightly. 'Next time'—he released me, stood back, but kept his hands on my shoulders—'wait for back-up.'

'There won't be a next time.' A shudder worked its way down my spine at what might've been. 'And, like Iris, hopefully, I've recorded it all too.' I waved my mobile phone in the air.

'Philly love,' said Stewart with a resigned grin. 'With you, there's always a next time. And if Dawkins here is going to be helping us out on the occasional cold case, I can't imagine you'll keep your nose out of it.'

'Me neither,' chuckled Robbie.

'Okay,' I conceded, 'you might have a point, but can I go home now? I've got a couple of dogs that will need letting out and a shop that has to be opened. I'll send you the recording – it should all be on there – and you can take my statement afterwards.'

Stewart shook his head in exasperation, but Robbie didn't attempt to hide his laughter. 'Right you are. Do you need me to drive you home?'

'I'll be fine,' I said briskly.

Stewart crossed his arms, his jaw tight. 'I think you should let Robbie drive you. You've been through a stressful experience and sometimes the shock can sneak up on you, can't it Robbie?'

'Stewart's right, it's perfectly normal after an incident like this for it to hit you later. I'm happy to drive you.'

Their concern was touching, but it was also beginning to crowd me. What I needed was space, quiet, and routine.

I needed to sit in my old trusty Libby and drive myself home. I needed everyone else out of my head – even if it was just for an hour. I needed to see my dog and I needed a shower and I needed to do all of that on my own. And then I needed to go to work.

Robbie watched all of that flick across my face and nodded. 'I understand. Call me if you need me.'

Placing my hand lightly on his arm in gratitude – for his offer, for being there when I needed him, for knowing that I needed to cuddle my dog and keep busy – I said, 'Thank you.'

Stewart would have argued but Robbie sent him a warning look.

'I'll come by later and update you,' Robbie place his hand under my elbow as he walked me to the car.

'I'll make sure Ginny saves you something,' I teased.

The forced grin lasted until I was back behind the wheel of Libby and out of sight. Only then did I pull over. My hands were shaking too hard to drive; my head slumped against the steering wheel until my breathing slowed. In. Hold. Out. Hold. In. Hold. Out. Hold. That had been too close.

Back home, both dogs were treated to extra-long greetings and subjected to cuddles. To his credit, Balthazar stood still while I crouched down and buried my face in his fur, Jess was happy to snuggle for longer.

The reaction had well and truly set in, so I stripped off and scrubbed my close shave with an early ending away, standing under the hot water for long minutes until I felt clean again. Even though the logical part of my brain argued that Marlene wouldn't have killed me, each time I closed my eyes, the barrel of the shotgun came back into view, and my heart sped up.

Feeling almost human again, I went to work where news – courtesy of Iris, who had called by to let everyone know I was likely to be late – of my lucky escape had already spread. I played it down as much as I could, but Ginny's sympathy and the Ashton's horror of the danger I'd been in almost brought me undone again. It was Bell who put a stop to it.

'She's here, she's alive, and I think she's overwhelmed, so how about we all let her get back to doing what she's here to do – sell antiques.' She gave me a most un-Bell-like gentle smile. 'And then she can tell us the entire story over a pint or three tonight.'

Ginny had hugged me one last time before reluctantly heading back to the café; Ambrose took my hand and patted it, not yet willing to lose his concerned frown, while Eugene forced a smile and said, 'I'm glad she didn't shoot you,' a comment which made Ambrose's frown deepen and which had me laughing.

'Thanks, Bell,' I said when they'd all gone.

'It's all good,' she said, her voice catching a little. 'As

long as you do tell us all the gory details later. Now,' she said to the dogs, 'are either of you going to keep me company today?'

Jess stood, her tail wagging and followed Bell into her shop – after taking a wide detour when Rochester appeared in the doorway of the Ashton's licking his paw menacingly.

After all that had happened this morning, it seemed anticlimactic to sell antiques, but that's what I did. A shopping bus tour was in from York, and between that and the sunny day, we were all kept busy. The Ashtons were over the moon with their sales – including a World War I periscope they'd been carrying for longer than they would've liked – and I'd had my best day this year, selling several items from the cabinets as well as a 'foster mother', or stoneware animal feeder I'd been considering taking to auction. Given it was wide enough to fit eight lambs or piglets around, how the buyer would get it back on the bus was anyone's guess.

When I had a break between customers, I phoned the hospital and checked in on Albert. Although he was resting, his daughter Jenny came to the phone and told me he was doing well.

'Thank you so much for finding him when you did,' she said. 'And for taking Jess – her name was the first word he spoke when he woke up, and he was so relieved when we said she'd gone home with you.'

'She's no trouble,' I said. 'She's fitting in well here at the shop and is welcome to stay as long as she needs to.'

It was almost four and the last of the customers had gone by the time Robbie came by, the shadows under his eyes telling me what sort of day he'd had. Ginny brought us in tea and sausage rolls and left us to talk.

'How are you feeling?' he asked simply, his expression inscrutable, but his eyes gentle.

'I'm fine,' I said. 'A little shaken still, but I'm fine. Tell me, have you charged anyone?'

He nodded wearily. 'Yes, all three with various offences.' He bit into a sausage roll and closed his eyes briefly. 'Where do I begin? We searched the stables after you left and found the items that had been reported stolen from the Willoughby's and it didn't take much questioning for Ashley to admit that he'd been responsible for that break-in – at Marlene's request. He was very quick to blame the other robberies on Ron Jackson though. At first, he said he had no idea what Ron had been up to, but we searched Ashley's house and found more of the items that had been reported stolen. Ron had obviously been staying there, and they had quite the stash of silverware they were waiting to release into auction houses. We still don't know the full extent of that, but it appears Ashley and Ron have been running this little operation for some time, with Ashley being the contact at the auction houses. Neither are that smart, though – we also found business cards in the house where Ron was purporting to be working as a dealer for whichever auction house Ashley was based at.' Robbie rolled his eyes before continuing. 'Then there's the issue of the Land Rover – Ron needed a vehicle, so Ashley thought he'd "borrow" his father's as he'd bought himself a new Range Rover.'

'Let me guess – he forgot to tell his father.'

Robbie nodded, his mouth too full of sausage roll to answer.

'And was it Ashley who I chased that night at Albert's and who followed me home?'

'Yes, and Ron was the driver. I asked why they followed you, and Ashley said he didn't know whether he'd been seen so they followed you in case you could identify them and they needed to come back and convince you to keep quiet.' Robbie grimaced at the thought of what the convincing might have involved. 'From what Ashley said – and he began talking once he knew we had him as an accomplice to the robberies – his father had hired Ron to cause the damage at the farms he'd identified, the same as what they'd done in Leeds before a stop had been put to that. Ashley says it was Ron's idea to also commit the robberies at those properties and sell the goods through the auction houses Ashley was working at. I suspect though, that was Ashley's idea as the robberies appear to have been going on for longer than the real estate scam. So when Charlie approached Ron about helping him with the real estate, Ron brought Ashley in to provide extra muscle.' He paused and took a mouthful of his tea. 'I get the impression that young Ashley is anxious to prove himself to his father.'

'Where does Marlene come into it?'

'She's been seeing Charlie Morrison for some time, and Charlie talked her into putting the farm up as security for finance to purchase additional real estate, the idea being they'd renovate the houses and convert the barns into holiday lets. The problem was Gordon. While he wanted more holiday lets, he wasn't keen for Marlene to take out a mortgage on the farm for it. Even though Marlene owned Wych Tree Farm and didn't need Gordon's permission, she wanted to divorce Gordon so she could be with Charlie—'

'—but if she divorced Gordon, she'd have to reach a settlement with him,' I finished.

Robbie nodded. 'If he was in jail for, say, arranging a burglary, she'd be able to sign the mortgage papers without him knowing anything about it. And what better way to set him up than arrange for Ron to do exactly what he'd previously done to Brenda. All she needed to do was plant the idea in your head and stand back while we descended on Gordon.'

I shook my head; the whole thing was so convoluted it was no wonder we'd had problems linking all the pieces. 'And Gordon?'

'He had nothing to do with any of it – his only crime was infidelity.' He chuckled. 'You should've seen his face when we knocked on the door this morning after arresting Marlene. He's come out in his bathrobe, had slept through the whole thing and couldn't believe what Marlene had done.'

I smiled at the picture of a perplexed Gordon finding out that while he'd been sleeping, his docile wife had been holding someone (me) at gunpoint in the tack room. 'Who killed Ron – was it Ashley?'

'Aye. Accidentally – if you believe him.'

'Do you believe him?'

'Aye, I've a mind to – it's so ridiculous it's got to be the truth. Marlene overheard Iris and co talking about how they'd set Ron up so she warned Ashley. He, in turn, told Ron that Albert's place would be empty on that night so they decided to take advantage of the situation. Ashley says he'd been mooching about in the shed and had picked up the table crank and had then come out to ask Ron if he knew what it was, but as he did, a noise from inside startled him – and also startled Ron, who was about to finish the artwork Ashley hadn't managed to start on their last visit – and as Ron ran from around the back of the shed he, in turn, surprised Ashley who lashed out in reaction.

'Ashley then panicked and went in search of the noise and found Albert in the kitchen so hit him from behind. He thought he'd killed him too, so he ran to Leeds and holed up at Chelsea's.'

'And Charlie Morrison?'

Robbie shrugged. 'We'll have our work cut out to make any charges stick. All the evidence against him is circumstantial. Let's say he's smarter than his son.' His smile was wry. 'And now you're all up to date.' He drained his tea but not before I surprised an almost wistful expression.

'Your last case, hey,' I guessed.

He nodded, a sombreness filling his face. 'My last case.'

'You're going out on a high, though.' He'd not only identified a case where there hadn't previously been one, but he'd solved it when the likelihood of doing so was small.

'Aye.'

'Are you rethinking retiring?' I rested my elbow on the desk and my head against the back of my fist.

At first he didn't answer, but finally he shook his head. 'No, it's time. I can't keep up with the DI Whitelys of the world.' He hesitated. 'Being a copper is all I know, that's all.'

I reached over and gripped his arm touched he trusted me with his vulnerability. 'I know. So does Stewart – and that's why I think he's serious about getting you back as a consultant.' I grinned. 'After all, you can only spend so long on your allotment.'

'Aye, you're right there.'

I hesitated and then asked gently, 'Had you and Audrey talked about what you'd do in retirement?' I knew Robbie didn't like to talk about his late wife but hoped our relationship had moved closer to being able to do just that.

He raised his eyes to mine, and for a few seconds, I didn't think he'd answer me. 'Not really,' he finally said. 'We thought we'd go to Australia and visit our Jim, maybe take a cruise … She always wanted to see the northern lights.' He shrugged. 'It doesn't seem the same without her.' Forcing a smile, he said, 'Who knows, maybe you might want to come along with me one day … as friends, of course.' His cheeks coloured as he added the last comment, and my face flushed with heat.

'Who knows? One day I might just do that.'

'Philly …' he began.

'Yes?'

'If you're going to help with future cases, you need to promise me you won't go to suspect's houses without back-up. I'm getting too old to be running about trying to save you.'

'It was you who saved me, was it? I think Iris would have something to say about that … besides, at the time of going there, I didn't know she was a suspect.' I crossed my fingers in my lap.

He tilted his head to the side and grinned. 'You can uncross your fingers too – you had every opportunity after Iris phoned not to follow Marlene into that tack room.'

I grinned back. 'I only did because I had every faith in you showing up.'

Ambrose and Eugene joined us, followed by Ginny and finally Bell with Jess.

'You'd all be waiting for a story?' I guessed.

'Aye, lass,' said Ambrose.

'The pub?' I suggested.

'The Chipwell Arms it is,' agreed Eugene.

Another thought struck me. 'Did you happen to recover the murder weapon?'

'Aye, it was at Ashley's house; why?'

'Albert will be needing it back – that table won't be worth as much without the matching crank … and the end buyer won't need to know it was used to kill someone.'

Robbie's rumbling belly laugh filled the shop.

Recipes

It would be remiss of me to end this novel without sharing a few of Philly's and Ginny's recipes. You can, of course, find more from this novel – and my others – at my website brookfordkitchendiaries.wordpress.com.

Grandma Goulash

Ingredients
- 1 kg hamburger mince. Don't buy the super lean beef mince – you need the one you'd make burgers with; mince with a little fat.
- 2 x 400 g cans crushed tomatoes
- 1 can corn kernels
- 1 tablespoon vegetable oil
- 1 heaped teaspoon curry powder
- 2 onions, finely diced
- 2 cloves garlic, grated
- Salt to taste
- 2 cups cooked noodles. I used fettuccine which

I broke up before cooking. This does, however, sometimes clump together like railroad tracks so feel free to use macaroni.
• Enough grated cheese for the top.

Method

Warm the oil in a large (wide) frypan and add the onions. Cook over medium-low heat for about five minutes until soft. Add the garlic and curry powder and cook for another minute before adding the mince. Turn the heat up and cook until it's browned and has lost its pinkness. You'll need to use your wooden spoon or a fork to break it up as you go.

Add the corn and the tomatoes, turn the heat down to medium, and cook for about 10 minutes, stirring occasionally, until the meat is cooked through.

While that's happening, preheat your oven to 180C and cook your pasta in boiling water in the usual way, remembering that it will have some more cooking in the oven, so al dente is all you need.

Introduce the pasta to the meat sauce and pour it into an oven-safe tray.

Toss over the cheese – enough to cover it – and pop it all in the oven. It should take about 30–40 minutes or until the cheesy top is golden brown and bubbling.

Philly's Goulash

A cheaper cut of meat is called for here; the stew is cooked long and slow, so you need something that's going to melt into richness over this period of time – and that means fat and sinew so one of the cheaper cuts. If you can get it, beef shin is perfect, but otherwise, chuck or gravy beef will do the job – or whatever it is you call stewing beef where you live. Needless to say, rump steak will be wasted on this one.

Ingredients
- 2 tablespoons oil
- 1 kg (or thereabouts) shin or gravy beef, trimmed, cut into 3 cm cubes
- 2 large brown onions, sliced into half moons
- 2 garlic cloves, crushed
- 2 large red or green capsicums (bell peppers), cut into 2 cm pieces
- 2 tablespoons plain (all-purpose) flour
- 3 tablespoons sweet paprika
- 1 teaspoon caraway seeds (ground)
- 1 teaspoon salt (or to taste)
- 1 teaspoon pepper (or to taste)
- 2 bay leaves
- 2 cups beef stock
- 400 g can chopped tomatoes or a 400 ml bottle of

tomato passata – whatever you have in the pantry
- Juice of a lemon
- Sour cream to serve
- Cooked egg noodles, spaetzle or potatoes (boiled or mashed – your call) to serve
- Chopped fresh flat-leaf parsley (or chives), to serve

Method

Preheat the oven to 140C.

Mix the paprika, salt and pepper, caraway seeds and flour into a large bowl and tip in the beef, tossing it until it's evenly coated. I think clean hands are the best tool for this job.

Heat the oil in a heavy-based oven-proof casserole dish over medium-high heat, and then brown the meat in batches, being careful not to crowd the pan. Remove when golden and crusted, and set aside.

Scrape the bottom of the pan and add the onions, adding a little more oil if necessary. Cook until soft and starting to brown, then stir the flour and spice mixture in the bottom of the bowl (the one you originally had the beef in) into the onions and cook for a couple of minutes, stirring. Tip the beef back into the pan and add the stock and tomato. Scrape the bottom of the pan again, stir through a couple of bay leaves, then put in the oven for about two and a half hours.

Stir the capsicum and lemon juice into the goulash

and cook for another half hour or until the meat is very tender – you can remove the lid to let the sauce reduce if you like it stewier rather than soupier. Check the seasoning and serve with sour cream, your carb of choice and parsley.

Ginny's Tomato and Lentil Soup

Ingredients
- A glug of olive oil (not your good extra virgin) or something like grapeseed, rapeseed or canola
- 1 onion, diced finely
- 1 garlic clove, grated
- A thumb-sized piece of ginger, grated
- 1 tablespoon cumin seeds
- 1 tablespoon garam masala
- 250 g dried red lentils
- 1 litre vegetable stock (fresh or from a cube)
- 500 g tomato passata
- 160 ml can coconut cream
- salt and pepper to taste

Method

Heat the oil in a large saucepan over medium heat and add the onions with a pinch of salt (the salt will stop them from taking on too much colour). Sweat them down for about five minutes until they become soft and translucent, then follow with the ginger and garlic and cook for another five minutes. Tip in the garam masala and cumin seeds and mix well. By now, your kitchen should be smelling amazing.

Add the lentils and stir them through everything, then pour in the passata, stock and coconut cream. Bring to a simmer and cook on a gentle heat for 20–25 minutes, stirring every now and then until the lentils are soft.

Ginny's Cauliflower Cheese Soup

Ingredients
- 35 g butter
- ½ tablespoon olive oil
- 2 sticks celery, diced
- 1 potato peeled and diced
- 2 onions, peeled and chopped
- 1 bay leaf
- 1 large cauliflower broken into florets
- 650 ml chicken or vegetable stock
- 350 ml dry cider
- Generous grating of fresh nutmeg
- A good dollop of double cream
- 115 g extra-mature cheddar, finely grated, plus more to serve
- 30 g parmesan, grated (to serve)
- 1 tablespoon parsley, finely chopped (optional)

Method

Heat the butter and oil in a heavy-based pan and sauté the celery, potato, onion and bay leaf gently for a couple of minutes, then add a splash of water, season with salt and pepper, and cover the pan. Sweat for about fifteen minutes, adding a splash of water occasionally to keep it moist.

Stir in the cauliflower, then the stock, cider, nutmeg and more seasoning. Bring to the boil, then simmer until the cauliflower is completely tender. Leave to cool.

Remove the bay leaf and whoosh it with a stick blender – or, for a smoother result, puree in batches in an upright blender – even though this can be a faff, you do get a lovely, velvety result.

Return to the pan, add the cream and cheddar and heat through without boiling, stirring from time to time, until the cheese has melted. Serve with parmesan and parsley (if using) on top.

Ginny's Cheddar and Rosemary Scones

It's no coincidence these come straight after the cauliflower cheese soup – they are perfect to eat with that. They're actually also perfect on top of a beef stew similar to the one I told you about in Philly's last adventure. If you don't have that book (available from your favourite online retailer), you'll find the recipe at brookfordkitchendiaries. wordpress.com.

If you don't have any wholemeal self-raising flour, feel free to use all white. Oh, and even though there's no butter in this recipe and the scones aren't as light and fluffy as a posh scone, the usual scone rules apply: keep everything cold – except the oven, which must be at temperature before you slide your scones in. And don't overwork the dough. I usually like to rest my scones for ten minutes before popping them in the oven, but with these, that isn't necessary.

Ingredients
- 125 g self-raising flour
- 125 g wholemeal self-raising flour
- 1 tablespoon finely chopped rosemary
- Pinch of salt
- 150 g cheddar
- 175 g full-fat milk
- 1 egg, beaten (for brushing)
- Plain flour for dusting

Method
Heat your oven to 220C (200 fan) and line a baking tray with baking parchment.

Tip the flour into a large mixing bowl. Add the salt, rosemary and 100 g of the grated cheese. Pour in most of the milk, mixing with your hand or a flat kitchen knife.

Make sure the mixture is evenly combined. Slowly add the remaining milk if needed (you mightn't need all the milk).

Turn the dough out onto a lightly floured surface and fold it together to form a soft dough.

Roll out, or gently pat with your hands, to about two fingers thick and stamp out using a floured 7 cm round cutter. Take care not to twist the cutter as it will impact the scone's ability to rise evenly. Pop onto the baking sheet spaced slightly apart. Reroll the trimmings until all the dough is used.

Brush the tops of the scones with the beaten egg and sprinkle with the remaining cheese. Bake for 15–20mins, until the scones have risen and are golden in colour.

Ginny's Apple and Cinnamon Scones

Ingredients
- 500 g self-raising flour
- 140 g butter, cubed, fridge-cold
- 90 g caster sugar
- 1 large apple, peeled and diced (I used a granny smith or cooking apple)
- 2 teaspoon ground cinnamon
- 1 egg, beaten, plus extra to glaze
- Approx 200 ml full-fat milk

Method

Preheat the oven to 210C (190 fan) and line a baking tray with baking paper

Sift the flour into a mixing bowl, tip in the cubed butter, and rub the butter into the flour with the tips of your fingers until it looks like sandy breadcrumbs. Work as quickly as you can with this to avoid melting or softening your butter too much. Stir in the sugar, apple and cinnamon and pop it in the fridge for ten minutes to cool down.

Add the beaten egg and begin to add the milk, mixing with a dinner knife until you have a soft dough. Remember, don't handle it any more than is necessary.

Turn the dough out onto a lightly floured surface and knead it gently into a ball – again, don't overwork it.

Roll out, or gently pat with your hands, to about two fingers thick and stamp out using a floured 7c m round cutter*. Take care not to twist the cutter as it will impact the scone's ability to rise evenly. Pop onto the baking sheet spaced slightly apart and reroll the trimmings until all the dough is used. Brush the tops with beaten egg and bake for 10–12 minutes until risen and golden brown.

*If you don't have a cutter, split the dough into three equal balls, flatten slightly then cut each into four triangles to give you 12 scones in total.

Before you go

If you enjoyed *Philly Barker Is On The Case* I'd love it if you left a review in the usual places. If you'd like to stay up to date with what Philly gets up to next, you can sign up for my newsletter at my website: https://joannetracey.com

You can also drop by and see me – virtually speaking, of course – here:

My blog: https://andanyways.com
Facebook: https://facebook.com/joannetraceywriter
Instagram: https://instagram.com/jotracey

Acknowledgements

I'm not the world's greatest finisher of things so the fact that here I am, writing the final words in what will be my eleventh book amazes me.

While it might sound trite, the truth is I *really* couldn't do it without the help of several people.

The usual thanks go to my fabulous editors – Nicola O'Shea and Jo Speirs. Not only do you make my words read so much better than they did when I first wrote them, you also inspire me to continue to improve my craft and push myself. To Nicola, I can't believe this is the eleventh book we've worked on together. Here's to many more. To Jo, I apologise for forgetting the difference between em and en dashes … and hyphens (there *is* a difference, isn't there?)

The feedback and support from my early reading team is invaluable, so thank you from the bottom of my heart to my sister-in-law Pieta (who has read every one of my books before anyone else) and the members of my simply stunning book club – Donna, Sue and Deb.

It goes without saying that I couldn't do what I do

without Grant and Sarah. Writing this book was especially challenging and more of a juggle with the day job than usual, so thanks for putting up with the weekends where I refused to do anything other than sit at my desk and pound out the words.

Mostly though my thanks are to you, dear reader, for supporting me and picking up this book to read when there are so many you could have chosen. It means the world to me.

About the author

Joanne Tracey lives on the Sunshine Coast in Queensland Australia with her husband and a cocker spaniel who takes her role as resident flop-dog and guardian of Jo's office very seriously. An unapologetic daydreamer, eternal optimist, and confirmed morning person, Jo writes contemporary romance, romantic comedy, women's fiction and cosy crime. When she isn't writing or day jobbing, Jo loves baking, reading, long walks along the beach, posting way too many photos of sunrises on Instagram and dreaming of the next destination and the next story.

Jo's life goals (apart from being a world-famous author) are to be an extra on *Midsomer Murders* and to cook her way through Nigella's books.